PRAISE FOR
THE SUBMISSIVE SERIES

The Collar

"Titillates and captivates from the very beginning."

—*Romantic Times* (top pick)

"Creative use of conflict. The character development was excellent. . . . Long story short, I'm adding Tara Sue Me to the auto-buy list. . . . If you're looking for an honest book about building trusting relationships while finding yourself, pick up *Seduced by Fire*."   —That's What I'm Talking About

"[Me] writes a well-flowing, easy-to-read book. . . . There are intense emotions and very expressive scenes . . . steamy."

—Harlequin Junkie

"I am awed by Tara Sue Me . . . a very powerful book written with grace and style. The characters were brought to life with a love story that will leave you wanting for more."

—Guilty Pleasures Book Reviews

"[An] erotic and edgy story line . . . that will end with a HEA (for now)."   —The Reading Cafe

continued . . .

"I can't say enough good things about how Tara Sue Me was able to just let this story flow out of her. And let the reader come along for the ride. It was so well written. . . . This is the kind of erotic writing that makes the genre amazing."

—Debbie's Book Bag

The Training

"Very passionate. . . . The characters are very easy to relate to and there is a depth to their feelings that is intriguing and engaging . . . intense and very, VERY H-O-T. Definitely worth reading!" —Harlequin Junkie

"Written with a good sense of literary flow, keeping the story moving forward, keeping the characters balanced. . . . There is great emotion here . . . quite compelling." —Book Binge

"Hot and intense. . . . [I] look forward to Tara Sue Me's future endeavors." —The Good, the Bad, and the Unread

"The story of Nathaniel and Abby continues, but with an interesting twist . . . fascinating." —Bookish Temptations

The Dominant

"I was blown away." —The Good, the Bad, and the Unread

"This was truly an amazing read, and I found myself staying up until three a.m. just to finish it." —Louisa's Reviews

"Steamy. . . . I was shocked at the depth of it!"

—Under the Covers

"I love it when an author writes from the male POV . . . completely worth it."
—Bookish Temptations

The Submissive

"For those *Fifty Shades* fans pining for a little more spice on their e-reader . . . the *Guardian* recommends Tara Sue Me's Submissive Trilogy, starring handsome CEO Nathaniel West, a man on the prowl for a new Submissive, and the librarian Abby, who is yearning for something more."
—*Los Angeles Times*

"This book is going to make you say 'Fifty What of What?' . . . [Me] is so talented and captivating." —Southern Fiction Review

"Very spicy . . . quite well written and certainly entertaining."
—Dear Author

"An interesting read."
—The Book Cellar

"Wonderfully done, full of emotion and intensity . . . different from so many others out there."
—The Good, the Bad, and the Unread

"I really enjoyed the *heck* out of it."
—Under the Covers

ALSO BY TARA SUE ME

The Exhibitionist

The Submissive Series

TARA SUE ME

NEW AMERICAN LIBRARY

NEW AMERICAN LIBRARY
Published by New American Library,
an imprint of Penguin Random House LLC
375 Hudson Street, New York, New York 10014

This book is an original publication of New American Library.

First Printing, November 2015

For more information about Penguin Random House, visit penguin.com.

LIBRARY OF CONGRESS CATALOGING-IN-PUBLICATION DATA:

Me, Tara Sue.
The exhibitionist/Tara Sue Me.
p. cm.—(Submissive series)
ISBN 978-0-451-47452-0 (softcover)
1. Sexual dominance and submission—Fiction.
2. Man-woman relationships—Fiction.   I. Title.
PS3613.E123E97 2015
813'.6—dc23   2015018146

Printed in the United States of America
1   3   5   7   9   10   8   6   4   2

Penguin
Random
House

To my sister,
my secret keeper, my cheerleader, and friend.

Acknowledgments

When I started *The Submissive* in January 2009, I thought maybe ten people would read it. It was a new venture for me. Up until that point, I'd never written anything more graphic than a kiss. Truthfully, if you had told me everything that would happen as a result, I'd have had a good laugh, slapped you on the back, and told you that was the funniest thing I'd ever heard.

Well, what can I say? Life is funny sometimes.

Since I took that step forward and opened the bedroom door in my writing, so many incredible things have happened. I've met some of my closest friends and I'm now able to spend my days doing what I love.

And though I never planned to write Nathaniel and Abby beyond *The Training*, it's been a lot of fun visiting with them again. Of course, I can't do this alone, and I'm forever thankful for the people who helped me.

Christin, who helped me with the German parts. Any error is all me.

Tina, who very graciously read and gave me feedback.

Elle, who is always there for me to brainstorm with, laugh with, and share stories with. (P.S. Cole's next!)

Claire, Jenn, and the entire team at NAL, whose enthusiasm for Nathaniel and Abby keeps me going.

Steve, who made this possible.

My children, who ensure I actually turn the laptop off at times.

You, my readers, who encourage me. I wish it were possible to meet every single one of you.

And Mr. Sue Me, who doesn't bat an eye when I blurt out, "OMG, I JUST REALIZED WHAT HAPPENS NEXT!"

The
Exhibitionist

Chapter One

ABBY

The smell of lust filled the room. In fact, the sexual tension was so high I would bet most of the women present longed to be in the place of the lovely redhead. Currently standing in front of Cole Johnson, the Partners in Play group's newest senior Dominant, the petite woman trembled slightly. Although she was fully clothed, she displayed a vulnerability I was all too familiar with.

"Daniel told me she's been having difficulties focusing," my husband and Dominant, Nathaniel, said. We were at a play party being held at a private residence. He stood behind me, and though we were somewhat removed from the group, he still whispered. "He said he hopes the session with Cole will help."

"With everyone watching?" I asked. "That seems unlikely."

"I guess we'll see."

We couldn't hear Cole's voice; he spoke too softly. The

submissive's gaze drifted from him to the watching crowd. Bad move. Quick as a lightning strike, Cole grabbed her chin and forced her to meet his eyes.

"On me," he said, the threat in his voice noticeable before it dropped back down to a whisper.

"Perhaps he believes if she can focus while in the middle of a crowd, she can focus during anything," Nathaniel said.

There was probably some truth to that. The submissive certainly didn't appear to be tempted to look our way again. Then again, Cole had placed his hands on her shoulders and started a slow stroke up and down her arms. All the while, he kept his eyes locked on hers. I doubted there were many women who would be able to think about anything else if he was looking at them like that.

After a few minutes, he stepped back and spoke to her again. "As far as you're concerned, you and I are the only people in this room. Understand?"

She answered with a softly spoken, "Yes, Sir."

"Louder," he said. "Own your words."

"Yes, Sir," she repeated, this time with more confidence.

"You are to keep your eyes on mine the entire time we're together unless I tell you to do otherwise."

"Yes, Sir."

"What's your safe word?" Cole asked.

"Red, Sir."

"Thank you. Take your shirt off."

Her gaze briefly flickered to the floor.

"That's one, sub," Cole said, and she sucked in a breath. "Tell me what you did."

"I looked at the floor, Sir."

"And what were you supposed to do?"

"Keep my eyes on yours."

Cole nodded. "Take your shirt off the proper way."

This time, she kept her focus on him while she unbuttoned and slid the shirt off her shoulders. It fluttered to the floor.

"Very nice," Cole said. "Now remove your bra."

I wasn't a Dominant by any stretch, but I'd been an active submissive for long enough to know and recognize hesitation. Hell, I'd done it often enough myself, but I always learned something new when I was an observer. It was certainly interesting seeing things from a different perspective.

Cole took a step toward her. "On the checklist you filled out, how do you have *public nudity* listed?"

"As *won't object*, Sir."

"And how else am I to interpret your hesitation as anything other than objecting?"

"I don't know, Sir."

"That's because there is no other way. That's two. Now remove the bra."

She quickly reached behind her back to unsnap her bra, but my own focus was suddenly shifted to my husband's two hands, which were unbuttoning my shirt.

His voice was rough in my ear while his fingers stroked my breasts. "You like watching, don't you?"

"Especially with you teasing me like that with your hands, Master."

"You like teasing?" he asked.

I realized what I'd said and how he'd probably interpret my words. "Uh, well . . ."

He chuckled. "Too late. I'm going to thoroughly enjoy teasing you tonight, but for right now, watch Master Johnson."

In front of us, Cole had bound his submissive for the night with her arms above her head. Two identical floggers sat on top of a bag off to the side of where they were standing. From the look of them, he'd be demonstrating Florentine flogging.

Cole went right into the scene with both floggers, warming up the submissive with light and easy strokes. Interesting. Whenever Nathaniel used two floggers, he'd start by warming me up with a single one first. But the technique appeared to be working. The submissive's expression transformed into a look of complete bliss, and by the time Cole started putting more power behind his swing, she was in subspace.

I was transfixed by the sight of them. It appeared almost like a choreographed dance, the way his arms moved in time with her side-to-side sway.

"Very nice," Cole said to her. "I'm going to bring you down. No climax for you tonight, since you didn't follow directions at the beginning of the scene."

She started to protest, but he cut her off. "Unless you want me to demo how to properly discipline with two floggers, you'll keep that comment to yourself."

She wisely didn't say anything else and Cole's movements grew slower and slower.

I jumped when Nathaniel slipped a hand down my skirt.

"Someone liked watching," he said.

I pressed back against him and wiggled my butt across his erection. "Yes, Master."

"I'm going to flog that wiggly ass. Let's go to the garage."

The garage was set aside for public play and filled with all sorts of fun toys. Plus, there were always people observing the play scenes. It would be our first time being in the garage, and I smiled at the thought of finally being a participant.

I walked in front of him, nodding and smiling at the people we passed on our way. The party had been going on for about an hour and a half, so the house was filled to capacity. About half of the partygoers were in the garage. A laughing couple pushed past us on their way into the popular play space. I feared the garage would be too crowded, but when we made our way inside, I was happy to see that wasn't the case.

The room was large and clean and there were no cars. Different play stations had been set up with plenty of room between the areas for people to stand and observe without getting in the way of the people playing. Also, next to each station was a basket filled with cleaning spray and paper towels.

"I like the cleaning stations," I said to Nathaniel.

"Yes, it's important."

I stood for a minute just inside the doorway and tried to take in the entire scene. Between fifteen and twenty people were in the garage, and of those, about eight were engaged in play. The two padded benches and the padded table were occupied, as was the St. Andrew's cross. Both the people playing and those watching were being observed by the group Dungeon Monitor. He saw us and nodded.

I looked to Nathaniel for instructions and he nodded toward one of the remaining free areas: a whipping post. "On your knees in front of the post."

I crossed the floor and knelt down while I waited. I closed my

eyes to focus myself on serving him. I thoroughly enjoyed playing in front of others, but I never wanted my focus to drift from
where it was supposed to be.

"So you like it when I tease you?" he asked.

"Most of the time, Master."

"Whereas I, on the other hand, always enjoy teasing you." He
took a few steps and stood behind me. "And I love to hear you
beg. So tonight, I'm going to start a scene and we're going to
finish it at home. How does that sound?"

"Like a long ride home, Master."

He laughed. "And if you don't want it to be an even longer
night, you'll behave."

"Yes, Master."

"Stand up and face the post."

I rose to my feet and turned to the post, imagining how I
looked to the crowd as I did, and positioning myself to please
Nathaniel.

He ran his hands up my back and situated my arms so they
were above my head. "You would enjoy this better if you were
naked, wouldn't you?" he asked.

"Most things involving you are better if I'm naked, Master."

He gave my ass a slap. "Someone feels a little sassy tonight,
doesn't she?"

"Maybe just a little." I wiggled my butt, hoping he'd spank it
again.

But he didn't. Instead he moved my hands to two grips on the
post. "Don't let go and no speaking unless I ask a question."

He hadn't brought his toy bag with him, so I couldn't imagine
what he was going to do.

"I'm going to lift your skirt," he said. "Are you wearing anything under it?"

He was the one who had picked out my outfit before we left. So he knew the only thing under the skirt was me.

"No, Master."

"Everyone's going to see your ass. The only thing better would be if everyone saw me spank you."

I tried not to think about how much that thought turned me on. He said he was going to tease me, which probably meant he wasn't going to let me climax at the party.

He drew my skirt above my waist and I expected him to continue his upward trail, but instead his fingers slipped behind me and he pinched my butt. I bit the inside of my cheek to keep from making a noise.

"You're being so good," he said, keeping one hand on my ass and shifting the other to stroke my breast.

I relaxed against the post, enjoying the feel of his hands on me, the experience made more erotic by the accompanying sound track of sighs, whimpers, and moans from other couples in the garage. Nathaniel's hands finally made their way between my legs and I held my breath, anticipating his touch right where I needed it and reminding myself that no matter how good it felt, I could not make a noise.

"I'm going to finger-fuck you." Nathaniel's warm breath kissed my ear. "You can't make a noise and you can't come. Do either of the two and I won't let you come for two weeks."

I wasn't about to let that happen. I took a deep breath and started reciting German in my head, my tried-and-true way of delaying orgasm.

"Are you doing your German, Abigail?" he said, moving his fingers lightly over my clit and making me rise on my toes. "Are you?"

"Yes, Master."

"Do you think the German alphabet is going to keep your mind off the fact that I have my fingers inside you?"

"No, Master. Not entirely. Just enough. . . ." I arched against him as his fingers found that spot inside me that felt so good. "Just enough to help me . . . be good."

"There's a man in the far corner. He's in the shadows, so I can't make out who he is. He's watching us."

I sucked in a breath and almost let out a moan before I remembered I couldn't make a sound. *Fuck.* When I knew I was being watched, my skin broke out in delicious shivers and I became a puddle at Nathaniel's feet.

"I know you like that. I know it gets you off." His fingers moved faster. Deeper. "Too bad he won't be able to watch you come."

He stroked over and over and my release built within me. I started conjugating German verbs. Translated the preamble to the Constitution into German. Anything. Just when I thought my body was going to fall apart all over him, he slowed his movements.

He slipped his fingers out and straightened my skirt. "Are you okay?"

"Yes, Master."

"You can let go of the straps and stand up."

I straightened and turned. He watched me with his intense green gaze.

"You did very well, Abigail," he said, and I felt my heart flutter at his praise. "I'm going to have to think of a suitable reward."

He dropped his head and gave me a soft kiss, but his lips didn't linger. Pulling back, he brought his finger to my mouth. Without being told, I sucked it inside and licked, tasting myself and cleaning him.

When I finished, he kissed me again. "Very nice, Abigail."

I sighed and Nathaniel tightened his arms around me. The pounding need to have him inside me was still there. Yet it was tempered by the knowledge that he would reward me once we were home. Or, more to the point, when we were back at the hotel we were staying in for the weekend.

A few months ago when we were in Wilmington, Delaware, for a conference that Nathaniel was speaking at, we fell in love with the area and people. According to him, the tax rate was wonderful, so we decided to buy a place. Initially, we'd looked at the coast, but we soon discovered most of our time was spent in Wilmington and it only made sense to buy there.

I loved our new house. It was from early in the last century and filled with character. But more than that, it would be the first place we'd live in as a family that Nathaniel and I bought together. He'd inherited our Hamptons estate from his parents and our New York City penthouse he'd bought when he was still a bachelor. I owned a chalet in Switzerland that he had given me as a wedding present, but we only ever visited there. I was excited to have a space that was "ours."

Wilmington, Delaware, was also where the Partners in Play BDSM group was. One of the group's core Doms, Jeff Parks, had rescued me one night from a raunchy nightclub I'd made the mistake of going to with a friend and without Nathaniel. Another Dom, Daniel Covington, was a colleague of Nathaniel's. That's how we met the group. Since then, I'd become friends with both of their submissives. Dena was now engaged to Jeff, and Julie had moved in with Daniel a few months ago.

A phone call from Jeff a week ago had led to our visit tonight. Jeff had wanted Nathaniel to come down because there had been trouble within the group lately. Namely with two relatively new Doms. Nathaniel had been asked to help.

Now Nathaniel took my hand and we left our little corner of the garage. I was tempted to look around and try to locate the man who had been observing us. Without much thought, I decided not to. Sometimes the fantasy was better than the real thing.

He squeezed my hand. "Would you like something to drink?"

"Yes, Master." And sometimes reality was better than fantasy.

Nathaniel and I made our way into the kitchen, greeting only a few people. Nathaniel took a bottle of water from a cooler and we walked into the living room.

He nodded to the floor and I sat at his feet while he sat on the couch. We were experimenting with different levels of protocol to see what we liked and what worked for us. Sitting at his feet was something we'd been trying lately and I was surprised to discover I liked it. In that position, I felt protected and secure.

He opened the bottle and pressed it to my lips.

"Thank you, Master," I said when I'd had my fill.

The door to the room's left opened and Cole and the red-headed submissive stepped out. He spoke to her softly and stroked her cheek. She left him with a smile on her face and a spring in her step.

Cole was still somewhat of an enigma to me. According to

Dena, he'd broken up with his long-term girlfriend several months earlier. He usually traveled for his work, and I gathered the breakup was his reason for staying in Delaware as long as he had. He was a journalist and a good one; I'd read some of his articles. I wrote for a national news blog, and since he was a writer, I was interested in getting to know him better.

Cole spotted us and headed our way.

"Master West," he said, shaking Nathaniel's hand.

"Master Johnson."

Cole inclined his head in my direction. "I haven't been formally introduced to your Abby yet."

I wasn't allowed to interact with Doms at a party unless Nathaniel gave me permission, so I remained where I was.

"We must correct that." Nathaniel smiled at me. "Come meet Master Johnson, Abigail."

I moved to my feet and waited to be introduced.

"Master Johnson, this is my Abby." Nathaniel lifted my hand and kissed my knuckles. "She is my everything."

I didn't miss the subtle lift of Cole's eyebrows or Nathaniel's slight nod. Granted permission to touch me, Cole held out his hand.

"Very nice to formally meet you Abby."

I shook his hand. "The feeling is mutual, Sir."

"I understand you're a writer," he said.

"I just write a blog for WNN, Sir," I said, slightly taken aback that he knew anything about me. It wasn't a secret, of course. It was just, he was a *writer* writer.

"You express yourself through written words. You're a writer."

"And a damn good one," Nathaniel added.

The corner of Cole's mouth lifted in what could only be called a devilish grin. "I know. I've read her blog."

"You have?" I nearly squeaked, and then remembered where I was and composed myself. "I mean, you have, Sir?"

He chuckled. "Yes. And you shouldn't demean it by saying it's only a blog."

"Thank you, Sir. I'll try to remember that." I wanted to return the praise. "I'm really enjoying the series of articles you're writing based on your time in India, Sir."

All traces of joviality left his expression, and darkness covered his face. I wasn't sure what I had said to upset him, but now I wished I hadn't spoken at all.

"It was a *unique* experience," he finally said.

"It's a unique country," I said.

"Yes. There are parts that are breathtakingly beautiful and I met some incredible people. But I think—" He looked pained. "I think I won't be going back."

I was momentarily stunned, since his articles seemed filled with a real love for India, but fortunately I was saved from any long, awkward silences by the appearance of Jeff and Dena.

"There you guys are," Dena said. She was holding hands with Jeff, and they both looked so happy I couldn't help smiling along with them. I spared a quick look back at Cole, but whatever had upset him was forgotten. The devilish grin had returned.

"What's going on?" Cole asked.

Dena spotted Daniel and Julie in the hallway and waved them over.

"What's happening?" Daniel asked.

"I'm wondering the same thing," Cole said.

Dena looked so excited I wouldn't have been surprised if she started bouncing up and down. "We set a date!" she finally said.

"A date for what?" Cole asked, and Dena's smile temporarily deflated. Nathaniel thumped him on the shoulder. "Just teasing, you guys. Congratulations!"

"I love weddings," I said. "Tell us when it is."

Jeff replied with a date less than two months away.

Dena held up her hands as we all started speaking at once. "I know it's short notice, but it'll be small. We thought about just having the justice of the peace do it, but since our collaring ceremony was private, we thought better of it."

Jeff slipped his arm around Dena and kissed her forehead. "I was the one pushing for a private ceremony."

"Thank goodness she didn't go for your idea," Daniel said. "I've been waiting on this day."

"But if she had," Jeff said, "we'd be married already."

"There is that," Daniel said.

Dena had stayed with us at our Hamptons estate recently. Jeff had been out of town caring for his terminally ill father, and because she'd been getting threats from a stalker, we'd offered for her to stay with us. She was a prosecutor and her father was a prominent politician, so no one was sure who was threatening her. That was all in the past now, but Dena and I had become good friends during the weeks she'd stayed with us and I knew exactly how happy she was to be marrying Jeff.

I didn't know Jeff quite as well, but I'd actually met him first, and one of the things I picked up on was an underlying sadness about him. There was no sadness now. Only joy and, as he gazed down at the woman who wore both his collar and his engagement ring, love.

It made me a bit nostalgic for the early days of my relationship with Nathaniel when everything was so new and we couldn't keep our hands off each other. Of course, we still didn't want to, but it was harder to find time to ourselves. I hoped the move to Delaware would mean more time at home for him and allow us to connect more.

"Angel," Jeff said, "didn't you want to talk to Abby and Julie privately?"

"Yes, as long as it's okay with Masters West and Covington."

"Of course," Daniel said, dropping a kiss on Julie's cheek. "Don't stay away too long. I have a new toy."

The brunette's eyes lit up. "Yes, Master."

"I don't have a new toy," Nathaniel whispered in my ear. "I just want to fuck you."

My knees almost turned to jelly. "Yes, Master."

"Hurry back to me," he said.

I would. I definitely would.

Dena took us up the stairs to the small bedroom that wasn't in use. The house belonged to William Greene, a Dominant I had only met in passing. The lack of furniture and minimal decorating led me to believe he lived alone.

"I wanted to wait until Sasha was here, too," Dena said. "But I'm not sure when all of us will be together. I'll tell you guys and will catch up with Sasha later."

"Everything's okay, right?" I asked.

Her eyes lit up, and I swore she was so excited they sparkled. "Everything's great. I'm pregnant."

Julie's hand flew to her mouth, and tears filled my eyes. Dena had already had one late-term miscarriage. She had told me part of her history with Jeff while she was living with us. I had been fortunate, both my pregnancies were trouble free and full term. I could only imagine how scary a pregnancy would be following a miscarriage. At the moment, though, she didn't look frightened. She positively glowed.

"I thought it was strange you didn't have a corset on tonight," Julie said, and then pulled the willowy blonde into a hug.

Dena smoothed a hand over her short skirt and cropped shirt. "Yes, this isn't my normal party outfit by any stretch, but my corsets are going into storage for the next eight months."

"What does Jeff think?" I asked.

"Jeff's completely besotted," she said. "He reads *Goodnight Moon* to my belly every night. I told him hearing hadn't developed yet, but he said since no one knew exactly when it did, there was no harm in it."

"I love watching strong men get all melty because of a baby," I said, remembering Nathaniel with our kids.

Dena nodded. "There is nothing hotter, that's for sure. We haven't publicly announced anything yet, so please don't tell anyone. I had to tell you guys, because, well, I just did."

"How are you doing?" Julie asked.

"Scared to death," Dena said with a tight laugh. "Trying to relax, but going crazy with each ache, pain, and cramp. Jeff's so good. He's a great listener and he gives the best back rubs. But I know it's hard for him, too."

"I imagine so," I said.

"I don't think I'll completely relax until I bring this baby home."

Julie reached for her hand. "I'm glad you told us. Now you have Jeff, Abby, and me to talk to."

"Thanks." Dena wiped a tear from her face. "Damn pregnancy hormones. Anyway, I also wanted to ask you guys if you'd stand with me at the wedding. I'm going to ask Sasha, too."

"Yes!" Julie nearly shouted, and I hugged Dena and told her I'd be honored.

"Jeff wants to get married before the baby's born. I told him that was fine, but I wasn't walking down the aisle looking like a whale."

"Oh, we'll go wedding dress shopping," Julie said. "All four of us."

"It'll have to be soon." Dena looked over at me. "Can you go this weekend, Abby?"

I shook my head. "No, we're starting the move this weekend. But don't let me hold you up. You go without me."

"We'll see how it goes. I hate for you not to be there," Dena said.

I hated to miss it. Wedding dress shopping was fun.

"What do your parents think about your wedding plans?" I asked.

"Mom wouldn't care who I married as long as it meant there would be the potential for grandchildren in the future. But she's taking her directions from Dad and he's not speaking with me."

I winced. "Sorry to hear that. Will they be at the wedding?"

"Only if I marry someone other than Jeff, but that's okay." I knew Dena's father was a bit of snob and didn't approve of Jeff's working-class background. "I stopped needing their approval a long time ago. And to be honest, it'll be better without them."

"I'm so happy for you guys," I said. "Everyone should be as happy as you two are."

"I think we both finally realized we deserved happiness."

If anyone deserved happiness, it was Jeff and Dena. They'd gone through so much to be together. But like with the journey Nathaniel and I were on, those hardships only served to make their relationship stronger.

"Okay," Julie said. "I hate to cut this short, but I'm dying to see what Daniel has planned for tonight."

We hugged good-bye and went our separate ways. Nathaniel was waiting at the foot of the stairs and crooked a finger at me when he saw me.

Oh yes, I couldn't wait to see his plans.

Chapter Two

NATHANIEL

"I want you to go inside the suite and head to the bedroom," I said when we pulled up to our hotel. "Kneel on the rug and while you wait, I want you to think about what I promised I'd do to you when we got home."

Her sharp intake of breath left no doubt in my mind that she remembered, but just because I wanted to hear her say it, I asked, "What am I going to do when I get into the bedroom, Abigail?"

"You said you would fuck me properly, Master."

"That's my plan."

She shifted her weight impatiently from side to side on the elevator ride and once I unlocked the door, I simply said, "Go."

While she got ready, I sat on the couch and wrote out my observations of the group party. The first thing that concerned me was how lax security had seemed. There was one member working the door and one Dungeon Monitor on duty. One person at the door was enough, but it seemed to be asking a lot for one person to oversee the entire party as DM.

I tapped my pen on the notebook. What we needed was a place with video cameras so DMs could keep an eye on every room at once. And more acting DMs. Hard to get more DMs when the group itself only numbered around twenty regular attendees, with an additional fifteen or so casual members. And the only person whose house had cameras was Daniel, and even he didn't have them installed inside. I couldn't very well make a recommendation that a host house had to have cameras.

Things to think on another day and time. For tonight, I belonged to Abby and I was going to focus my attention and time on her.

She waited for me the way I'd requested, nude and kneeling in the middle of the floor. Her breathing was deep and even and her posture was relaxed, yet still at attention, so I knew she was waiting for me to speak.

There were no words to describe how I felt whenever I saw her waiting for me like this. Through the years, I'd tried to come up with them, but they somehow always fell short of capturing the emotion that swelled in my chest and the humility I felt at receiving her submission.

"You are amazing," I said to her. "Absolute perfection."

She didn't say anything because I hadn't given her permission to speak, but I saw her cheeks flush. Everything that was beautiful was captured in her. She would point to her breasts that weren't as firm as they used to be since she'd had two children, or she'd mention her belly that wasn't as perfectly flat, even though she worked out hard trying to make it so. I saw those things, too, and thought they made her even more beautiful because they were the markings of a body that had grown, nourished, and created the new life that was our children. To me, they were the badges of her love for me.

My need for her grew, and the group's troubles left my mind. "On your back with your ass at the edge of the bed."

She rose gracefully and moved to the bed. Her hips swayed seductively and the curve of her ass begged me to spank it. I'd have to do that later. She climbed onto the bed and got into position. When we'd checked in, she mentioned how much she liked the white bedding. Personally, I thought it was ironic—all that pure white bedding as a backdrop for all the wicked things I would do to her body.

"Touch yourself," I told her. "Are you still wet after being flogged?"

I could see she was, but I wanted to see her finger herself. I unbuckled my pants and stepped out of them.

"Look at me," I commanded. I fisted my cock and gave it a few pumps with my hand. "Are you wet?"

"Yes, Master." Her voice was heavy with lust and need.

"Being tied up and flogged turned you on."

The evidence of her arousal was slick against her upper thighs. I wanted to taste her, but feared that might push her over the edge. She'd been holding back her orgasm for over an hour by now. I moved to stand between her legs and slipped two fingers inside.

"Hell, yes. Feel that. How wet you are."

Her lower body strained with the effort to remain still. Just that small movement showed how much she trusted me. She purposely held off letting herself orgasm because she trusted me to let her come when I knew it would bring her the most pleasure. Even now, holding still, she did it because it was what I expected and she wanted to please me. And she knew in doing so, I would please her.

I removed my fingers and brought them up to her mouth. "Suck them. Prove how much you want me. How much you want my cock."

She took me deep inside her mouth, running her tongue around and between my fingers.

With my free hand I cupped her breast and while she gave my fingers a hard suck, I pinched her nipple. "It's been too long since I've had clamps on you. I think the next weekend the kids are gone, I'm going to have you go topless all day and every so often I'll decorate you with clamps and then have you go about your day, your breasts marked for my viewing pleasure."

Her soft moan told me she would like that.

"Maybe I'll have you go topless to the next group meeting, wearing only my clamps." I pinched her other nipple. "Or maybe I'll use clamps with bells and then fuck you, so every time I push inside your pussy, they ring. Would you like that?"

"Yes, Master. Yes to both."

I loved playing with her breasts. I wished I had my crop with me. It would be fun to flick the tip of the crop against her nipples. But, unfortunately, I hadn't brought my toy bag with me for the weekend and all my implements were back in New York. I smiled. Good thing I knew how to improvise.

Instead I flicked her nipples with my fingers. It wasn't expected and she gasped. Feeling slightly evil, I held one breast and flicked the nipple again and again.

"Oh, God. Oh, *fuck*," she panted almost in time with my flicks.

Her positive response turned me on and I wanted to drive

her even more out of her mind with pleasure. I brought my knee up to rest between her legs, pushing against her slightly, and she moaned at the unexpected sensation.

"You're so wet. So needy." I pressed it harder. "I bet I could make you come just like this."

I moved my knee back and forth, making sure to hit her in different spots and every so often, rubbing her clit. Then I gave her nipple a flick with every stroke of her clit until she was writhing under me.

"I like watching you squirm. Rocking your body with the pleasure I give you. Makes me so hard. Fucking turns me on."

I switched to her other breast and flicked that nipple, still pressing my knee where I knew it would drive her mad.

"That's it. Push against me. Show me how much you need me to fill that pussy." She wiggled against me, desperate for more. "You want it? You want my cock?"

"Yes. Please, Master."

"Since you asked so nicely." I put my foot back on the floor. I lifted her hips, brought them in line with my cock, and slowly eased into her.

Her breasts were red from my earlier attention. *Mine.* I loved taking her after a play session when my marks were still visible on her skin. Loved how it showed she was mine and mine alone and I would take her knowing she would never wear another man's marks.

With that thought consuming my mind, I thrust into her completely. *Fuck. So good* competed with *Mine, only and forever mine.*

"Oh, my God. Yes," she said, bucking upward to draw me deeper.

I held tightly to her waist and pulled out so only the tip of me was left inside. Because I still felt a little evil, I made shallow thrusts, bouncing the tip in and out of her.

She whined.

"Who decides how much cock you get?"

"You do, Master."

"That's right." I pulled out completely and watched her struggle not to beg. To be even more mean, I took my cock in one hand and slapped it a few times against her clit. "Maybe I think that's all the cock you'll get. What about that?"

She gyrated against the bed. "Please."

"Please more?" I rubbed my length along her slit and across the sensitive bundle of nerves there. Then I ended it with another handful of slaps. "How long do you think I can torment your little clit until you come?"

"Not long, Master." Her eyes captured mine and I saw how hard she was working to hold back her climax.

"I think you've been a very good girl today. So I'm going to give you all of my cock." I put the head right at her entrance again. "All at once," I said, driving into her fully.

"Damn." Her eyes fluttered shut. "Fuck. Me."

"Come when you want."

I pulled out and thrust over and over, going deeper inside with each forward motion into her body. She arched her back and pushed her hips toward mine, in time with me, drawing me even farther inside.

"I never want to stop being inside you." I thrust again. "There's nowhere else my dick would rather be."

Her climax shook her body on my next push into her.

"Such a good girl. Coming all over my dick." I took some lube I had put on the bed earlier and squeezed it over a finger. "I want you to come again."

"Oh God. Oh God. Oh God," she chanted as I pushed a finger into her ass.

"It's only a finger," I said. "Not nearly as big as a cock. Of course, when I do this . . ." I hooked my finger a bit so it stroked me as I moved within her. The feel of her inner walls separating my cock and finger was amazing. I could only imagine how it felt for her. "I feel my cock fucking your pussy."

She was lost in sensation and bliss. Pleasure filled her eyes. I added a second finger.

"Maybe I'll fuck your ass and finger my cock through your pussy."

At my words, she gave a lazy nod. I thrust deeper inside.

"I'm going to come," she whispered.

"Yes, you are."

Her second climax was just as intense as her first. As her inner muscles squeezed me, I knew I couldn't hold back any longer. I gasped as I released inside her. *Fuck.* It'd been a long time since I came so hard. We were both still and breathing hard for a long time.

Finally, I drew her close and kissed her. "You made me so proud tonight." She sighed and burrowed into my arms, mumbling something under her breath I couldn't make out.

"What was that?" I asked.

"Love you."

I smiled. "Love you, too."

Chapter Three

ABBY

The following weekend, I made my way to our bedroom, running the obstacle course comprising moving boxes, bubble wrap, and tape. The packers we'd hired had been busy all day getting together the items we planned to take to Delaware. Most of the boxes were half-filled, though a few had already been taped up. Several empty ones lined the hallway. But no matter how much they held, they all had one thing in common—they were brown.

"I've decided brown is my least favorite color," I announced to Nathaniel as I finally made it into our room.

"The most boring of all colors," he agreed. He stood beside the bed, going through an open box. "Did Elizabeth settle down?"

"Yes, she wants to know when Jeff and Dena's baby will be able to play and she didn't quite grasp there were still seven months until he or she is born. And then she wanted to know how the baby got into Dena's belly in the first place."

Nathaniel laughed. "I wasn't expecting that conversation just yet. I thought we had a few more years."

I rummaged through my drawer, looking for pajamas. "You've got ten hours. I told her to ask you in the morning." He stopped laughing and I giggled at his expression. "I'm kidding. I told her we'd talk about it later, that it was too late tonight. Have you seen my blue-striped pajamas?"

He nodded. "I put them in with the winter clothes yesterday. They're in a box somewhere."

I shut the drawer closed with more force than was necessary. "Everything's in disarray. Nothing's where I can find it."

It was a slight exaggeration. We weren't packing everything. And *we* technically weren't packing anything. We'd hired a company to do that for us. But it still didn't take away from the fact that I couldn't put my hands on my favorite set of pajamas when I wanted them.

"In about another hour you won't need pajamas anyway," he said, taking the box off the bed.

He was right, of course. It was a Friday night and he'd collared me a few hours ago. We were experimenting with lower protocol outside the playroom. A useful thing, since thus far our scheduled collar time had consisted of boxes, trying to get the kids to sleep, boxes, taking Apollo outside, and boxes.

"But I'd like to wear something comfortable until then," I said, and then quickly added, "Sir."

I needed a few hours in the playroom. Needed to let him take over and make all the decisions. I felt stressed and frazzled. When I got that way, there was one thing guaranteed to make it all better: kneeling at Nathaniel's feet.

My phone buzzed with an incoming e-mail. I pulled my cell out of my pocket and sighed when I saw it was from Meagan, my boss. A few months ago, the blog I wrote detailing my submissive journey came to the attention of a large media network. They offered me a job writing content for the women's sexuality section of their Web site, as well as posts about BDSM for their late-night talk show on women's health. Occasionally, I'd also appear on the show to answer questions.

I scanned Meagan's e-mail. The topic for Monday night's live episode had been changed, thanks to a particularly virulent case of the flu hitting several of the guests scheduled to talk. That meant the blog post I'd prepared wouldn't work.

"Damn," I said. "I told her we were moving starting this weekend. A new post will take a ton of research. I don't know how she expects me to fit four days of work into one."

"Will you need to work tomorrow?" Nathaniel asked.

"At some point," I said with a huff, rubbing my forehead. "Damn. Damn. Damn. Like I didn't have five thousand other things to do, now I have five thousand and one."

"Look at it this way, now you have an entire week's work done for a future show."

I sighed. "Since Linda's watching the kids while we finish up packing this weekend, I really wanted to enjoy some alone time with you. Especially since tomorrow night will be our last night here." Thank goodness for Nathaniel's aunt. I wasn't sure what we were going to do in Delaware without her.

A strange look crossed his face, surprise or maybe guilt. "It's not our last night by any stretch of the imagination."

I waved my hand. "You know what I mean," I said, looking for another pair of pajamas.

"Abigail."

I looked up.

"This will all work out. I have to go into the city tomorrow for work, and because my meeting is so late, I'll spend the night."

"What?" He was going to leave me with a half-packed house?

"I have a late meeting with Charlene. Linda will still get the kids, so you'll have time to do your work."

All the stress of the move suddenly mixed together with my irritation at having to rewrite the work I'd done, and Nathaniel's late-night meeting with Charlene was the cherry on top of an ice-cream sundae of total crap.

"When were you planning on telling me?" I asked.

"I just found out this afternoon."

"That woman has got some nerve setting up a meeting for our last weekend home, when I'm wearing your collar, and she *knows* we're moving." I crossed my arms. "It's like she's a mind reader and knows exactly what to do to piss me off."

"Abigail." His voice was a warning, but Charlene was like a trigger for me.

"Tell her you'll meet her Monday night."

"You'll be at the station. And Linda can't keep the kids then."

I crossed my arms. "There has to be something you can do."

"Oh, there is." He spoke calmly, but we'd been married enough years for me to know he could conceal his anger behind a mask of calm.

"Then do it."

His voice was low and soft when he spoke. "Kneel."

His command caught me off guard, but one look at his tense expression let me know he meant business. I abandoned my search for pajamas and dropped to my knees.

"Just to make sure we're both on the same page, are you currently wearing my collar?"

I swallowed. *Damn it.* Charlene had a way of getting me in trouble without even being here. "Yes, Master."

"I know we're experimenting with some lower protocol, but that does not give you free rein to speak however you wish. I know you have issues with Charlene. You have not made this a secret."

Damn straight I haven't made it a secret.

"This is after you have repeatedly stated that you trust my choice of employee and that you trust me around her. Isn't that correct?"

"Yes, Master," I admitted begrudgingly.

"Furthermore, why do you assume it was Charlene who set up the meeting?"

I didn't have a response to that.

"I set up the meeting," he continued. "She wanted to meet Monday night. I told her that wouldn't work because you would be at the station and I knew the kids would be with Linda tomorrow and one of us needed to be home. I *actually* thought I was doing you a favor by giving you some time to yourself. I know this week has been hectic for you."

"May I speak, Master?" It seemed prudent to slip back into higher protocol.

"Yes."

"I appreciate the fact that you were thinking about me and wanted to give me some alone time tomorrow, and I understand why you didn't want to meet with her on Monday night." I paused, trying to formulate in my head how to word the next bit. "But you are also aware of how I feel about her, and it just raises the question, how did you think I'd react?"

"Have you or have you not told me you trust my choice of employee and you trust me enough to know I would never break my vows to you?"

My stomach sank as I picked up on where he was going. "Yes, Master. I've said that."

"In fact, you've said that repeatedly. Correct?"

"Yes, Master."

"*That* is why I thought you might have a different response."

He was right, I'd told him that several times. But saying it was different from living it. "I'm sorry, Master."

He was silent for several seconds. "I'm not sure what it's going to take in order for you to understand that Charlene is not a threat to us. What is a threat is this jealousy that is completely unfounded. It makes you seem petty, and you're not a petty person."

He hadn't asked a question, so I didn't speak. I almost apologized again but changed my mind. He didn't seem to be in a mood for multiple apologies.

"I'm not sure what your writing schedule looks like tomorrow, but I want you to take time to write out ten things you can do to overcome your issues with Charlene."

"Yes, Master."

"Then you are to draft a schedule for implementing them. We will discuss both on Tuesday."

I nodded.

"That's tomorrow, though," he said. "For tonight, I want you in the playroom in five minutes."

He left the bedroom. Probably to prepare for whatever it was he had in mind. I wasn't sure if he'd had a scene planned before my outburst about Charlene or not. If he had, I was willing to bet it'd changed.

I undressed quickly and walked to the playroom. Nathaniel was there already, his back to me as he worked with something in a far cabinet. I closed and locked the door behind me, shooting a quick glance to a nearby shelf where the steady green lights of the child monitors ensured that we'd hear either child if one needed us. Elizabeth was four and typically slept through the night, but almost-two-year-old Henry had a history of ear infections and never slept well.

Nathaniel hadn't moved and didn't say anything, so I made my way to the middle of the room and knelt. I looked down at the floor and fell almost immediately into my yoga breathing. I breathed in the calm of the playroom and exhaled the stress of my jealousy.

He didn't come to me immediately, perhaps allowing me time to get in my headspace. When he did walk toward me, I heard him place several things behind me.

"This is not a discipline session; it's a lesson in trust," he said. "However, because it's a lesson and not a play scene, you're not allowed to come. Understand?"

"Yes, Master." *Damn it.*

"I'm also going to film our session," he said. "Stand for me, Abigail."

He'd recently installed a video camera in the playroom and occasionally filmed our time together. It added another layer of excitement for me. I hurried to my feet and he took down the chains above my head and buckled my wrists into the cuffs. He walked to stand in front of me.

"This is going to be intense." He reached above my head and wrapped my fingers around a bell. "Drop it to safe word."

My heart pounded. There was only one reason he'd give me a bell to stop the scene. My suspicion was confirmed when he took a ball gag out of his pocket. *Holy hell.* It'd been a long time since we used a gag. Even though he told me I wouldn't be coming, arousal warmed low in my belly.

"Open," he said, and slid the gag into place.

Next he withdrew a blindfold and covered my eyes. I thought he'd start the scene, but instead he brushed my hair back and pulled it into a low ponytail.

"I've taken away your sight, and your ability to talk and move. Now I'm going to take your hearing. You will be totally and completely at both my mercy and disposal. Nod if you understand."

I normally loved this type of scene, but normally I was given permission to orgasm. I wasn't nearly as excited as I typically would be. I nodded.

"You have the bell to drop if this becomes too much. Drop it and we stop immediately."

He normally didn't take so much time reminding me of my

safe words or in this case, safe out signal. For the first time in a long while, I felt a twinge of nervousness.

"If you don't have any objection, I'm going to insert the earplugs."

My fist tightened on the bell. I didn't want to drop it, but I felt reassured just knowing it was there.

He waited a few more seconds and then I was plunged into total nothingness.

Everything was already black from the blindfold, but it wasn't until the earplugs were put in that I felt truly vulnerable.

There was nothing but silent darkness and I was naked and exposed. I allowed the feelings of being in such a position to wash over me, only relishing the fear because I felt completely safe.

I waited for Nathaniel's touch. When I'd been in similar positions before, I'd jump when he touched me, and this time I wanted to be prepared. I waited for his touch, anticipating it on my back, or my breasts, or my ass. But there was nothing.

There was no movement at all that I could perceive. Just stillness and darkness and silence. Nathaniel would never leave me alone in such a state. I knew he had to be in the room somewhere. But my mind wandered. He *could* have walked out of the room and left me all alone. I wouldn't have been able to tell.

The silence became deafening, and I imagined I heard the shuffling of feet or a creak of the floorboard. The stillness hummed inside my head and I heard my heart beating and felt the movement of air in and out of my lungs. It was the only thing to grasp on to, so I focused on my breathing.

Even though I said I would anticipate his touch, the first sweep of his fingers down my back made me jump. He pressed against me, and his body shook with laughter. I smiled. Some things never changed. With a quick kiss to the nape of my neck, he was gone.

I was prepared for his touch, but the sharp press of metal along my upper arm almost made me drop the bell.

Is that a knife?

I knew it wasn't. Blood play was one of my hard limits. But it felt like a knife and it had stung and, holy shit, there was something wet on my skin. Panic clawed at my throat.

The feel of metal left my skin and his arms surrounded me, hugging me tight.

I was safe. I was safe. I was safe.

I repeated the words over and over in my head, and relaxed into his arms. Gradually, my racing heart slowed and the panic disappeared. He took a step back and the sharp pain returned, skimming along the other arm. I lifted myself up on my toes and twisted to get away from it, but he slapped my butt as a reminder I was to be still.

I argued with myself. It felt so much like a knife, it had to be a knife. But just as certainly, I knew it couldn't be. He would never go against my hard limits.

Trust him. The scene was all about trusting him. And I trusted him enough to know beyond a shadow of doubt, he wasn't cutting me.

I felt the next sweep of whatever instrument it was around my breast, and though I'd told myself it wasn't a knife, it again felt sharp. I tried to protest around the gag in my mouth. But of course I couldn't. He dragged whatever it was up across my nipple. It hurt, but it wasn't a constant pain. I sucked in my breath. That meant it wasn't a knife, right? I couldn't decide. For long seconds there was nothing, just my mantra repeating in my head: *I'm safe, I'm safe, I'm safe.*

He circled the other breast and, *fuck it all*, it felt as if he was slicing my skin. My fingers tightened around the ball. But right before I dropped it, I realized the liquid couldn't be blood; there wasn't enough.

I waited for the next pass and he surprised me by pressing it down my side. I gasped around the gag. He didn't stop, but brought it around my back and up the other side. I jerked against the pressure, but he wouldn't stop unless I dropped the bell.

Trust.

Trust.

Trust.

I focused on that one word, and before long, I was drifting in my head. I trusted him with my life. He held my soul in his hands and would protect me.

I wasn't sure how much time passed before I realized he was simply holding me. He'd somehow managed to unbuckle me without me noticing. He stood behind me, his arms once more wrapped tightly around me.

His hands came up and gently, one at a time, he removed the earplugs. Sound came back to me in a loud whoosh. But it was his voice I listened for, and when it came it was low and husky.

"I'm so proud of you. I know that was intense."

I still had the gag on, so I couldn't speak, but I nodded to show him I'd heard.

"I'm going to remove the gag now," he said.

It fell away and I worked my jaw open and closed several times. He wiped my mouth with a soft cloth. "Are you okay?"

"Yes, Master." I couldn't say much else because I felt I was still on sensory overload.

"I'm going to remove the blindfold."

I closed my eyes, knowing even the dimly lit playroom would appear bright after I'd been in the darkness for so long. Even when the blindfold was removed, I kept my eyes closed for a minute. Then I slowly eased them open.

The first thing I did was look down at my body. I couldn't help it. As I suspected, there were no cuts, only faint red lines that appeared to be fading quickly.

"Go ahead and look," he said. "I don't blame you at all."

My mouth felt as if I'd eaten cotton for dinner, but I managed to get out "What *was* that, Master?"

His only reply was a chuckle. "Top-secret Dom tool."

I turned in his arms. "I knew you wouldn't cut me, Master." And as I said the words out loud, their significance hit me.

He wouldn't cut me emotionally, either.

Chapter Four

NATHANIEL

I arrived at my New York City office about three hours before my meeting with Charlene. I'd planned to get some work done while I waited, but I found myself unable to concentrate. My mind kept returning to the night before. I felt at a loss because I didn't know how to break through and alleviate Abby's suspicions about Charlene.

I gave up on working and walked over to the large picture window in my office. I watched the general flow of people on the street far below and decided I needed some air.

I'd always felt there was something to be said for allowing oneself to get lost in the city, to become one with the crush of people. The city was alive, and to mix in and become part of it was to feel that life seep into your soul and revive the sluggish parts.

For the next forty-five minutes I simply walked. The last time I'd gone for a pleasure walk in New York was in December when Abby and I had gone Christmas shopping. Now I walked by a few of Abby's favorite shops, wishing she was with me. Before I knew it, I found myself going into a rare-book store that she loved.

Though my parents had been avid book collectors and had built the estate's massive library, it wasn't until I shared the space with Abby that I truly learned to appreciate it. We had added a few volumes to the collection over the years, but we were always looking for more.

The shopkeeper, Jeremiah, saw me and waved me over. He was an older gentleman with white hair and walked with a hunch. Perhaps from spending so much time bent over one of his beloved books.

"Mr. West," he said with a grin when I made it to the worn wooden counter. "I was going to call your wife. I had a book come in earlier this week that I think she would like."

I didn't doubt him. Before we had kids, Abby and I would visit the shop on weekends and she would go through boxes of books with Jeremiah. I'd enjoyed simply standing nearby and watching her joy at new discoveries.

"What do you have?" I asked, peering over the counter.

"First-edition Lord Byron—1815 *Hebrew Melodies*." He stated it with pride.

I looked over the well-kept volume. "An excellent find."

He craned his neck to look over my shoulder. "Is Mrs. West with you this afternoon?"

"No, unfortunately, she's at home. Had some work to catch up on." I was already reaching for my credit card. "But this is just the thing for me to give her tomorrow since I have to stay in the city overnight."

Jeremiah's white head nodded as he rang me up and wrapped the book. I, meanwhile, was thinking back to a cold winter night.

A night I'd entered the library to find Abby, who'd only been my sexual submissive at the time, combing through the poetry section. What followed was a game of quotes that ended with her naked in my lap and a moment of passion that forever changed me.

"Mr. West?" Jeremiah held the book up.

"Thank you," I said, taking the package from him and promising to give Abby his regards.

I made my way back to the office and pulled out my notes for the upcoming meeting with Charlene. The trip to the bookstore had made me melancholy and I thought about driving home after we'd finished. Once there, I could take Abby back into the playroom for a different kind of scene from what I'd done last night.

But she had work she had to do, and even though she probably wouldn't want to admit it, I was willing to bet she was looking forward to some alone time. With two kids, her job, and our playtime, she didn't have much time that was hers alone. My fingers hovered above my phone and I thought about calling, but a sharp knock on my office door stopped me.

"Charlene," I said, opening the door. "Thank you for meeting with me on a Saturday."

"Don't mention it," she said, breezing past me. "I'm just glad we were able to work something out before I left town."

I tried to imagine her from Abby's perspective. Charlene was a lovely woman, with blond hair and blue eyes. I was sure other men would find her attractive, but she didn't even compare to my Abby. I'd hired Charlene to run my late uncle's nonprofit because my involvement had gotten unmanageable and I counted myself fortunate to have found her. She was a hard worker and had done more in a few months than I could have accomplished in a year.

I motioned to the couch near the large window and we sat down.

For the next few hours we went through the accounts and I signed all the papers she'd brought for me. When we finished, I leaned back in my seat.

"Can I get you something to drink?" I asked.

"You can do better than that," she said, putting her documents inside her tote bag. "I'm free for dinner."

"I better not." It was certainly tempting, since I was otherwise eating alone and Charlene was a delightful conversationalist. Still, even though I knew nothing would ever happen between the two of us, there were several reasons it wasn't a good decision to go out to dinner with her. For one, Abby wouldn't like it and two, people would see us together.

"Just saying." She tucked a piece of hair behind her ear. "A bit of company would be preferable to an empty penthouse."

"Charlene," I said with more force than necessary. "I do not enjoy repeating myself endlessly, nor do I like being badgered. I'm having dinner alone tonight. Do you understand?"

Her eyes had grown dark. "Yes, sir."

It was not unheard of for employees to call me *sir*. However, I had been a Dominant long enough to know the difference between a business associate using the title and a submissive's yielding. Our eyes locked and a moment of recognition passed between us as we each acknowledged what the other person was.

Knowledge was a good thing. Wisdom a better thing. And I had the only submissive I wanted or needed in Abby. I nonchalantly reached for my cell phone. "The *sir* isn't necessary. You know I prefer *Nathaniel*."

She shook herself, as if waking from a trance. "Right. Sorry."

"Don't worry about it."

Of course, saying not to worry about it is quite different from not worrying about it myself. As I ate dinner in the penthouse that night, watching the lights of the city, I wondered if somehow I had known all along. Had I been drawn to hire Charlene because I somehow instinctively recognized her submissive nature?

I didn't believe that to be the case. I felt certain that in all my years of business, I had worked with people who identified themselves as submissives and I was none the wiser. After all, I didn't tell my business associates I was a Dominant.

Which led me to another question: did I tell Abby?

She made no secret of her dislike of Charlene. But I was around submissive women all the time when we met with our BDSM groups, and she had never reacted toward them the way she did toward Charlene. Abby was normally a very sensible woman who rarely made rash judgments.

I stood up from the table, cleaned the kitchen, and took a shower. By the time I got out and dried off, it was after ten. Abby was probably either working on the assignment I gave her or writing the revised piece for the blog. On any other Saturday night, we'd be headed to the playroom. I'd spend the next few hours working her into a frenzy of pleasure, driving us both to the highs we craved so much. I missed her.

I glanced once more at the clock and picked up my phone.

She answered on the first ring. "Hello, Master."

"Abigail." My body immediately relaxed at the sound of her voice. "How was your day?"

"Productive, Master. I accomplished a lot. I did the writing assignment you asked for and then I did my new piece for work."

"You did all that today?"

"Only because I found some things I'd written while researching other posts. I was able to use some of it for the new piece. That cut down on the time I had to spend working."

"Sounds like you were very productive. I think you deserve a reward."

"Thank you, Sir."

She had to be on edge after not being able to come the night before. "Where are you right now?"

"I'm reading in bed, Master."

"What are you reading?"

"A dirty, filthy erotic novel and thinking about you."

I was already hard, and hearing her mention the book she was reading made me uncomfortably so. I undid my pants. "What are you wearing?"

"One of your white dress shirts."

I groaned. My plan was to have her strip, but the image of her in my shirt had me pushing my boxer briefs down. "Leave it on. Are you wearing panties?"

"Just a tiny pair."

"Take them off."

There was a rustle of clothes from the other end of the phone and then her breathless "Done, Master."

"Very nice. Now I have to warn you, you still aren't allowed to come. But tell me about the last sex scene you read."

"It was hot, Master."

"How so?"

"The hero had the heroine in front of a group of people. She was blindfolded and he was explaining to the crowd all the various positions he could take her in."

"Interesting."

"And he made her get into all of them, but he just teased her and never took her."

"Never?"

"I haven't finished reading the scene yet. I'm sure he will soon, though. He'd just taken his cock out when you called."

I chuckled. "Bad timing, huh?"

"Not really, Master. With you on the phone, I can pretend you and your cock are here in bed with me."

"So why don't you tell me what you would do to my cock if I was in the bed with you right now?"

"Mmm, your cock in bed right now. Don't I wish?" She sighed. "I'm assuming you're already naked in this scenario, by the way, Master."

"That's fine."

"I think the first thing I'd do is pour a bit of lubrication into my hands. And I'd stroke it all over your cock."

"Fuck, I like where this is going." I was surprised by the mention of lube. She liked anal sex, but not really enough for it to make an appearance in a fantasy.

"It's not going *there*, so don't get too excited, Master."

"I'll try to curtail my enthusiasm."

"*Curtail* and *enthusiasm*, Master?" she asked. "Not exactly the kind of sex talk I'm used to."

"Sorry, is that killing the mood?"

"Slightly."

"Okay, so my cock is all lubed up, but apparently it's not going in the orifice I thought."

"It's not actually going in any orifice."

She was fantasizing about giving me a hand job? "I'll be quiet now and won't assume anything. You can continue."

"I move up the bed and get on my back. Then I ask you to hold on to the headboard."

I pictured it in my mind, still not sure about where the fantasy was headed. "Okay."

"Once you're in position, I take your cock and slip it between my breasts. Then I hold them all—"

"Motherfucking hell, Abigail."

"You like?"

I took myself in hand. "Fuck yes. Go on."

"So, I hold them together real tight and tell you to fuck my tits."

I stoked myself, imagining. "Damn, I love doing that."

"It's an odd feeling, but I like it. I like watching you slide in and out. And you're on top of me, so I can't really move and it's all about you and your pleasure and your cock feels so good."

"Just thinking about it makes me so hard. I'm not going to last long."

"I can tell by the way you're thrusting and I whisper, 'Use them, Master. Fuck them hard.'"

"Abigail," I moaned, stroking faster and harder.

"I feel your cock twitch, so I say, 'Come on then, Master. Mark me with your come.'"

"Fuck. Fuck. Fuck."

"I want to feel it all over my skin and then I'm going to have you watch while I lick it off."

The image she painted in my mind had me thrusting my hips and working my cock harder. I didn't even try to hold my release back. "I'm coming, Abigail. Coming so hard all over those gorgeous tits."

"Yes, I feel it. It feels so good. Mmm, I'm trying to get some in my mouth because you taste so good and I move a bit and suck you in my mouth, not wanting to miss one drop. And, damn, your cock tastes good, too."

I was breathing heavily as I took a washcloth and cleaned up the best I could. "Damn, that was hot."

"Thank you, Master."

I pictured her in bed, still aroused and not able to do anything about it without my permission. "And how are you, Abigail?"

"Horny as fucking hell, Master."

"I'm not going to let you come tonight, either." I wanted her on the edge and so ready for her release that she could hardly stand it. I very rarely withheld orgasms from her, but after her blowup concerning Charlene, I wanted the point made very clear that only good behavior was rewarded.

"That's okay, Master. I enjoyed getting you off."

I would probably make her wait until next weekend. She had gone that long before, but it had been a while.

We spoke a bit more about the move and the kids and then I decided to push her closer to the edge.

"Now, let me tell you just how I'm going to fuck you the first time in our new house."

Chapter Five

ABBY

The move to Wilmington and the unpacking that followed proved to be uneventful. With the people we'd hired doing the bulk of the work, I wasn't surrounded by boxes for too long. Elizabeth and Henry thought the entire move was a grand adventure and they seemed to like the new house.

I had to admit, I thoroughly enjoyed showing it off and I didn't hesitate to say yes when Dena asked to stop by.

"Come in," I said, leading her inside the weekend after our move. "How are you doing?"

"Good." She looked around. "This is gorgeous."

"Thanks. We really like it, especially now that we're settling in."

"You're going to have to give me a tour. Oh." She lifted up a basket. "These are for you. Pumpkin nut muffins."

"Thanks. I love pumpkin nut. You'll have to give me your recipe."

She laughed. "I don't cook. Jeff made them."

"Then thank him for me. I'll go put these in the kitchen and then I'll show you around."

"I'll go with you. I want to see what the kitchen looks like."

As we walked down the hall, I pointed to the various rooms we passed. "That's the library and office, currently nice and clean, just waiting for me to clutter it with papers. Farther this way is the dining room. We haven't eaten in here yet, but I love it. Need to set up a dinner party or something. And in here's the kitchen."

"Look at this kitchen," she said as we stepped inside. "It's gorgeous."

"And box free for the longest time," I said. "It was the first room we tackled. I knew if I got the bedroom and kitchen unpacked, I'd feel a lot better."

"All this counter space." She ran her hand across the granite we'd picked out.

"We had that put in. Doesn't it have the most beautiful quartz running through it?"

She nodded. "This room is so gorgeous, I can't wait to see how you decorate the rest of the house."

"You might be waiting awhile. I'm not much of a decorator. These smell so good." I placed the basket down and peeked in. "I think I want one now. Join me?" At her nod I poured us water and we sat down at the kitchen table with a couple of Jeff's muffins to nibble on.

"Where are the kids?" she asked.

"Henry's taking a nap and Elizabeth is up in her room 'unpacking.' She said she wanted to set up everything herself."

Dena laughed. "You're awfully brave."

"Nah, I put her markers and crayons away. She's trying to decide which dolls she wants where and how to arrange her stuffed animals."

"Is Henry's favorite toy still the trash can?"

I laughed. While Dena stayed with us in New York, Henry discovered the trash can and loved to see how many things he could throw away.

"No, we finally had to put a childproof lock on it. There were just too many ways for him to get hurt. You should have seen him when he tried to open it after we put it on. He told me it was broken and begged Nathaniel to fix it."

"Your kids are a riot."

My chest swelled with pride and love. "They are wonderful. They really are. Even when they play in the trash can." I nodded toward her still-flat belly. "How are you doing?"

Her hand dropped to her tummy and she rubbed it. "Great. I'm trying not to be so neurotic and my doctor's been wonderful and doesn't mind when I call her in a panic over something. Little one here looked good on the last ultrasound."

"And Jeff?"

Her eyes darted to mine and then down to her belly. "Jeff's good. He's always done the cooking and he rubs my feet and reads *Goodnight Moon*, and—"

"I sense a 'but' in there somewhere."

"He won't touch me. You know? Really touch me."

"Sex?"

"Out of the question."

"Oh."

"Yeah." She leaned back in the chair with a huff. "I know it's personal, and you can tell me to fuck off, but you have two kids. Did you?"

I raised an eyebrow. "Stop having sex when I was pregnant? No. Not at all."

"Jeff said it was too dangerous and he wasn't going to do anything that could potentially lead to problems. I know he's trying to keep everyone safe and I love him even more for it, but I dream about sex. And it's so vivid! I'm almost positive I orgasmed in my sleep last week."

"I've heard pregnancy has that effect on some women."

She took a drink of water and reached for another muffin. "He's miserable, too. I can see it. I even offered to lend a hand, or a mouth, and he wouldn't take me up on it."

"I can't speak for every couple, but you know Nathaniel. Mr. Conservative when it comes to safety, and I love that, don't get me wrong. When we found out we were pregnant with Elizabeth, he did hours of research and then we sat down and talked about how our play would change."

"That sounds like him."

"A lot of the things he said weren't negotiable. He wouldn't bind me in any way while I was pregnant. There were no scenes with me on my back. He checked in with me more often than normal and he extended aftercare. He limited anal play, too." I closed my eyes, but it really shouldn't have been that hard to remember. Henry wasn't that old. "I'm sure I have something written down or on my blog I could look through and find for you."

"If you don't mind. That'd be great." She sighed. "Part of me feels it's stupid. I mean, it's sex, right? I can live without it for a few months."

"Of course you could," I assured her. "But why do it if you don't have to? Sex is a need, and it doesn't go away simply because you're pregnant."

"Thanks, Abby."

"Don't even think about it. I'll do some digging tonight and see what I can find." I drummed my fingers on the table as another thought came to me. "You know, I could talk to Nathaniel. See if he could have a chat with Jeff."

"I don't want to put him on the spot and I don't want him to feel like I'm using him."

I waved my hand, brushing away her comment. "It's no big deal. I'd actually suggest a group talk on the topic if you weren't the only pregnant couple and probably the only couple that will be any time soon."

"Yeah," she said with a half laugh. "That would be awkward."

"Maybe one day, if the group gets a few more long-term couples that move in that direction."

"This is why I'm so glad you and Nathaniel are joining the group. You guys have been through things a lot of us haven't."

"Right? That's why I should at least put a bug in Nathaniel's ear about talking to Jeff. He can make it sound like it's his idea. Just kind of a 'So, how's it going with the pregnancy?' thing."

"I think that would be great. Thank you and thank him for me."

I winked at her. "I will."

"I have something else I want to talk to you about," she said, her face growing serious.

"What's up?"

"Jeff said you and Nathaniel were going to be looking at ways to make the group safer and more secure."

I nodded. "Nathaniel mostly. I'm just going to be giving him my opinion as a submissive."

"That's perfect. I need a submissive's viewpoint on this. At least one that isn't as personally involved as I am."

I waited for her to continue, horribly curious as to where this was going.

"This is group knowledge, so I'm not breaking anyone's confidentiality in telling you this. You know Julie's business partner, Sasha?" she asked me.

"Yes, we met before. Briefly." I knew from listening to various murmurings around the group that Sasha had been whipped badly.

"She was with one of the group's Doms, Peter." She raised an eyebrow in question.

I nodded. I'd seen him at a group meeting, but had never been introduced.

"He wanted to do a scene with her," she continued. "I'm not sure of all the details, but what ended up happening was she was bound and gagged while he used a bullwhip on her. And he didn't give her a way to safe word."

I fell back against my seat, and my jaw dropped. It was inconceivable to me that a Dom could possibly do that. I finally asked, "She didn't say anything to him before he started?"

"From what I gather, he had mentioned collaring her. She'd never been collared and thought it was romantic that they could play without safe words."

"Holy hell."

"Right? She wound up in the hospital and dropped out of the group." Dena's forehead wrinkled in thought. "She did come to a group meeting shortly after, but she had a panic attack and never came back."

"That's horrible."

Dena nodded. "I recommended a therapist and she's been seeing her for a while now."

"Is she better?"

"That's what I wanted to talk to you about. When I went by her place to ask her to stand with me at the wedding and told her about the baby, she mentioned she was kicking around the idea of rejoining the group."

I could see both the positive and negative in that. For her to have not only the desire, but the strength and courage to face coming back to the group was amazing. On the other hand, with Peter also around, it would be hard. "I think I see where you're going."

"I worry for her."

I put my hand over hers. "I'm sure you do."

"I want her to be back in the group, because she's a submissive and she needs it. But I'm so scared something's going to happen that will leave her in a worse place than she was before."

"And since Nathaniel's going to be working toward restructuring things . . ." I let the statement hang in the air.

"I know keeping everyone safe is his top priority," she said. "I just thought it'd be a good idea for you to know in more detail *who* you're keeping safe."

I thought for a few seconds. "Do you think she wants back in the group for social reasons or physical? I mean, do you see her wanting to play?"

"To be honest, for a long time, I thought she'd never want to play again. It seemed like men were the lowest thing on her priority list. And I can't say I blame her. But recently, she expressed interest in a Dom."

"Oh, well, that sounds positive."

"You don't know who she expressed interest in."

"Is he a bad Dom? Do we need to kick him out of the group?"

"No, nothing like that. He's just"—she searched for the right word—"tough. I'm not sure that's what Sasha needs."

But tough with a purpose could be beneficial. "Or it might be exactly what she needs."

"As long as she's with someone kind." Dena smiled. "Jeff can be tough, but I've never doubted his inherent kindness."

"Funny, I normally don't associate kindness with a Dom, but I think you're right. At least with Nathaniel. He can be a grade-A ass, but I know inside I'm the most important thing to him."

She nodded. "That's what I want for Sasha."

Sasha was a fortunate woman to have such a good friend in Dena. And Julie was fiercely devoted to her as well. Both women would be needed for support, if and when Sasha rejoined the group. "I'd like to spend some more time with Sasha. Get to know her."

"I know! I was going to go by their shop this weekend. Why don't I come by here first and pick you up? We can go together."

"That's a great idea," I said. "I just need to make sure Nathaniel can watch the kids." We really needed to find a sitter in Delaware. I added that to my mental to-do list.

"Sounds great. Just call me." She looked at her watch. "I better be going. Jeff and I have a date tonight. He's taking me to a new bistro. They have fish stew on the menu. With calamari. I don't know, must be the baby."

I laughed. "I craved peaches."

I stood to walk her to the door. I'd wanted to ask her for her opinion about Charlene, to see if I was overreacting, but it wasn't going to happen today. I felt that it was more important to discuss her concerns about pregnancy. And Sasha was important, too. Especially since Nathaniel would be working in the group to hopefully avoid situations like hers. Compared to that, my problem with Charlene seemed very small.

It was fortunate I had the extra week of work done from the previous weekend, because I found that even though the boxes weren't around for long, there was still plenty to do. The night after Dena stopped by, I collapsed into the couch in our new living room.

"The kids are in bed," I announced to Nathaniel. "I'm ready to do nothing for about three hours. Scratch that. Make it thirty."

He slipped his arm around me and kissed my forehead. "You know, I was thinking. We might need to rethink our position on hiring a nanny. Especially when we're in Delaware. It's not like we have Linda nearby to take them."

I nodded. "The thought's crossed my mind a few times, too. I think it's a good idea."

"We need to decide if we want a live-in or not."

I thought about the bedroom we were in the process of converting to a playroom. It was almost complete. "Off the top of my head, I'm thinking no live-in. It's not like we need a babysitter every day."

"True, but if you had a little help, it'd be easier for you to work on the blog and show."

"That would be nice." Those benefits of a live-in would be great. "I just don't think I'm at the point where I want someone unrelated to us in the house twenty-four/seven."

"Just think about it. Since I'll be having a driver take me into the city when we're here, I don't want you to be without any nearby help."

I saw his point. "But someone *living* here, I just don't know."

"We could always start with a scheduled time for someone to come by either every day or most days. See how that goes. Then if it works for all of us and we need to, we could look into a live-in situation."

I nodded. "I like that idea."

"You want to ask around and see if you can get a few names? Then we can schedule some time for us to interview some people?"

"I know you'll be at home most days, but I don't want to set up a time that's not good for you."

He stood up and held out a hand to me, and pulled me up to stand in front of him when I took it. "Whatever you set up, I'll make work," he said.

Damn, he looked so good. He was wearing soft cotton lounge pants and nothing else. I ran my hands over his chest. "That's very accommodating of you."

He gave me a sultry smile and pressed against me. "I pride myself on being extremely accommodating where you're concerned."

"Is that right?" I slid my hand down to cup his ass. "Maybe I should return the favor. How can I accommodate you?"

"Why don't you go upstairs and slip into something more comfortable?"

"Why would I go all the way up to our room? I can be accommodating here." After nearly two weeks of no sex, if he was hinting what I thought he was, I didn't want to waste a minute.

"Shh." He put a finger to my lips. "Upstairs."

If going upstairs meant I'd get sex, I'd go upstairs. I huffed so he knew I wasn't thrilled about having to change before we did anything, and started upstairs. He didn't move.

I looked over my shoulder. "You coming?"

Mischief danced in his eyes. "I'll be up shortly."

"Don't wait too long."

I walked up the stairs and down the hall to our bedroom, all the while thinking he must have something in mind. Normally, he was all over spontaneous sex. The fact that he wasn't tonight told me there was something going on.

I walked into the bedroom and my mouth went dry at the sight of my nightstand.

Usually bare except for a lamp, it now also had my black leather collar on top.

Yes.

After our first trip to Wilmington, we'd decided to make a few changes. Up until then, we'd only been playing about once a month. Compared to how often I wore his collar before the kids, it felt like a rare occurrence and we both agreed we weren't fully satisfied. Now I wore his collar every weekend, with necessary low-protocol times built in because of the day-to-day routines with the children. With the move and settling in, he hadn't collared me yet this weekend.

But one of the other things we'd agreed to was the ability for one of us to ask for playtime during the week. Nathaniel's method for letting me know he wanted to move into our Dominant/submissive roles was to place my collar on my nightstand.

Though I had the ability to turn him down if I wanted, saying no tonight didn't even cross my mind. Just the sight of my collar on the nightstand had me desperate to kneel before him and sent waves of arousal through my body.

If I decided I wanted his collar, his request that I slip into something more comfortable really meant "get naked." My fingers trembled with excitement as I unbuttoned my shirt and pushed my jeans down. Once undressed, I knelt in the middle of the room and waited.

He entered minutes later.

"Very nice," he said. "I see you liked my suggestion."

"I decided it was much better than staying downstairs."

He laughed quietly and walked to the nightstand to get my collar. "I thought I might let you come finally, but that it would be on my terms if I did." He buckled the collar around my neck. "Kiss my feet in thanks."

I slid forward and brushed my lips across first one foot and then the other. "Thank you, Master," I said before moving back into my waiting position.

"So polite this evening. Someone must really want to come."

I didn't say anything. I believed that was fairly obvious.

"Get on the bed. Face the headboard and hold on to it."

I moved quickly while still trying to be graceful and seductive. As I settled into position, I caught sight of my reflection in the mirror to the right of the bed. I turned and watched as he got behind me.

It turned me on like nothing else to watch him take me. To observe while at the same time feeling his possession. I groaned just thinking about it.

He pushed down on my shoulders a bit, kicked my knees apart. The entire time I watched him in the mirror. He situated me the way he wanted and then caught my gaze.

"You like seeing me get you into the position I want?" he asked. "Making sure your body is accessible and open for me?"

"The only thing better is watching you actually take me, Master."

"Mmm," he hummed. "I think we need mirrors in the playroom."

"I like that idea, Master."

"I thought you might, you wicked girl." He rocked his hips against me but didn't enter me yet. He cupped my backside and squeezed. "I want you to imagine something with me."

I was so impatient for him to fuck me, but I knew if I did as he instructed, it would be so much better in the end.

"See yourself in the mirror?" he asked. I lifted my head and took in what I saw. Naked, bent over, and waiting for him to take me. I thought I looked sexy as hell. Of course, that was due in part to him. On his knees behind me with that look in his eyes, he made the very air in the room feel sexy. "See?"

"Yes, Master," I said.

"Imagine we're in front of a group of people. That you're bent over and begging to be fucked in front of a group. Do you see what they would see?" He slapped my ass. "Do you?"

"Yes, Master." I could easily picture the three men we'd played in front of in Delaware months ago. Simon, Jeff, and a Dom I only knew as Master DeVaan.

He slipped a finger inside me, ensuring that I was ready. "What do they see?"

My eyes locked on our image in the mirror. He moved closer to me, cock in hand, and oh so slowly, pressed forward. Before us, we both watched as he entered me.

"They see you, Master," I said. "They see you taking me. Ohhh, fuck. Yes."

"You feel so damn good." He ran his hands over my back, cupped my breasts, and stroked down to my hips. His fingers dug into my flesh as he held tight to my waist and thrust fully inside.

I couldn't tear my gaze from the mirror and I watched him pump in and out. In my mind, there were more than the three men watching. There were lots more and many were strangers. Watching Nathaniel move inside me turned them on.

"They can't keep their eyes off you. How your pussy takes my cock. Spreading to take it all. The men wish they could feel how tight you are." His hips moved in a slow rhythmic stroke, going deep and retreating. "I'm fucking you slowly to give them more time to picture it. Love watching you stretch so you can take my dick. Next time I'm fucking your ass and I'll have you watch that."

My body shivered at the thought. I loved watching him use my body for his pleasure and was certain watching him take me there would be a complete turn-on.

"You like that idea, Abigail?" he asked, and instead of waiting for an answer, he picked up his pace. "But the truth is, no matter how vividly they imagine it, it'll never compare to the real thing." He paused, worked himself deeper, and then started again with short strokes.

I arched my back, trying to get more of him inside me. When that didn't work, I moved my hips in time with his thrusts. But he was still holding back.

"Hold still," he said. "See how my cock's claiming you? Do you feel it?"

"Yes, Master."

He positioned himself for better balance and I knew I was in trouble. His eyes met mine in the mirror. "Hold on."

I took a tighter grip on the headboard. He pulled out just a bit and then thrust into me hard and deep and it felt so good. I couldn't stop the moan that escaped my lips.

It was all the encouragement he needed. He withdrew again and pulled my hips to meet his thrusts. "Eyes open and on the mirror. Watch me ride you."

I shifted my eyes to our reflection, and the sight of him

working his hips to get as far inside me as possible, the way his muscles flexed, his entire body moving with one goal, was almost enough to send me over the edge.

He was beyond talking now, his entire being focused on his body and what it wanted. My orgasm continued to build and I looked at where our bodies joined. He was hard and long and the sight of him pounding into me, and the way I opened for him, was quite possibly the most erotic thing I'd ever seen. His hands gripped my hips even harder as he repeatedly drove into me. He held still and shifted his hips again, hitting the spot he knew would set me off. He spoke only one word.

"Beg."

"Please, Master, let me come. Please. Please."

"Yes."

"Oh . . . holy . . . fuck!" I panted, and my orgasm, so long denied, crashed over me, shaking my body. It seemed to last forever, rolling through me in wave after wave. I savored every second of it, transported in a way I hadn't been before. When my breathing calmed, I whispered, "Thank you, Master. Thank you."

"I'm going to come so hard." He was still pumping in and out of me. "Turn around. I want you to swallow."

He pulled out and I barely had time to turn around before he pushed me down on the bed and within seconds, he thrust himself into my open mouth.

"Yes," he hissed. He pumped in and out two or three more times and then held still. "Fucking swallow all of it."

I gulped hard, not wanting to spill anything. He finally stopped coming and slipped from my mouth. With a heavy sigh, he lowered himself down to the bed and took me in his arms.

"Feel better?" he asked.

"Yes, Master. Thank you."

"I think I will install mirrors in the playroom."

"I like that idea, Master. But you know, the mirrors were hot and it was a turn-on watching, but the real thing is hotter."

He cocked an eyebrow at me. "That wasn't real? Because I feel like I ran half a marathon."

"Not *that* part, Master. I mean the part about people watching."

He smiled and pushed the hair out of my eyes. "Little did I know when I took you at the Super Bowl that you would turn into such an exhibitionist."

"I like it when people watch, Master."

"Yes, I'm learning you like it very much."

I settled back into his arms. "The Super Bowl, the men in Delaware, the play parties. Especially the parties at our house, Master. I like it all. There's something about being watched, but knowing no one can touch me, that is such a turn-on."

"Tell me," he said, and his voice was serious. "Is a threesome something you want to experience? Something like the afternoon we had Jeff over, but with the third being more active?"

I had to think about that. The novels I read made it sound interesting and hot and fun. I'd enjoyed the afternoon Jeff was invited to play with us. But that was a long cry from someone other than Nathaniel touching me sexually.

"I don't think so," I answered honestly. "I don't think I'm ready for more than just you at the moment. Right now, this very second, there's only one Dom I want to serve and only one Dom I want to control me."

"You'll let me know if you change your mind?"

"Of course."

We stayed silent for a few minutes. His hand stroked slowly up and down my arm and I turned my head to kiss his shoulder. He lifted my chin and captured my lips with his. His mouth was so strong and yet he somehow managed to convey his love and adoration with his kiss. I turned, facing him, and wrapped my arms around him, kissing him again.

He moved forward, lowering me to the bed, his hands moving to my neck and unbuckling the collar.

"Wait," I said. "I thought—"

"Not this time," he whispered against my lips.

"Why?"

"Because I decided that what I want to do now is make love to my wife."

He had never uncollared me so quickly and I wondered for a second if our talk about threesomes had been what changed his mind. Then he lowered his head and peppered kisses along the top of my breasts and I decided whatever changed his mind wasn't important.

He was strong and commanding as my Dominant, but he was equally as passionate and loving as my husband and lover. Nights like this, when he took me slow and gently, almost reverently, weren't very common, but I loved them just as much as when he took control of our joining. Either way, my body was always hungry for him.

Right before he entered me, he switched positions. "Ride me, Abby."

And though being on top wasn't my favorite, I moved to straddle him and lowered myself onto his cock.

"You're beautiful," he whispered. "All feminine and strong."

He took hold of my waist, but unlike the way he held me before, this time his hands were gentle. His goal wasn't to control, but to simply touch me.

"I could watch you forever," he said. "I'll never grow tired of seeing you."

"Good thing," I said. "I'm never going anywhere."

I moved up and down on him, mesmerized by his expression. His eyes were filled with something I couldn't quite put my finger on. Lust, certainly, but something that spoke of his love and warmed me. Then he moved his hands up and fondled my breasts.

"Every inch of you is gorgeous," he whispered sweetly, and I continued to move on him, working my hips to get the most friction where I wanted it. When he threw his head back and arched his back, I knew I'd hit the right spot.

"I love watching you in this mood, too," I said. "Seeing you take a different kind of pleasure in me." I stopped speaking as my orgasm built and concentrated only on the heat that came from our joined bodies.

"You make me come so hard." His voice was a strained combination of lust, love, and desire. He reached down and played with my clit. "I want to see how hard you come."

His hand was what I needed to push me over the cliff of my approaching orgasm. I sucked in a breath and let it wash over me. Nathaniel wasn't far behind and he came seconds after I did.

Afterward, he pulled me down and kissed me. "I love you," he said, spooning himself behind me.

"Love you, too."

"Does Nathaniel have the kids?" Dena asked the next Saturday as she drove us to Julie and Sasha's floral shop, the Petal Pushers. She'd called earlier in the day to invite me to go with her for lunch.

"Yes. They're going to explore our land some more. Last time they went out, he showed them our apple trees."

"Your kids are great." Dena's hand swept across her belly. "You'll be exploring with your own before you know it."

"It's hard to picture it. I'm still trying to decide what I want to do about my job after the baby comes."

"You still have time," I assured her.

"Yes, and I'm grateful I have the option to stay at home if I want to. I know not everyone has that."

"You and Jeff will find what works best for you and your family," I said to her.

"It's scary to think about the future. I'm so afraid we'll make all these plans and I'll lose this one as well."

"When you have thoughts like that, you need to remember what's true. The ultrasounds have been positive and the doctors have all said there's no reason to expect that whatever caused your loss before will affect this pregnancy."

She nodded, but I knew she wasn't convinced. And there wasn't anything anyone could do or say to change that. Anyone in her position would worry, and only time and giving birth to a healthy baby would calm her fears.

A few minutes later, we pulled up in front of a storefront building in the downtown area of Wilmington. The display window was filled with white and light pink flowers, a reminder to those passing by that wedding season was approaching.

"I didn't realize it was a restored building," I said.

"Sasha said they were able to negotiate a great price because the seller didn't want to deal with any of the repairs." She pointed above the front door. "They actually own the second floor as well. Sasha's living there."

I opened the door and held it for Dena. When we went inside, we found a large room filled with light and the colors and scents of beautiful flowers. Julie sat in front of a computer and Sasha sat beside her.

They looked up as the door chime announced our arrival.

"Dena, hey. And, Abby. I wasn't expecting you." Julie moved out from behind the counter and gave us hugs.

Sasha stood and came over to where we were. She was shorter than Julie and her dark hair was styled with spikes. A hard wind would have blown her away. She was so thin she looked gaunt.

I held out my hand. "Hey, Sasha."

"Nice to see you again," she said, shaking my hand.

"Everything going well?" I asked, and she nodded.

Dena gave Sasha a hug. "Let's just eat here instead of going out. I'll order pizza. That's what I'm craving today."

"Sounds good to me," I said. "As long as it's decent. I haven't had decent pizza since we left New York."

"Are you a pizza snob?" Julie asked.

"After living in New York City for years, I'm most definitely a pizza snob," I answered. "I'm not a snob about most things, but I can't take bad pizza."

Dena shook her head. "No worries, my first date with Jeff

was at an Italian restaurant and they have wonderful pizza. Trust me."

"We can go upstairs and eat once it's delivered," Sasha said. "It'll be more comfortable."

Thirty minutes later, we sat in Sasha's apartment, eating a delicious lunch. Julie and Dena were as jovial as ever, but Sasha was more withdrawn. I wondered if it was because I was there or if she was still suffering from depression because of what had happened with the bullwhip.

"Everyone going to the play party next weekend?" Julie asked.

Dena had a silly grin on her face. "Yes, your place, right?"

Julie giggled. "My place, I like that."

"I knew you would," Dena said. "Jeff and I will be there."

"I'll be there," I said.

"I'm thinking about going." Sasha spoke with trepidation and all three of us looked at her. "What? I talked with my therapist. I'm not ready to play or anything. Hell, I don't even want to date. But I think it's time for me to go to a party."

"Have you spoken to any senior members about it?" Julie asked.

"Does Dena being here and listening to me count?"

"Probably not," Julie said with a raised eyebrow to Dena.

"We talked about it briefly when I came by a week or so ago," Dena said. "But I'll admit, I didn't think you'd be interested in attending this soon."

"What are the concerns about Sasha attending?" I asked.

"The last time she went, she had a panic attack," Julie said.

Sasha shot a glare at Julie. "That was months ago."

I couldn't tear my focus away from the two friends. Since we would be joining the group, I was particularly interested in Julie's reaction to Sasha mentioning attending. And, I'd admit, I felt a bit like a mother hen, especially toward Julie, what with her being so new to the lifestyle.

Julie walked to where Sasha sat on the couch and knelt before her, taking her hands in hers. "You showed up at my house after, crying, shaking, and told me you were never going back. I sat by your side for weeks with you giving only one-word, yes-or-no answers. I love you like a sister and I finally have you back. I'm scared if you go to the party, the real you will disappear again."

"The real me won't return until I reclaim that part of my life."

"What if going sets you back another three months?"

"What if it doesn't?" Sasha squeezed Julie's hands. "Don't you see, I have to find out. I have to try. I see you and Daniel and how happy you are and I think, *That's due in part to me.* I'm the one who urged you to join the group and I've watched you grow into a satisfied submissive and find peace with it. So call me jealous or greedy or whatever you want, but I had that once and I want it back. I need it back."

Silent tears ran down Julie's cheeks. "Promise me you won't disappear inside yourself again."

"I promise." One lone tear escaped from Sasha's eye. "If I feel a panic attack coming on, I know what to do. I'm not defenseless."

Listening to her talk and seeing how she responded to Julie, I believed Sasha was ready. I vividly remembered how it was to long for domination and not have it. It was time for Sasha to return to the group. I glanced out of the corner of my eye to Dena, and she caught the movement and looked my way. I tilted my head toward Julie and Sasha and nodded. Dena smiled and returned the nod. She thought so, too. I would have to give my opinion to Nathaniel.

Julie stood. "Dena, will you talk to Jeff about Sasha attending? I'll do the same with Daniel. And, Abby, you and Nathaniel will be revising the requirements for inclusion in group?"

"Yes," I said. "I'll talk to him about being sure there are rules in place that will allow Sasha to feel safe when she attends."

"Thank you," Sasha whispered.

"I feel like I've been out of it the last few weeks," Dena said. "Is Peter still in the group? Will he be there?"

Sasha cringed at Peter's name.

Julie sat down at Sasha's side. "Yes, he's still in the group. Master Greene hasn't released him from mentoring yet, and he could come to the party. I don't know if he will."

"Maybe I'll suggest to Nathaniel that it'd be a good idea for Master Greene to keep Peter from attending this party." I looked over to Sasha. "Or is that overstepping my bounds? I think if I were in your place, I wouldn't want him there the first time I returned."

Relief washed over her expression. "If you don't mind, that would be great. My fear of running into him again is part of what's held me back. I know I have to face him, but it's all about baby steps. I think it'll be easier to meet with the group and then deal with him than to deal with him and then meet with the group."

I nodded. "I agree. You shouldn't do them both at the same time, and group first makes sense to me."

"We'll all be there for support, Sasha," Julie said. "You won't be alone."

"You guys are the best." Sasha looked as if she might cry again, but she blinked and nothing rolled down her cheek. "Now let's talk about something fun. Dena, tell us about all your wedding plans."

Chapter Six

NATHANIEL

Abby was out with Dena and her other friends from the Partners group, and I was having a tea party with Elizabeth and Henry. The children had somehow lured Apollo into joining us and they'd grown too quiet in the few minutes I stepped out of the room to make a quick call.

There were hushed whispers as I returned to Elizabeth's room, but then I heard Henry squeal, "Pretty!" and I knew I'd come to Apollo's rescue just in time. I stepped inside to find Apollo with a pink feather boa around his neck, a pink "Princess" sash draped over his shoulders, and a sparkling pink tiara tied to his head. He looked at me as if to say, *Pink really isn't my color. Make them stop.*

"How's the tea party going?" I asked Elizabeth, who was dressed in a princess gown and a pair of Abby's old shoes.

"Henry won't wear his crown," she said.

At the mention of his name, Henry smiled and pointed to Apollo. "Dada, he's pretty!"

"Yes, Apollo certainly looks very pretty, but I think he needs to rest now. He's old, you know, and playing princess tea party is hard work."

"Is Apollo really, really old?" Elizabeth asked. "Like ten?"

"He's closer to twelve," I said, laughing inside that ten was *really, really old.*

"That is old." She walked to Apollo as best she could in the shoes and started de-princessing him. "Go rest with Daddy, Apollo. We can play tea party later."

Once he was no longer decked out in pink, Apollo stood up and shook, then trotted over to me. "Let's go take Apollo outside and we can play on the swings."

"Cookie. Please," Henry said.

I glanced at my watch. "Too close to dinner. Mommy wouldn't like it if I let you have a cookie now. Eat a good dinner and we'll see."

"I have cookies," Elizabeth said, pushing an empty plate toward him.

Henry looked down and, realizing they were only imaginary cookies, told her, "Fix it."

Elizabeth tried to explain why imaginary cookies were better and Henry didn't believe her one bit. But he didn't complain. They played together really well, at least most of the time.

Growing up as an only child, I'd always wanted a brother or sister. Then my parents died when I was ten and I lived with my aunt and uncle. Their son, Jackson, had been like the brother I'd never had. I'd always known that if I ever had children, I'd want at least two.

"Let's go." I picked Henry up to carry him down the stairs and Elizabeth followed with Apollo.

Later that evening, after Abby returned home from lunch with her friends, I pulled into Daniel's driveway. He'd called while the women were at lunch and asked if I could stop by his house for a little bit. I'd just gotten out of the car when I heard voices near the patio.

"How long is Cole going to be at the guesthouse?" The question was voiced by a woman I didn't recognize.

"I don't know." That sounded like Julie. "He's been gone a lot. Traveling different places. I really can't keep up with him."

"Does he have a lot of . . . people over?"

"By *people*, do you mean women?"

There was a tight laugh and then, "Yeah, that's what I meant."

"I haven't seen anyone stay overnight, but that doesn't mean he's not inviting women over to play."

"Just wondering."

Julie sighed. "You know Cole's reputation in the playroom, don't you, Sasha?"

"I've heard some things."

"From what I've picked up on, they're all true," Julie said. "Do you think about playing when you picture yourself back with the group?"

There was nothing from Sasha and I wanted to make my presence known before they started chatting again. I walked quickly,

covering the distance in a few long strides. Turning the corner, I
found them working in the garden that ran along the front porch.

"Hey, guys," I said.

Julie sat back on her heels and smiled. "Hey, Nathaniel. Daniel said you were coming over. He's in the sunroom at the back
of the house. If you follow the walkway around, you'll find him."

"Thank you, Julie." I glanced at Sasha. She'd put her shovel
down and was looking at the dirt. Abby had told me about her
conversations with Dena. I still had reservations about Sasha
rejoining, but wasn't sure exactly why. "Hello, Sasha."

She didn't look up. "Hello, Sir."

"I prefer *Nathaniel* when we're not with the group."

She lifted her head, and a mischievous grin crept across her
lips. "Does anyone ever call you *Nate*?"

"Not if they want a reply."

"I didn't think you looked like a Nate."

I grinned. "What does a Nate look like?"

She shrugged. "I'm not sure. I just know it's not like you."

"Sasha," Julie said. "Come help me carry these empty plant-
ers to the greenhouse."

The two women went back to their gardening and I followed
the path around the house to the sunroom, finding Daniel exactly
where Julie said he'd be.

He saw me and opened the door. "Hey, Nathaniel. Come on in."

We took our seats at the dining table and I noticed a pile of
paperwork at Daniel's place. He picked it up and flipped through
the stack.

"I've pulled the paperwork from all active members," he said.

"I thought if you were going to be redoing the application process, we might as well have everyone fill out paperwork and resubmit."

"I was actually going to suggest that. I was thinking it was a good idea because Peter had been out of the mentor program for a while and Ron was still in it when he harassed Dena, so it's not like we can point to one thing to identify as the breakdown."

He leaned back in his chair. "I know you and Abby are coming to the party tomorrow night. I'll be interested in hearing your thoughts after."

I'd been to the group's play parties before, but always as a guest. This coming weekend, Abby and I would attend as members. But more than that, we'd be looking for ways to improve safety and security for all members.

"Abby mentioned Sasha wanted to attend this weekend's party," I said. "What are your thoughts?"

"I talked to her when she came over to help Julie in the garden. I won't lie to you, after what happened with Peter, I thought she would never join the group again."

"She was that bad off?" At first, I'd been alarmed when I saw her. She still looked depressed. She was too thin and her eyes had the look of a person who didn't sleep very well. But her comeback on the Nate thing showed me she had more fire inside than it at first appeared.

"Yes. She wouldn't even stay and watch when I collared Julie."

"But when you talked to her this afternoon?"

"She's in a better place. I'm okay with her attending tomorrow night, but I'd like for us all to keep an eye on her and be there if she needs us."

Sasha's paperwork was on the top of the pile. I picked it up and glanced over it. "Abby said she wasn't planning to play."

"No, I know she won't tomorrow. But I think it'd be good for us to be proactive and have a plan ready for when she is."

A noise from outside caused us both to turn our heads. The two women had moved to the side of the house with their gardening. Cole stood with them holding a flat of flowers. But what had captured everyone's attention was the petite woman at his side.

"Cole has company," Daniel said. "First time I've known him to have someone over. Maybe he's finally getting Kate out of his system."

"She could be his editor."

As we watched, he passed the flowers to Julie and then slipped his hand to rest low on the unknown woman's ass.

"Or not," I added.

"Yeah, I'm guessing not his editor. Wonder why he brought those back to Julie? I had them delivered to the guesthouse because that's where she wanted them planted."

"I saw her and Sasha working by the driveway."

"She wanted to add some new plants and I want her to think of this as her home, too." He laughed. "Though I told her I'd like it better if she planted in the nude."

I chuckled, then glanced back outside. Cole and his friend had left, heading toward the guesthouse. Julie and Sasha appeared to be arguing. Julie looked up and Daniel motioned for her to come inside. She put the container down and walked toward us. Sasha followed, not looking happy at all.

"Hey," Julie said, once inside. She sounded a bit huffy, and was clearly agitated.

"Did Cole have a problem with the plants?" Daniel asked.

"No, he thought they brought them to the guesthouse by mistake. He was going to take them back, but I told him to leave them. I wanted to fertilize them anyway. Then we can plant them."

"There's no *we*," Sasha said, crossing her arms.

"Honestly, Sasha. I want to get these in the ground today."

"I'll do all the other plants."

"You're being absurd."

Daniel cleared his throat. "Nathaniel, can you get me one of the blank checklists from the bottom of that pile?"

I took the pile of papers and gave Daniel a sheet from the bottom. I lifted an eyebrow. Sasha's demeanor had changed from when I first arrived. If I didn't know better, I would say she was being bratty because she was jealous. The look on her face reminded me so much of one Abby got when Charlene's name was mentioned. Daniel nodded. He'd picked up on it, too.

"Sasha," he said. "I need you to fill out a new checklist. You can give it to either me or Nathaniel at the next play party."

Her cheeks were flushed when she took the paper. I hadn't realized how pale she was until I saw the dark splotches on her cheeks.

"Thank you, Sir," she said. "I was going to ask for a new one." She looked back at Julie. "I'm going to fill this out. I'll be back in a bit."

Julie shook her head as Sasha walked away, but gave Daniel a quick kiss and headed back outside to finish.

"There's something else I wanted to talk to you about," Daniel said. "There's a tri-state BDSM chapter starting and they're looking for someone to lead some demos. I don't think Julie's ready for something like that, but I was wondering if you and Abby might be interested."

"When and where are the meetings?" I asked, thinking it might be a fun way to further explore Abby's exhibitionist side.

"The schedule's still being worked on, but the first meeting is in Pennsylvania. I can give you the name and number of the person in charge if you think it's something you'd be interested in."

"That would be great. I'll definitely talk to Abby about it."

As I thought, Abby was excited about the possibility of the demos. I waited until we'd put the kids to bed and she came downstairs to the living room, where I was preparing for work the next day. I looked up as she entered and smiled when I saw what she had on.

"You look sexy as hell," I said, appreciating the long silver gown she'd changed into.

She shot me a sultry smile and sat on the floor near my feet. I ran a free hand through her hair.

She hummed and leaned into my touch. "Mmm, thank you. I thought you might like this."

"I like it very much."

We sat in the stillness for several minutes. It was one of those rare and precious moments when everything seemed right, and I wanted to drink it in. My children and my wife, all together with me, healthy and happy. There was nothing more I wanted.

"How'd it go at Daniel and Julie's today?" she asked, breaking the silence.

"Good. Sasha was there. And Cole. With a woman."

"Oh?"

I shrugged. "I didn't meet her; they were going to the guest-house." I tapped her shoulder. "Come sit up here for a minute."

She rose gracefully and curled up on the couch beside me. I wrapped my arm around her and inhaled deeply, smelling her hair.

"I did want to talk to you about something Daniel brought up."

She looked up, expectantly.

"There's a tri-state BDSM chapter starting up and they're looking for couples to do a few demos." I didn't miss her look of excitement at the word "demo." "It seems like you're craving exhibitionism, and I thought this might be a good way to meet that need."

"I have been fantasizing about playing in public a lot lately. I don't know why."

"Whatever reason there is, if it's something you need right now, I want you to have it."

"I don't know if it's a need or just a recurring fantasy."

I ran my knuckles over her cheekbones. "Do you want to do the demos, regardless of why you're fantasizing about it?"

"Yes."

"Then we'll do it." I twisted a piece of loose hair around my fingers. "I'll call the organizers tomorrow and get more information."

"Do you know what they want us to demo?"

"Daniel said bullwhip was one. That's why they called him first."

Her excitement dwindled a bit at the mention of the bull-whip. "You've never used one on me."

"True, but I have one and I know how to use it. I'll just need some practice before I use it on you." I tilted my head. "Does that make you not want to do the demo?"

"Oh no. I'm still very interested."

"Even with the bullwhip?"

She leaned in for a kiss. "I trust you completely."

That was what sometimes scared me. Not that she trusted me not to hurt her, but that she trusted me to fulfill all her desires and fantasies.

What if I failed?

I'd always enjoyed play parties. The way they vibrated with the sometimes subtle, sometimes blatant undercurrent of the power exchange we were all a part of. And I'd never stop enjoying the diversity of the participants. In one room you could happen across a Dom with two male submissives, and in another find a submissive being led by a leash. And there were those who looked as if they just finished shopping with the girls or had come straight from work.

Tonight, Abby and I were only observing to see if we noticed anything happening that was a concern. There were fewer people present than there had been at previous parties we'd attended with the group. Space wasn't an issue, though. Daniel's house was more than sufficient for the people in attendance. He and Julie weren't doing a demo tonight, but when we arrived, he'd had her pressed against a wall, holding her hands above her head and saying something that had her eyes heavy with desire.

Jeff stood off by himself, watching Dena. The vivacious blonde was in the middle of a group of three women who'd come expressing interest in the lifestyle. She spoke animatedly, but with a smile and a demeanor that left the women looking calm and at ease. Not always an easy thing to do.

"You're a lucky man," I said to Jeff.

He smiled. "That I am. She's something else."

One of the women pointed to Dena's collar, causing her to look over her shoulder to where we were. Jeff waved.

"Baby doing well?" I asked. At Abby's request, I'd called him a few days ago and casually brought up playing during pregnancy.

"Yes," he replied. "And thank you for the talk the other day. I spoke with Dena and we're going to try a few things. I'm still nervous, but I feel better. And it made me realize that I was being unfair not only to her, but to our relationship as well."

We stood quietly for a few minutes. Master Greene hurried past us with a brief "hello" and wave. He was the acting Dungeon Monitor and obviously on his way down to Daniel's playroom. Several people followed in his wake. I thought again that the responsibility was too much for one person.

I scanned the room, looking for Abby, and found her at the living room's entryway. We'd arrived together, but decided to split up for the first thirty minutes to observe separately. At her side was Sasha, looking paler than she had appeared days before. Papers were clutched in her hand.

"I hope it wasn't a mistake letting her come tonight," I said, inclining my head toward the pair.

"I wish you could have seen her before," Jeff said. "She was always so full of life and, from what I've heard from those who played with her, borderline insolent."

She certainly didn't look insolent now. Her eyes were wide and she was nodding at whatever Abby was saying. Abby caught sight of me and, at the tilt of my head, crossed the room in our direction with Sasha following.

I slipped my hand up to the back of Abby's neck when she made it to my side, fingering her collar. "Sasha, it's good to see you."

"Thank you, Master West." She held out a wrinkled paper. "I filled out my checklist like you asked."

I took the paper. "Very good. I'll make sure it's entered into the system." Abby and I had talked when I got home from Daniel's the day before and she'd suggested the idea of loading group member information into an electronic database. She'd mentioned it might be a good way to pair up unattached members based on interest. I wasn't sure we wanted to do anything electronically, but she brought up listing everyone by a number instead of putting personal information in the computer. I told her I'd think about it. I did like the idea of matching people up.

Looking at Sasha at that moment, I found it hard to believe she'd want to be matched up any time soon. Just as well. Since tonight was her first party in a long time, it was best she took things slowly. Once she had a few meetings and parties under her belt, maybe we'd think about pairing her with a Dom, if that was what she wanted.

Jeff looked at his watch. "Cole's demo is starting in about five minutes. Dena and I aren't going to watch, but you and Abby might want to."

I raised an eyebrow at Abby. "Let's go see Cole. Sasha, you can come with us."

Sasha's mouth opened, as if she was going to say something, but she only nodded. Abby must have sensed something. She put a hand on Sasha's upper arm and gently asked her, "Are you sure?"

"Yes," Sasha replied, and her voice shook a bit. "I'll be fine."

Abby would have picked up on the fact that I wanted Sasha with us. So her double check meant there was something going on with Sasha that I had missed.

We made our way down the stairs to Daniel's playroom. I led the way and held the door open for the women. "Sasha," I said when she walked by. "Is everything okay?"

She looked me in the eye. "Yes, Sir. I'm fine."

There was a glimmer of something in her expression that hinted otherwise and she couldn't hold my gaze for long. "If you don't want to watch, Abby can sit with you upstairs."

"I'm fine, Sir. Really."

There wasn't much else I could do. I'd asked if she was okay and I'd given her an out. If she wanted to stay in the playroom, I would let her. "Stay near Abby."

She nodded and stood next to Abby. I kept my eyes on Sasha instead of paying attention to the setup for the demo. She spoke quietly to Abby, but when she turned to observe the middle of the room, she jerked in shock.

Curious, I followed her line of sight and saw Cole and the petite woman he'd brought to the guesthouse. She knelt at his feet while Cole waited for everyone to make it inside and close the door. Once the crowd settled down and he was satisfied, he began by introducing himself, the submissive, and what his plans were. I worried for just a bit when he told the crowd he'd be using a violet wand. While I knew Sasha had been hurt with a bullwhip, I wasn't sure how she'd do watching an electrical scene. A quick glance showed her relaxed and calm, though.

Cole had the submissive move to the top of a table, and while she got into place, he went over safety information with the crowd. When he finished, he shifted so he faced both her and those of us watching. He looked over the people gathered, and it wasn't my imagination when he did a brief double take at seeing Sasha.

Then he turned his attention to the woman before him, and I thought we all held our breath as he spoke quietly to her and turned the wand on. The lights were dim in the room, which served to showcase the bluish purple light of the wand and tiny spark of electricity that licked the submissive's skin.

Cole's face was a mask of concentration. He'd told us before he started he would only use a low setting tonight, but it was enough. The submissive he worked with held perfectly still, letting out only the slightest moans in pleasure.

He stopped for a second to check in with her after she'd been quiet for a few minutes, and it wasn't until she nodded and he started again that it hit me how loud the room had been with the combination of wand and submissive. I shot a quick glance to Sasha, hoping she didn't feel overwhelmed, but she appeared transfixed by the scene before her.

Her cheeks were flushed and her breathing rapid, but her lips parted in what looked like desire. I imagined she must be picturing herself in the submissive's place, yet when I followed her line of sight, she wasn't captivated by the submissive, but Cole.

At the same moment I realized where her attention was, Cole did as well. He looked up briefly and caught Sasha's gaze. The corner of his mouth uplifted just a bit in a smug half smile.

Sasha gasped and I braced myself, waiting to see if she'd turn and leave the room. But she stood where she was, simply dropping her eyes to the glowing wand.

I looked over at Abby and saw she'd picked up on Sasha's reaction, too.

Definitely a discussion for later.

Chapter Seven

ABBY

We had a leisurely breakfast the next morning, thanks to Linda taking the kids for the weekend. She'd picked them up yesterday before the play party, saying she'd missed them horribly since we moved.

Nathaniel had us sit at the kitchen table. Whenever I had his collar on and he wanted me to speak freely, we'd sit there. I made him bananas Foster French toast. It was a recipe I'd created while I was still single and he loved it. I didn't often have time to cook it, though. One look at Nathaniel's expression when I set his plate down made me vow to do it more often.

"This looks great," he said.

"Thank you, Master. I'm sorry it's been so long, I'll have to make it more often."

"Maybe once we hire a nanny, things will settle down a bit." He took a bite and closed his eyes in bliss.

I sat down, smiling inwardly as I typically did whenever I saw his joy at my cooking. He was an outstanding cook as well, so it really stoked my ego for him to like something I made.

"Tomorrow morning I'm cooking breakfast for you," he said.

I still had his collar on and it wasn't typical of him to cook when I did. "That's unexpected, Sir." I ate a bit of toast, making sure I got a piece of banana.

"I'm fairly certain you'll be otherwise occupied."

I couldn't even start to imagine what he meant by that, so I just nodded. "I look forward to it, Sir. I'll welcome whatever you have me do."

"Mmm."

I didn't think he believed me. I wasn't sure I blamed him.

"Would you like some orange juice, Sir?" I asked.

"No, the coffee's fine. But thank you." He took a bite of banana. "Any thoughts about the meeting last night?"

"Yes, I really want to tell you what I've been thinking. I didn't see anything inherently wrong with their setup. They just seem like a normal group, and in fact I think they have more fun and interesting members than most groups. I like a lot of them, and I'm looking forward to getting to know them better and becoming friends. If you think about the two men who were problems, one was an experienced Dom. The other was a newbie. So I don't think the problems are related."

"Right, and I know Jeff ran background checks. Nothing turned up on either man. I looked over them myself. There's nothing that would have raised a flag for me."

I tapped my fingers on the tabletop. "I wonder if either man would have been invited to join if we'd asked for references."

"The problem with references, though, is you can pick who provides them for you and you obviously won't pick someone who might say something negative."

"What if you had to get a reference from someone already in the group?"

The corner of his mouth lifted and he jotted a note down on the pad at his side. "I like that."

"At least that way, a new member wouldn't be a complete unknown. And since everyone is having to resubmit their paperwork, we'd trust them."

"I wonder if we should go a step further and, even after a group recommendation, there should be a provisional period."

"Like a test?"

"No, I was just thinking more like a probationary period before they are fully accepted as members. It's important we get to know new people before we trust them, isn't it? In fact, maybe something else we should do is have new members meet the senior Dominants. We could stipulate that they meet together over dinner or something. So we can get to know potential members personally."

"That might be a good thing to put in place before they even attend a group meeting," I suggested.

He wrote that down. "I think it'd be good for experienced players if their first play scene or two were observed by a senior member."

"Would senior submissives be allowed to observe the newcomers?"

"Yes, even the submissives."

"Do you think a potential Dom member would take issue

with being observed by one of the submissive senior members?"
I asked.

"If they did, I think that would give us all the insight into
their character we needed, don't you?"

I smiled. "Yes, Sir. Very much so."

"In fact, it might be a good idea to get a sub's thoughts on a
potential Dominant."

"Do you think you'd work it the other way? Have a senior
Dom observe a sub?"

"Fair is fair, right?" he asked through a chuckle.

"That would only be for experienced people. What are your
thoughts for the new ones?"

"I think new members should be made to go through a man-
datory mentor training with a senior member."

"You're putting a lot of responsibility on the senior members.
It's going to take a lot of time to clear a new member."

"But if it works, the tradeoff would be worth it because we'll
know we can trust that person."

"True, but all this will make it harder to join the group, so it
won't get much bigger."

"I'd thought about that," he said. "But again, isn't it worth it
if it keeps everyone safe?"

I watched him for a minute. He was wearing jeans and a soft
T-shirt in a green hue that matched his eyes. It was one of those
everyday moments that took my breath away. Just the joy of a
simple moment, sharing a meal and talking. The way his smile
danced across lips.

The smile deepened. "What?" he asked.

"You." I reached across the table and took his hand. "How

everything comes back to safety. How you won't put up with attitude from a Dom." I dropped my voice. "How damn hot you look in that T-shirt, how it pulls across your chest, and how your face is all scruffy because you haven't shaved yet."

He lifted my hand to his lips and kissed my knuckles. "You're making it very hard for me to concentrate on the group when you say things like that."

"Good, because we've already made a really good start and I think we should put it aside for now and continue with our weekend, Sir."

He tilted his head.

"I did say *Sir*," I reminded him. "And we're at the kitchen table."

"I wasn't going to reprimand you."

I let out a breath. "Oh."

"I was going to say, look at how damn hot *you* are in that T-shirt."

His words were so unexpected, I laughed. "With all due respect, Sir, I find that hard to believe."

"You're right. I was going to agree with you. It *is* time to continue our weekend."

Something about his expression made desire swell low in my belly.

But he was full of surprises. "First thing is a jog."

A jog? Was he serious?

My disappointment must have been obvious. He laughed. "There'll be plenty of time later in the day for what you're thinking. It's been a while since we've jogged together and I know I need a good workout."

I nearly huffed. Sex. Sex was a workout.

"Later, Abigail."

Two weeks later, I stood in front of the large gathering of people for the tri-state conference. Nathaniel and I had driven up for the evening, since it was being held in Philadelphia at a private club. There were easily one hundred people present, and only a handful of them were from our Partners in Play group.

The St. Andrew's cross Nathaniel requested stood behind me. He'd told me he wanted me nude, and though there were parts of my body I didn't like, at the moment I felt sexy and sultry. Being in a BDSM demo, having the opportunity to play in front of people never made me feel self-conscious. When we were in a scene and Nathaniel was controlling me, it was as if I saw myself through his eyes. Even when he didn't say anything, I could see how he felt just by looking in his eyes.

I doubted anyone other than Nathaniel noticed my nervousness. Or at least, I hoped they didn't. They had all smiled warmly and welcomed us when we arrived earlier. I felt the urge to fidget, but forced myself to remain still. Nathaniel placed a hand at the small of my back and I took a deep breath.

"Are you okay?" he asked.

"Yes, Master. Just a few butterflies at being in front of a new group. But overall I'm excited." Sometimes I wondered if it was the excitement that helped turn me on.

"Kneel for me," he said, and I dropped to my knees.

He called the group to order and introduced us.

"Abigail is going to help me demonstrate the use of a bullwhip. Now, there are several ways to use one and while most people associate them with punishment, I want to demonstrate how they can be used for sensual pleasure."

I watched his feet turn back to me. "Ready, my lovely?"

"Yes, Master."

"Thank you. Go stand and face the cross."

My nerves dissolved into erotic excitement as I stood and made my way to the large wooden X. Nathaniel took his time binding me: running his hands along my body and trailing kisses along the inside of my elbow before securing me.

"Before you use a single tail and especially in a nonpunishment scene, you'll want to warm the submissive's skin up with a flogging or something similar." He picked up a waiting flogger and gently started working it along my backside.

I loved floggings. Especially when he worked the flogger seductively across my body, easing me gently into subspace. His strokes grew harder and I fell into my yoga breathing.

"Abigail," he said, "are you with us?"

"Green, Master," I said.

I heard him address the crowd again, but since he wasn't talking to me, I didn't pay attention to what he said. Instead I returned to that blissful place in my mind.

A sharp lick of pain hit my right butt cheek and I knew he had switched to the bullwhip, but the sensation soon diffused into vibrations of pleasure and I couldn't help the moan of contentment that slipped from me.

"Very nice, Abigail."

After a few more strokes he asked, "How are you doing? What color are you at?"

"Green, green, green, Master."

The whip started landing higher up my body and at times I could have sworn he was using two. But it felt so good, I wanted to concentrate on the pleasure and not worry about breaking down everything he was doing.

I got lost in subspace then and was surprised when a few minutes later—or what seemed like just a few minutes later—he said, "So good, Abigail. You did so good."

I wanted to protest because I wasn't ready for it to be over. I wanted more. But I trusted him to know what I needed. He switched the whip out for a flogger and I sighed as I came back down from my subspace high. He didn't say anything when he put the flogger down and ran his hands up and down my body.

Yes! I shouted in my head. This was what I needed, too. His hands on me so I could feel the way he spoke through touch alone.

"You did so well, my lovely," he finally whispered, pressing himself against my back. He undid the buckles attaching me to the cross. "You looked incredible. You made me so proud."

"Thank you, Master."

He placed soft kisses along the back of my neck. I was faintly aware of the quiet shuffle of people and then there was nothing.

"How did it feel?" he asked.

"It felt so good, Master." I still felt warm and floaty inside.

"I'm so glad, baby."

"I thought it would only be painful. I wasn't expecting it to feel so good."

He lifted me in his arms and carried me to a padded table in the corner of the room. As we went, I realized everyone had left.

Once he put me down, he climbed up beside me and pulled a fluffy blanket over both of us. I pushed back against him.

He whispered against the skin at the nape of my neck, "Do you want to come, Abigail?"

"Yes, Master." I was starting to wake up. "So much."

He kissed the spot right at the top of my spine, the one he knew would drive me wild. I shivered when he licked it and bit it softly. Ever so slowly, his hand slid between my legs and teased me.

"You looked so hot being worked over by a whip. You handled it so well. Such a good girl." He continued softly praising me as he worked his finger deeper and started stroking my clit. "When I get you home, I'm going to fuck you properly. For now, I'm going to make you come with my fingers. Come for me. Come all over my fingers like you would my dick."

Granted permission to come, I moved my hips in an attempt to get his fingers deeper.

"There you go," he said. "Work for it. Work those hips and give that needy pussy what it wants. What it needs."

I gyrated my hips. "I need you, Master."

"For now, you're just getting my fingers. My fingers fucking that pussy. Do you want more? Do you want to come? Fuck them like you mean it."

I sucked in a breath and he worked his fingers deeper inside.

"Oh yeah," he said. "You feel so good and my cock is jealous. It can't wait to fuck you. To sink inside and pull out and pound back into you over and over and over." He whispered in my ear, "Are you going to make my cock happy when we get home?"

"Yes, Master."

He pressed his fingers into the spot inside that always got me off. With a grunt, I pushed back hard against him and came around his fingers.

"That's it. That's the way," he said before pulling me close and tight in his arms. My eyes started to grow heavy and I was barely awake to hear him whisper, "Close your eyes and rest now."

"Thank you, Master."

I didn't doze long. It felt like merely minutes later when I became aware of him kissing my back.

I groaned, realizing he was kissing the marks left by whip. "Feels good to have your lips on me, Master."

"Then let me keep doing it."

By the time he'd kissed each and every line, I was once more warm and tingly and desperate for him. But he pulled back again. "I need to dress this."

"I think I prefer your kisses, Master."

"I know I prefer kissing you, but I need to do this." He placed one last kiss on my back. "Get on your stomach."

I rolled over, fully showing him my back. He put cream of some sort on one of the lash lines and I sucked in a breath.

"Does it hurt?" he asked.

"No, not really." I thought about it. "It's just . . . there."

But when he applied ointment to another line, there was a definite sting.

"Okay, it hurts a bit," I confessed. "Which is a bit of a surprise. It didn't hurt at all while you were doing it."

"It didn't?"

"I expected it to, but instead it felt like little tiny bites all over and they kind of shot through me. Almost as if there were a million teeth nibbling at me." I turned my head and looked up at him. "That doesn't make sense. I'm not explaining it right. I know it was only the one single tail. You only used one, right?"

"Right."

"It was amazing."

He placed a soft kiss to my lips. "I'm glad you enjoyed it. That was what I wanted. You know, if you feel up to it, there's a party going on."

I rose on an elbow. "Now?"

Partying sounded fun, but when I went to sit up at his nod, I was sorer than I'd thought. "Ugh. On second thought, maybe we should skip it, Master. I don't want anyone accidentally bumping into my back."

His eyes gleamed with wicked secrets. "I have just the thing in mind."

He climbed off the table and reached for my hand to help me down. Waiting on a nearby table was a thick black robe. Nathaniel held it open for me and I sighed when I put it on, it was so soft.

"Does it hurt your back?" he asked.

"No, Master."

He nodded. "Follow me."

We made our way out the door to a set of elevator banks.

"There's a courtyard out those French doors." He pointed to the end of the hallway. "And there are private rooms that overlook it."

We took the elevator up two stories and exited on the third floor. Nathaniel took my hand and led me to the last door at the end of the hallway. He punched in a security code on the door's keypad.

I peeked inside. It looked like the typical room I'd seen in the

BDSM clubs we'd been to before. A bed took up a large portion of the floor space. But at the back of the room were large French doors.

"Take the robe off and kneel in the middle of the floor," he said just as a knock sounded on the door.

I dropped to my knees and waited. I wondered if he'd invited someone to watch as he had the first time we went to Delaware. I kind of hoped he did; I'd enjoyed those two sessions.

My back was to the door, so I couldn't see anyone, but I strained my ears to hear. There was only minimal chatter, though. Whoever it was didn't stay, but Nathaniel didn't come back to me immediately after they left. I heard his footsteps and the sliding of the French door and he did something outside before joining me.

"Stand up and let's go out on the balcony and have some wine."

The temperature was in the mid-sixties, so it wasn't too cold to be outside naked. There was only one chair, but someone, I assumed Nathaniel, had placed a soft blanket on the floor. As I knelt beside the chair, I noticed there was only one wineglass. I smiled. I liked sharing.

He followed right behind me and sat in the chair. While I waited, he poured the wine, then pressed the glass to my lips.

"Good?" he asked.

"Beyond good. It's my favorite."

He stroked my cheek. "I know."

Loud, pounding music drifted up from the courtyard below. I couldn't see anything from my spot on the floor. The rail was made of solid stone and there were no places to see through.

I leaned back against Nathaniel's legs and sighed. He placed his hand on my shoulder. *This.* This right here, on the balcony felt right. Him and me together. He pressed the glass to my lips and I took another sip. I loved simple moments like this.

We sat there for some time, listening to the music, sipping wine, and simply enjoying being in each other's company. The music grew softer and in its place came the sounds of play: moans, sighs, leather against flesh, and the occasional cry of someone climaxing. The wine made my body feel all warm and buoyant and it was turning me on more and more hearing the sounds of sex, but not being able to see anything.

Nathaniel leaned forward when I started to fidget in arousal and cupped my breast. "Sounds like people are doing more than dancing now, wouldn't you say?"

I rubbed my chest against his hand. "Mmm." He felt so good. "Yes, Master."

He pinched my nipple. "None of that right now."

It was sweet torture having him sit with his hand on my breast and not being able to move.

"There's an interesting scene setting up in the far left corner."

I looked that way, as if the stone in front of me would part and allow me to see. I stifled my sigh.

"Can you see, Abigail?" he asked.

"No, Master."

"Go stand against the railing."

I rose to my feet and as I moved toward the rail, I realized night had fallen completely. The way the balcony was situated, with the darkness covering everything, no one would be able to see me. It would be a lot hotter if we *could* be seen or, better yet, if we were down in the courtyard.

My heart pounded as I took my place. The stone was cool

against my skin. Perfect actually, since I suddenly felt flushed. I looked over the edge and couldn't take my eyes off what I saw.

Below us were about thirty people, most of whom were in various stages of undress and participating in various BDSM play. I scanned the crowd. Two men were talking to each other while one had a naked woman at his feet, giving him a blow job. A large post stood in the middle of the courtyard and at the moment, two female submissives were bound to it while their Dom lightly flogged them.

I hadn't been at the rail long when I felt Nathaniel press along my back. His clothes were rough against me and I couldn't hold back my moan.

"You can't be too loud or else we'll become the main attraction. Though I know you might like that, it's not exactly what I had in mind for tonight."

"I'll be quiet, Master. Or at least, I'll try to. It's hard to be too quiet when what you're doing feels so good."

He laughed and gave my ass a slap. "Can you see the scene I was talking about now?"

I scanned the floor and looked in the direction he'd mentioned earlier. There didn't seem to be much going on other than a very interesting setup in the far corner.

"The two men and the woman?" I asked.

"Yes," he said. "That one." He moved his hands along my body with the long sensual strokes, teasing and tempting me. The two men below us were similarly touching the bound woman. I tried to imagine myself in her place. Having not two, but four hands working to bring me pleasure.

"They're preparing her," Nathaniel finally said, breaking the silence. "Making sure she's ready to take both of them. Maybe she's never serviced two men before."

The two men were talking. I could see their mouths moving, but I couldn't make out what they were saying. At one point, the woman turned her head and spoke to one of them. He reached down and pushed his thumb into her mouth.

Nathaniel peppered kisses along my spine, and gooseflesh rose in the wake of his lips. I couldn't keep my eyes from the trio below us as he slid a finger into me and slowly began pumping. One of the men unbuttoned his pants and the woman took him in her mouth. I gasped as Nathaniel rocked his hips into me.

"Open," he said, pressing the finger that had been inside me against my lips.

I sucked it deep into my mouth, tasting myself and the salt from his skin.

"Do you taste how turned on you are?" He circled his hips again and the action caused my pelvis to hit the wall of the balcony. The coolness from the stone rubbed my clit and sent shock waves through my body.

"Oh, fuck," I said, but tried to hit the spot again.

Nathaniel took my hips and pulled me back. "Not yet, greedy girl. We've just started. Might want to go ahead and think about what you're going to translate into German tonight."

"Please, Master. I can't think about anything but how much I want you inside me."

"I'm not quite ready to fuck you yet. How about if you watch the trio downstairs and tell me what they're doing? In German."

"*Du bis so gemein, Meister,*" I said, telling him he was mean.

"You might want to rethink that, Abigail," he said, and took a step back as if to prove his point. "I can show you mean if you'd like."

"Sorry, Master."

"Besides, I'm not mean."

"Right, Master."

"I'm fucking diabolical." He spoke the last word as he pushed three fingers inside me. "Don't move."

I whimpered. *Holy shit,* he felt so good. I wanted to move and get more of him inside me, but I forced myself to be still.

"Now tell me what they're doing," he said.

I murmured in perfect German that she had one in her mouth.

"Always a good idea to keep a sub's mouth occupied." He hooked his fingers up, touching that spot that drove me crazy. "I'd fuck yours, but you have German to work on. Tell me what the other one is doing."

I replied that his head was between her legs.

"Ah, he's tasting her." He removed his fingers abruptly and I heard him lick them. "Mmm," he hummed.

I expected him to finger-fuck me again, so I was surprised when his hands came up to my shoulders.

"I want you leaning over the stone so that when I fuck you, your nipples scrape the railing. Can you do that?"

"Yes, Master." I readjusted my stance, aided by his hands, pushing me into place.

"Tell me what the two men are doing now."

"The one guy has stopped licking her and he's penetrating her now. She's arching, but the other one is holding her head still while he uses her mouth."

Nathaniel spanked my ass. Hard. *Ow. Fuck.*

"What was wrong with how you answered?" he asked.

Shit.

"I didn't answer in German, Master."

"Right, so answer the question again the right way."

I repeated my answer as he instructed.

"Good girl," he said. "I think that deserves a reward."

I held still, not trusting myself not to move. *"Ich danke dir, Meister."*

He took hold of my waist and then entered me with just the tip of his cock. It was torture, feeling him *right there* but not any farther. I could imagine how good it was going to feel when he finally took me.

But what the hell was he waiting for?

Holding his hips steady, he inched his hands up my body, brushing along my breasts, easing across my shoulders. Ever so gently he wove his fingers through my hair, caressing my scalp. It was slow and sensual and my muscles relaxed under his touch. I anticipated him entering me the exact same way. I sighed in bliss.

Before I finished my sigh, he grabbed my hair, jerked my head back, and thrust inside with one powerful stroke. I almost climaxed and stopped myself just in time.

"Holy shit, Master." I forced myself to take long, deep breaths because I was still dangerously close to coming.

He held still and I gulped at how big he felt inside me. I wasn't sure if it was the angle or our positions or what. But *damn.*

He rolled his hips, going deeper and hitting different spots. I gasped and blindly clutched the wall before me. Holy hell.

"Been too long, hasn't it?" he said, and his voice was coarser than I'd expected.

"What?" My mind was overwhelmed by the physical sensations he'd created in my body. It couldn't process anything requiring something as mundane as thought, much less conversation.

"Since I've taken you like this," he explained. "Hard and fast and with the potential of people watching."

"Yes," I said in a half groan, half moan as he rolled his hips again. "Too long." And I wished we were downstairs on the courtyard, where there was more than just the potential of people watching. It was a guarantee.

He gave a thrust and my chest scraped against the stone just as he said it would. It was just the right amount of *ouch* mixed with *yes* and *please, again more.*

"Tell me what they're doing now."

"In German, Master?"

"Of course."

I took a deep breath and opened my eyes, though they almost fluttered closed as he moved inside me again. My body shivered in response. Parts of me that had been dormant for far too long were waking up and I had to force myself to focus on the trio below us. If I didn't, I knew I wouldn't be able to hold back my climax.

"Tell me," he repeated.

I worked through the German words in my mind and that was enough to keep my climax at bay. "One's fucking her and the other just came in her mouth. Now he's fondling her breasts."

It probably felt similar to what I was experiencing with the stone wall. Though I did wonder if he was stroking or pinching. Was he being rough? As I watched, she let out a yelp. I saw her mouth move and his evil-looking smile at her response. Yes, he was rough and judging by her expression, she loved it.

Behind me, Nathaniel drove into me again and I let out my own yelp.

"You see her getting fucked? You're in a similar situation, except with only one Dom." He started moving faster and I panted in short, choppy breaths.

The woman's head turned slightly and she seemed to look our way. I didn't think we were visible, especially to those in the courtyard. Probably all she saw were moving shadows. But whatever she saw caused a smile to cover her face and she said something to the two men. They answered but didn't look our way. However, I did notice the one started thrusting harder.

Or maybe that was Nathaniel.

Damn, I needed to come. But he had been right, he was acting diabolical and teasing every last ounce of pleasure possible from my body and it was taking all my self-control not to give in to my need to climax. Even translating the actions of the trio into German hadn't helped that much.

"Need to come, Master."

He didn't pause in his thrusting. "You can come after she does."

I almost whined. The big bulk of a man currently driving into the woman didn't appear to be anywhere near reaching his own climax, nor did he seem to be concerned about when she had hers.

Nathaniel slowed down, but if I thought him doing so was going to give me any sort of reprieve, I quickly learned I was mistaken. Slowing down only allowed him to be more intent with his movements.

He took hold of the rail on each side of me and I upturned my hand. Knowing what I needed, he entwined his fingers with mine. We'd been in more intimate settings. We'd done kinkier things. And yet being on that balcony, feeling his presence around me and inside me, hit me with an emotional force that I'd never felt before. Perhaps because it was so close to being a very public scene and yet it was still very intimate and private.

After several long moments of Nathaniel's seductive and sensual thrusts, he once more sped up. I glanced at the trio. They, too, appeared to be nearing release.

"Sie kommen, Herr," I whispered in both relief and regret. *They're coming, Sir.* Relief because that meant it would soon hopefully be time for my own release. Regret because the moment had been so perfect and there were never enough perfect moments.

"I see them," he said. "You're free to come as soon as she does."

The Dom behind her took another handful of hair and pulled her head. Even sitting on the balcony, I clearly saw her back arch and her chest rise and fall in a deep sigh as his mouth formed the unmistakable shape of one word.

"Come."

At his command, she relaxed into her climax. Her eyes fluttered several times and her body shook slightly. The man behind her kept thrusting through her release and wasn't far behind with his own.

"Jetzt kann ich kommen, Meister?" I said, asking if I could come, and at his "Yes," I loosened my grip on the tiny thread of self-control that had been keeping me from my orgasm. At the next pass of his body into mine, he dropped our clasped hands between my legs and rubbed my clit.

"Feel this," he whispered, and moved our hands slightly so I felt him pushing in and out of me. "Feel me fuck you. Feel me as you come all over me. Squeezing me deep inside. Like you don't ever want me to leave your body."

His words were just the thing I needed to send me soaring over the cliff into my climax.

"There we go," he said, still pumping his hips. He grunted as he went deep. "Come hard for me. Never get tired of feeling you come apart." He held still inside while he rode out his own release.

He gently let go of my hands and rubbed my shoulders, slipping down the front of me to cup my breasts. "Sore?"

"Only pleasantly so, Master." The dull ache of my nipples and between my legs was a welcome reminder of what we'd just shared.

"Come here." He pulled me back to sit in his lap. From beside the chair, he took a warm blanket and draped it over my shoulders.

I sighed as contentment settled over me like the blanket. The intimacy of our time by the rail carried over to the chair and I snuggled deeper into arms. Usually, he'd hold me, but I lifted my head slightly and found his lips waiting to take mine in a kiss.

It was soft and gentle and he spoke in whispers against my mouth before cupping my head and slanting his own so he could kiss me fully. I lifted my arms to encircle his neck, feeling his muscles and basking in his warmth. He parted his lips and I followed, kissing him long and deep.

He pulled back and gave me a last quick kiss on the lips. "Better stop for a while. I'm not as young as I used to be."

"You couldn't be in better shape, Master." He certainly had the stamina of a teenager.

His forehead crinkled a bit as he smiled. "Thank you, my lovely."

I ran a hand down his chest, frowning slightly when I realized he still had his shirt on. "Of course, I could get a much better look and make a more accurate observation if you'd take your shirt off."

"You do it."

I looked around for a clock. "How long do we have the room, Master?"

"For as long as we want."

"Good." I kissed his neck. "Then I can take my time."

He let my hands wander down his chest and I caressed him through the material. Teasing him. It wasn't often when I wore his collar that I had free rein to touch him any way I wanted. The shirt he had on was a light blue dress one. I started at the top and unbuttoned the first button, leaning in to lick the skin it exposed.

"You taste good, Master."

"Probably taste like salt."

"Whatever it is, I could taste it every day and not grow tired of it."

He chuckled lightly, but sucked in a breath when I undid the second button and nipped the skin. "Fuck, Abigail."

"We did that already, Master."

"Keep that up and we'll be doing it again. Sooner rather than later."

I kept my mouth to myself while I undid the rest of his buttons. I found, however, that once he was all unbuttoned, I couldn't stop myself. I dropped my head and inhaled the scent of him, reminding me of oak and cedar.

He let out his breath in a low hiss. "Your breath is so warm."

"Are you cold, Master?"

"Not with you in my lap. It's only when you take a deep breath like that, it's all hot and I imagine it lower."

"I can go lower."

He cocked an eyebrow. "I know you can."

And since I had his collar on, if he wanted me to, he'd tell me. But for whatever reason, he seemed content with the way things were, so I stayed in his lap. With one fingertip, I traced one of his nipples, watching as gooseflesh pebbled his skin. He still didn't tell me to stop, so I lowered my head and licked along the path my finger had taken. Then I sucked as much as I could into my mouth and bit him lightly.

He shifted in his seat but didn't move.

"What are you thinking, Master?" It was a question he asked me often in the middle of a scene.

"Thinking about how much longer I'm going to sit here and let you play with me."

"What have you decided?" I asked, nibbling along his neck once more.

"I'm not sure. I'm certainly enjoying your hands on me at the moment."

And for the rest of our time in the private room, we stayed like that. Me in his lap, simply enjoying being close to each other and letting our fingers tease and touch. A simple way to pass the time and yet one we didn't take advantage of often enough.

I wasn't sure how long we stayed on the balcony, but by the time we left, the night had grown darker and most of the party-goers below had left. And though we hadn't done anything public, I felt satisfied and blissful.

Chapter Eight

ABBY

A few days after the tri-state meeting, I'd just sat down at my laptop to do research on an upcoming blog post when my phone rang. It was a New York number I didn't recognize. I glanced at the clock—just after two. Both kids would probably sleep for at least another thirty minutes.

"Hello," I said.

"Abby?" The voice was friendly, but I didn't recognize it any more than I did the phone number.

"Yes."

"This is Lynne. How are you doing?"

"Oh, Lynne, hey. I didn't recognize your voice. How are you?" Lynne belonged to our New York BDSM group. We weren't what I would call close friends, but we were more than passing acquaintances. Before the move, some months ago, her Dom, Simon, had participated in a scene Nathaniel set up in Wilmington.

"To tell you the truth, I've been better," she said with a sigh. "That's why I'm calling."

Her reply made me curious about why she called. "What can I do to help?"

"You remember I worked as an admin for a legal firm, right?" she asked.

"Yes, sure," I said. The firm wasn't one of the largest in the city, but it was well known and had an impressive staff.

"They've had a rough few months and have decided to cut jobs. I've been let go as of last Friday."

"Oh, Lynne, I'm so sorry to hear that." Already my mind was spinning with how I'd be able to help. Nathaniel was my first thought. Surely with a corporation as large as his, he'd be able to find something for her to do.

"I've actually decided it's the kick in the pants I needed to push me to do what I've been wanting to do."

"Oh? What's that?"

"I've always dreamed of being a teacher, but I never did anything about it. Now I'm thinking that maybe I should. I can't right now, obviously. I mean, I don't even have a job and I don't have the money saved for school. But I heard you were looking for a nanny."

It took my brain a few seconds to catch up with her words. "Yes," I finally said. "Yes, we are."

"If you haven't found anyone, I'd appreciate the opportunity to interview for the position."

"The position is still available." We had yet to find someone we connected with who also connected with Elizabeth and Henry. "You know we're living part-time in Wilmington, Delaware, now?"

"Yes, I have family about twenty miles from there. So I'm familiar with the area."

The more I thought about it, the more and more I liked the idea of Lynne working for us as a nanny. I'd always liked her, and having someone in the lifestyle would make many things easier for us. "Are you free this weekend?" I asked. "Would you be willing to come to Delaware to meet with me and Nathaniel and be introduced to Elizabeth and Henry?"

"This weekend would be perfect!" Her voice nearly hummed with relief.

"Great! Let me confirm a time with Nathaniel and I'll e-mail you details." No sooner had I spoken the words than a thought hit me. "What will Simon think about you being in Wilmington?"

She didn't answer and the silence was so absolute I looked at the phone to make sure she hadn't hung up.

"Simon broke up with me," she finally said.

"Oh, Lynne, I'm so sorry to hear that."

"I know we were only together for a little while, but I really liked him. We tried playing a bit, but he said I wasn't ready. He thought I wasn't really a submissive."

I didn't know Simon very well, but it didn't sound like him to break up with her so suddenly. Something else must've been going on with them—or at least with him.

She sighed. "I don't know what I did wrong. And then when I asked him about it, he wouldn't talk."

"That really doesn't sound like Simon. Something's going on. I'll have to talk with Nathaniel." Nathaniel knew him better than I did, so I hoped he might be able to find out what was going on.

"Oh no, don't do that. I don't want Simon to know I was talking about him."

"He won't know. I'll just ask Nathaniel if he knows what's going on." She didn't say anything, so I continued, "I promise Simon won't know you were talking about him."

"Thank you."

"No problem." The monitor at my desk crackled with Henry's babbles. "I have to go, kids are up. I'll be in touch."

I jogged up the stairs, elated because I was willing to bet I'd just found our nanny.

Later that night, after the kids were asleep, Nathaniel and I were relaxing together by the indoor pool. We'd just finished doing laps and were sitting in our deck chairs, both wrapped in robes. We'd turned on a few low lights and lit some candles I kept out by the pool, so the room was bathed in simmering shadows.

"Something must have happened with Simon," he agreed after I told him about my conversation with Lynne. "I only wish I knew what."

"When was the last time you talked with him?"

"I hate to admit how long it's been," he said, shaking his head. "I haven't kept up with anyone the way I should. Especially those in our New York BDSM group."

"Please don't tell him Lynne called. I promised we wouldn't let him know she had mentioned him to me."

"I won't. I'll just call him to catch up. I've been meaning to do it anyway." He ran a towel over his hair, drying it further. "I think it'd make a lot of sense if we hired her to be our nanny and she moved in with us. That way she can put aside money for school instead of paying rent. *And* she's familiar with the life-style. . . ." I nodded at his reasoning. "So she wouldn't be surprised if she came across us doing something in the middle of the night or if she stumbled into the living room and saw you kneeling at my feet while we watched the news."

"Exactly," I said.

"Why don't you call her tomorrow and see when she can come meet with us and the kids? If she doesn't get along with them, there's no reason to move forward."

"This is going to work out. I just have a feeling."

"I hope you're right. It would make things easier for us."

"There is one more thing," I said. "I want to hire Jeff to do a background. I mean, I've always liked her and she was in our New York group, so you would think everything's fine, but we really don't know her that well. . . ."

"You can never be too safe. I agree. Let me know what she says after you talk to her and I'll have Jeff run a preliminary before she comes to Wilmington. If that one comes out well, we'll have her sign paperwork for a more in-depth one."

I nodded. "That would make me feel a lot better. I'm glad you don't think I'm being too cautious."

"There's no such thing when it comes to my family's safety."

His voice was low and gruff and turning me on. Especially the way he was sitting, all wet and half-naked. I glanced up at the clock. Only nine forty-five. Not too late . . .

"Come here for a minute." His voice was downright husky now and I forgot all about the clock.

Perplexed, I walked over to his chair and he scooted over to make room for me.

"What's up?" I asked.

"I set the video camera up in the bedroom." His fingers untied my bikini top and pinched a nipple.

My mouth grew dry. Holy hell, I loved it when he set up a camera. "You did?"

He pinched harder.

"Oh God, Nathaniel . . ."

He dipped his head and nibbled my neck while he slipped a hand between my legs and teased the material aside so he could stroke my entrance.

"Go upstairs and wait for me on the bed."

I groaned. He was making me feel too good to stop and move upstairs. But he had the camera set up and I knew that would be fun, so I made myself move away from him and took my time getting to our room. While I walked, I thought about how I was going to act.

He found me a few minutes later, standing at the foot of the bed.

"I thought I said *on* the bed?" he asked, arms crossed.

"Don't want to," I said. I didn't have his collar on and I felt like playing hard to get. "I don't want you to fuck me."

He lifted an eyebrow.

I winked at him, then said, "You better let me out of this room."

He took two long steps to me and put his hand around my throat. Not tight, but there. "You're not going anywhere, naughty virgin maiden. I've captured you and you're going to bend over that bed and let me fuck you."

Barbarian and captured virgin maiden . . . we hadn't done that one in a while.

"Please, Sir," I said, batting my eyelashes. "If my betrothed finds out I'm not pure, he won't marry me."

"Not my problem, wench," he said, getting into his role. "Your father should have thought about that before he allowed you to go off by yourself into the woods." He swept a finger across my breast. "And he should have warned you about the dangers of swimming naked."

"I didn't know anyone was watching."

"I don't believe you. I think you knew I was there."

"I didn't. I—"

"Silence," he said. "You're mine now and you have to serve me."

"But, Sir." I blinked my eyes. "I'm a virgin maiden. I don't know how."

"I'll instruct you. And if you do a good job, I'll keep you to myself. Do a poor job and I'll give you over to my guards to do with you what they want."

"No, anything but that." I tried to look properly subdued. "Tell me what to do, Sir."

He pointed to the floor. "Kneel here and remove my drawers."

I snickered. "Your drawers? Have you turned into a dresser?"

"Knickers?" he suggested.

"Maybe loincloth?" We both laughed, and I moved to my knees and pulled his bathing suit down over his hips, revealing his erection. I gasped. "My heavens, Sir. What is that?"

"It's my cock."

"It's so big. Why's it standing up like that?"

"It has to be hard and stand up so I can push it inside your pussy."

I kept my eyes on his massive length. "My what?"

"Your sex. The hole between your legs."

"The one tingling right now?" I asked.

"Yes. That tingle is your body getting your sex ready to take my cock inside you."

"I don't think it'll fit. It's huge. Surely it'll split me open."

"It'll be tight and I'll have to push hard." He fisted himself and I swore he grew bigger. "No doubt it'll hurt when I break through your maidenhead, but you will allow me to do it and you will take my cock all the way inside."

"Let's say you're able to get that thing inside me. What will you do then?"

"Touch it," he commanded, ignoring my question. "Feel how hard it is."

I reached out and ran my finger around the head. "I touched it. Now tell me what happens once it's inside me."

"Call it by its name. It's a cock. Not *that thing*."

"Please, Sir. Tell me what happens once your cock is inside me?"

"Very good," he said. "That's when the real fun starts. Then I get to fuck you. And I'm going to fuck you hard and as deep as possible. And you will not be pure and your betrothed will not marry you, but you won't care because you'll only care about my cock from this day forward."

"Please, Sir. No."

"I'm tired of this conversation. My cock is hard and ready. I'll fuck you now or give you over to the guards. The decision is yours."

"Please don't make me. It won't fit."

"Enough. I'll call the guards to take you away so they can all take turns fucking you."

I made my eyes wide. "No, Sir. Please. Not that. I'll do anything."

"Anything?"

I nodded.

"Say it."

"I'll do anything, Sir."

"Very well. First, you're going to kiss my cock and then I'll show you how I'll fuck your pussy by taking your mouth. After that you're going to bend over the bed so I can take you."

"Yes, Sir."

"But that's not all. You said anything. So you're also going to offer your ass to me."

I faltered just a bit. There wasn't any lube out. Of course, that didn't mean he couldn't get some out of a drawer. I knew he'd never take my ass without it, but the thought pulled me out of my role for a minute.

"Guard!" he said with a smirk.

I jumped, not expecting him to call out like that. But one look at his face and I knew he'd said that about my ass because he knew it'd stun me momentarily. I could have begged him not to call the guards, but since I'd already done that a few times, I decided to do something to momentarily stun him.

I gave him a smirk of my own, leaned forward, and kissed the head of his cock. "Mmm, you taste like cotton candy, Sir. Do all cocks taste like sweet sugary treats?"

He choked out a laugh. "Come here," he said, pulling me up from the floor and gathering me in his arms. He cupped the back of my neck and pulled me close for a kiss.

"No more barbarian?" I said against his lips.

"Not right now." He nibbled my ear. "Maybe later."

"Good," I said. "I like your cock too much to act like a proper virgin."

"Just as well. I doubt I could be gentle enough for a virgin." He kissed me once more, then pulled back. "Since we couldn't stay in role for the role play, we'll have to do something else. You have two minutes to make me come with your mouth. I want those hot lips around my cock. I want you to take me in your throat as far as you can and when I come, I want your eyes on me as you swallow."

It was more than his voice or his command that turned me on. It was more than the role play and the anticipation of what was coming next. It was the thought that I was being filmed, that there was another presence in the room besides the two of us. "Nothing would give me more pleasure."

He brushed my cheek once more. "One minute, fifty seconds."

Shit.

I dropped to my knees and engulfed him in my mouth, sucking hard, and taking him deep. I grabbed his ass and held him to me. He pumped his hips in and out.

"I love fucking your mouth. Feeling you hot and wet around me."

I wasn't sure how much time I had left, but I knew if he was still talking in complete sentences, I probably wasn't going to make his time limit. In all honesty, that might have been his plan. But he didn't count on one thing. . . .

I lightly stroked the skin leading to his anus.

"Damn it," he said, jerking in my mouth.

I did it a second time and when he thrust forward again, I circled his opening. I couldn't insert my finger without lube, but I pressed gently and gave the illusion I might.

"Fuck!" he said again, and he grabbed my hair tight, holding my head still as he came.

After cleaning him off, I dropped back to my knees and waited. I didn't have to wait long.

"Bed. Now."

I climbed up on the bed. I didn't have his collar on, but it still turned me on to submit to him. It used to bother me that I liked it so much. Now, though, I simply accepted it. It was who I was, just like my hair color.

He moved to the end of the bed, his eyes hungry as they raked over my naked body. "I want you to work yourself to where you're on the verge of coming and I want you to be vocal while you do it. Get into proper position so I can watch."

I shifted and got on my back, spreading my knees slightly, allowing him an unobstructed view. "Can you see how much I want you when I'm like this?"

"Yes. Very nice. Show me how you like me to touch you."

I circled my breasts with both hands. "I love your hands on me. When you come to me urgently and you need me. How you turn me on simply by playing with my breasts. Sucking my nipples." I plucked one. He'd only used clamps on me once since Henry's birth and that was in Delaware before we moved. "I wonder if Master would like to decorate my nipples with his clamps sometime soon."

"Yes, I think so. It's been too long since I've seen those tits taking the teeth of my clamp. Watching how you try to get away when I pull their chain."

He wasn't lying. Those things had fucking hurt when he first put them on. When he connected them with a chain and pulled, the shock flew through my body and centered right on my clit. For the first few seconds, I'd fight it. Try to get away from the pain, but Nathaniel knew better and wouldn't let me. He knew the pleasure headed my way if I simply gave in and let the feeling complete its path.

"I would welcome you pulling the chain."

"Pinch those nipples. Pull at them."

I obeyed. My breasts were so sensitive I hoped he had me move forward relatively soon. Just thinking about him using the clamps turned me on, and when I added the way he watched me as I pulled and pinched, I feared I couldn't hold back my release.

"Slip your hands down between your legs. See how wet you are."

I groaned, knowing I was going from one form of torture to another. But I slid my hands down my body and slipped them inside. "So wet."

I glanced up and he was watching me intently, his hand stroking his cock. "So wet for me?"

"Yes."

"But you were a naughty girl when you had my cock in your mouth, weren't you?"

"I was? But I made you come in less than two minutes."

His hand was working faster, his erection growing as a result. "Ah, but were those my only instructions?"

"I think so?" I thought back. Hadn't they been?

"I believe my command was to make me come in two minutes with your mouth."

Oh, fuck.

"And how did you make me come?" he asked.

"With my fingers."

"Yes, my wicked girl. You thought you'd get me off faster if you played with my ass, didn't you?"

"Yes, and apparently it worked." I couldn't let him forget that.

"True, but you didn't follow my specific directions, wouldn't you agree?"

He was right, damn it all. "I suppose."

"What would I have said if it'd been appropriate to use your fingers?"

"You've have said, 'Make me come in under two minutes.'"

He slowed his hands. His erection was once more thick and long. "Since you didn't follow instructions and decided to play with my ass instead, I'm going to fuck yours."

I waited for him to say I couldn't come, but he didn't. I was going to make damn sure I heard every word he said from now on.

"I'm going to get on the bed and you're going to lower your ass onto my cock." He nodded toward the nightstand. "Get the lube. It's in the top drawer."

I rolled to the side and rummaged in his nightstand drawer for the lube. By the time I found it and rolled back to the middle, he was lying down on the bed, fisting his cock, his hand moving up and down. Knowing it would soon be in me.

Oh, fuck yes.

"Don't sit there looking at it," he said with a smile. "Get it ready for your ass."

I took the lube and squeezed some into my palm. I rubbed my hands together and then started on his cock.

"Straddle me," he said, and I hurried into place, with a knee on either side of his body. "Put some in my hand."

I put a good-sized amount in the palm of his hands and went back to his cock.

"There you go. Get that cock ready. Get it ready to take your tight ass."

Fuck, when he talked like that, I couldn't wait to get him inside me. One of his fingers started playing with my anus. I resisted the temptation to push against his finger.

"Have you been using your plugs?" he asked.

"Yes, of course." After forgetting to use the plugs the month before our honeymoon, I'd never made that mistake again. The only time I hadn't used a plug on a regular basis was when I was pregnant. Nathaniel limited our anal play then.

"You love it, don't you?" he asked, dipping a finger inside. "Servicing my cock with your ass. Letting me fuck you there?"

"Yes, so much." He knew I did. I loved how it exhibited my submission to him. Offering that part of myself to him, that part that no one else had ever taken. I wouldn't have believed it possible before I met him, but over the years, I'd had some of my most intense orgasms from anal sex.

In fact, the first time he'd taken me there, he'd also used a vibrator. The closest I'd ever get to double penetration. I remembered the books I'd been reading and how I'd imagined being between two men, servicing two Doms.

"What was that thought, Abby?" he asked, pushing his finger deeper and rubbing one of my nipples with the other.

"You let me experience, sort of, what double penetration would be like. When you use a vibrator, when you, *oh, fuck yes.*" I momentarily lost track of my thoughts when he hooked his finger inside me.

He looked smug. "Yes, it's the best I can do, since I don't have two cocks."

I was impaled by his finger and I knew what would soon be replacing it. I wanted it. Badly.

"Now," he said, "I think it's about time you mounted up so I can fuck you properly."

I rose above him slightly, knowing he was lining himself up. I looked down so I could watch as I lowered myself.

"There you go. Take that cock," he said. "Going to fuck that ass."

I closed my eyes when I felt him start to enter me and I couldn't stop the moan that escaped my lips. That first penetration was always the best. The most intense. The initial stretch, followed by the push inside, finally feeling him fill me so completely; there wasn't room for anything other than him. Even my thoughts belonged to him.

"Oh, fuck yes," he said. "Ride me."

He went so deep in this position. I felt him everywhere. For a second I wasn't sure I could move. His hands grabbed my waist and he started lifting me and then bringing me back down on him.

"Ah. Ah. Ah," I panted in time with our movements.

He worked his hips harder and faster. "Yes, damn it. You like me fucking your ass, don't you?"

I made some sort of sound, it didn't sound like anything to

me, but Nathaniel knew exactly how I felt and reacted. I worked my body in time with his hands, needing him harder and deeper.

"Naughty girls love cock and take it anywhere their man wants to put it." His voice was rough. "Look to your right, Abigail. See how naughty you are."

I knew what I'd see when I turned my head. I'd planned the bedroom after all. I was the one who decided to place a mirror exactly where it'd be possible to see ourselves. Even then, it was still somewhat of a shock to see me wanton and free, fucking myself with his cock.

"See it?" he asked. "See how naughty you are?" His hand drifted to my breasts and he fondled me roughly.

Watching us in the mirror was even better than watching us on film. With the mirror, I felt every thrust of his hips, every pinch of his fingers on my sensitive nipples. My eyes threatened to roll back in my head, but he wouldn't allow it.

"Don't even think about closing your eyes," he said. "I want you to watch as I come inside you. Hold still."

I held still suspended above him, bracing myself for what I knew was coming. "Please let me come," I begged.

"Yes," he said, right before he began punishing thrusts that hit me oh so right. Over and over he stroked in and out of me and my release was rushing toward me, unstoppable.

"Fuck, fuck, oh, holy fucking shit." The movement of him within me, the sight of us in the mirror, was too much and I gave in to the building need and let my climax crash over me.

"Yes. Damn it." They were the only words he could manage as his own climax made him stiffen and press deep inside me.

I fell on top of him, exhausted, but he held me tight in his arms, kissing my hair and murmuring his love. I lifted my head for a soft kiss. It wasn't until we were both almost asleep that I realized I needed to call Lynne back. Too tired to move and knowing it was too late, I put it on my mental to-do list for the next day.

Chapter Nine

ABBY

Nathaniel had business meetings in Wilmington the following afternoon, so he was working from home in the morning. We all ate breakfast together and he went with me to drop the kids off at preschool. Then we came home to find my supervisor, Meagan, waiting for me. Nathaniel nodded her way to welcome her before closing himself in his office to work.

He wasn't one to hold grudges, but I'd wound up in a bad situation a few months ago and he blamed Meagan.

"He's never going to like me, is he?" she asked as I led her into the library.

I decided to treat that as a rhetorical question. "I can't believe you're here this early. When you said you'd stop by today, I thought it'd be closer to lunchtime."

"I spent the night in a little bed-and-breakfast nearby," she said. "I do that sometimes, just take a night and get out of the city. It clears my head."

We chatted in the library for a while about work, discussing the show and possibilities for the Web site. She asked to see the house and I was giving her a tour when the doorbell rang.

"Nathaniel's in a conference call. I need to get that," I said to Meagan, hurrying from the kitchen to get the door.

"No problem," she said. "I need to be heading back to the city anyway. I'll walk with you."

We made our way to the front door. As expected, Nathaniel's office door was closed as we walked by and I heard someone speaking on the speakerphone.

"I don't think he was expecting anyone," I said. "He would have told me if he was."

Apollo sat by the front door, waiting, but trotted up to Meagan when he saw her. He was timid around most people, but he liked her. Meagan had told me once that she always had a golden retriever growing up, but her current apartment wouldn't allow dogs.

I peeked through the peephole, surprised at who I saw. I unlocked the door and opened it.

"Mr. DeVaan," I said. "Please come in."

I'd met Master DeVaan the first time Nathaniel and I went to Wilmington. He owned an art gallery there, but I also found out that he was a photographer. One of his specialties was erotic photos.

"Thank you, Abby," he said. "Sorry to just drop by like this, but your portrait was delivered yesterday. I thought I'd bring it over myself."

"Luke?" Meagan asked in a voice so strained that I turned my entire attention to her. She was so pale she looked as if she'd seen a ghost. For a second she looked as if she just might be one herself.

DeVaan seemed to notice for the first time that we weren't alone. "Meagan? Is that you?"

An uneasy silence fell across the room, broken only by Nathaniel coming to the door.

"DeVaan," he said. "I just got your text. I'm sorry I didn't reply. I've been in teleconferences most of the morning." He made it into the foyer and immediately noticed the tension between Meagan and DeVaan. "I would introduce you, but it appears you might already know Meagan."

Meagan smiled a little too sweetly. "Our paths crossed years ago," she said, and I got the impression she wanted to speak before DeVaan did. "Isn't that right, Luke?"

So that was his first name. Funny, he didn't look like how I pictured a Luke. He was quite handsome with blue eyes that always seemed as if they were in on a secret. At Meagan's question, his voice took on the soft, seductive tone I remembered from when we'd meet in Delaware.

"If that's what you want to call it, sweetheart," he said, and Meagan flinched.

Oh yes, there was something there. In the few short moments since I opened the door, Luke had gone from average ordinary man to a hunter and it was crystal clear to everyone that Meagan was his prey.

Nathaniel cleared his throat. "Your text said you had Abby's portrait?"

Luke held up the package in his right hand. "Yes, would you like to see?"

Nathaniel looked over at me. He hadn't told me which picture he'd selected from the photography session he'd arranged not too long ago. "Why don't you follow me?" he said, and the two men went down the hall. Luke didn't turn back.

"And with that, I'm out of here," Meagan said.

Of course, I had two thousand questions I wanted to ask her, but she clearly didn't want to talk, so I only nodded.

I held the door open for her while she rummaged in her purse for her keys. "Damn it," she said, digging in her pockets. "I think I left them in the library."

"I can go get them," I said. "If you want to wait here."

"I'll go with you."

I thought the two guys would be in the office, so I was surprised to find it empty when we walked past. That meant they were probably in the library, because I doubted Nathaniel took him upstairs to the playroom.

And in fact, the two men were standing by the very chairs we'd recently vacated. I glanced at Meagan, prepared to offer to go get her keys by myself. But she pushed her shoulders back and held her head high, and I knew she was going to follow me inside.

She didn't follow me, though. She walked right past me, into the library, and up to the two men. "I left my keys."

Luke snorted. "Likely."

Meagan glared at him. "Don't even go getting a big head. I left them here before I knew it was you at the door."

"I thought you might want to see me," Luke said. "It's been what? Two years?"

"You know where to find me. I'm at the club almost every weekend."

Luke crossed his arms and leaned against the table at his side. "You still hang out at that dive?"

"It's not that bad," Meagan said. I really wanted to interrupt and say yes, it was that bad, but I wasn't about to remind Meagan of the bad experience I'd had there the one time she took me.

"It's horrible," Luke said. "But not for long. I've put a bid in to buy it."

Meagan almost dropped her keys again. "You what?"

"I've decided to diversify. Open up a new business venture. Someone needs to shake that place up."

"I guess I'll have to enjoy it while I can then, before you go and ruin it like you do everything else." Meagan nodded toward me and Nathaniel. "See you two later. Luke, see you in another two years. Three, if I'm lucky."

She took a step toward the library door, but Luke blocked her. "If all goes according to plan, the club will be under my management in two months. I'll send you an invitation to the opening."

"I'm busy that weekend."

He smirked and then his voice dropped. "We'll play it your way for now, sweetheart."

She started to say something, but instead flipped her hair over her shoulder and marched out of the library. He watched her retreating figure and when she disappeared, he let out his breath in a long exhale before turning around.

Nathaniel raised an eyebrow at him. "That was interesting."

Luke gave a half smile. "Meagan and I have a bit of unresolved business," he said, turning back to the package, clearly signaling he didn't want to discuss it any further. "Let's get this portrait out. I want to see what you think."

My heart pounded. I normally didn't like pictures of myself, but I was really curious to see how this one had turned out. Master DeVaan was a real artist, which was why we had asked him to take my photograph. I remembered the photos he had in the back room of his gallery. They were subtly erotic and graceful.

He slid my framed photo out of the box, but all that was visible was the back. "I went ahead and framed it. Thought that would be easier for hanging."

Yes, whatever. Just let me see it.

Luke smiled. "I have to say, I'm really pleased with the way this turned out."

He slowly turned it around and I forgot how to breathe.

It was stunning.

I couldn't believe what I saw. The image was so perfect, so beautiful, so . . . there weren't words.

"I know it was only to be Abby's portrait, but when I saw this proof, I just knew," Luke said.

"I've never seen anything so exquisitely beautiful," Nathaniel whispered. "The angle . . ."

The image of us was in black-and-white and somehow taken from above. It showed my back, my hair pulled to one side to showcase my collar, and the rope binding my arms behind me. That alone would have made a gorgeous picture, but the addition of Nathaniel was what set it apart.

His head rested in the middle of my lower back, and looking at the picture, I could almost feel his lips pressing against my skin. His hands were splayed across my shoulder blades, highlighting the rings he wore: his wedding band on his left, the ring I gave him to symbolize our D/s relationship on his right.

"I can't stop looking at it," I said.

"That's the highest praise you could possibly give me," Luke said.

"I love it," Nathaniel said. "I never imagined it being so incredible." He slipped an arm around my waist. "And thank you for asking us to pose. This is so much better than what I had imagined."

"Too bad we have to leave it in the playroom. I'd love to show it off."

"And shock all our family members?"

"Nah," I joked. "Just a few of them."

"You know," Luke said, "if the bid I put in on the shady BDSM club goes through, I'll need to redecorate. Would you be opposed to me using some of the other pictures from the session? I can ensure that your identity is protected."

Nathaniel's smile faded just a bit. "I'll have to think about that."

"Take your time. I'll give you access to the file so you can see the other pictures."

Even though we'd agreed the pictures would be for us alone, I kind of liked the idea of showing them off. After all, they were beautiful and Luke said there was no away to identify us from them. I looked forward to talking to Nathaniel about them.

Luke shook Nathaniel's hand and nodded in my direction. "I need to be on my way. I'm so glad you like the picture. It was an honor to be invited into your playroom."

"I'll walk you out," Nathaniel said.

While he did that, I stayed in the library, looking at the

photograph. A few minutes later, Nathaniel came back into the room and slipped his arms around me from behind.

"I still can't stop looking at it," I said, leaning back into his embrace.

"It has a hypnotic power about it."

"It's so intense and yet tender at the same time."

He swept my hair to the side, baring my neck. "Just like us?" he asked before dropping a kiss on the nape of my neck.

"Mmm, exactly."

"What do you think of Luke putting some of our pictures up around the club?"

His lips were still moving against my skin and it prickled in response. "I like the idea actually," I said.

I could feel his smile. "Why doesn't that surprise me?"

"Because you know me and you know being watched turns me on." I took a deep breath. "But I understand if you don't want him to use them. If you think it's too invasive."

He turned me to face him. "There are two ways to look at it. For one, if someone's looking at the picture, they're in the club, right?"

"Right, but some might say you have more to lose."

"Even if the picture was seen outside the club, all someone would know is it was of a couple with dark hair."

I took his right hand. "As long as you ensure that this isn't seen," I said, twisting his ring. It was platinum and engraved with a unique pattern.

"True, there's only one of these."

"But other than that, I say we at least look at the other pictures. We can tell him which ones we wouldn't mind him using."

"Okay. I'll let you know when he sends me the other shots."

I nodded and he looked down at his watch. "I have another meeting starting in twenty minutes. When are you leaving to get the kids?"

"Not for another couple of hours."

"Let's go find a place in the playroom for this."

"If you think you'll have time." My heart pounded just thinking about going into the playroom together, even though I knew we weren't going to be doing anything.

He played with a strand of my hair. "I think I can spare a few minutes to hang a picture." Then his voice dropped seductively. "Who knows? It might be that it only takes five minutes to hang the picture. Then I'll have an entire fifteen minutes to fill."

I took his hand and we made our way upstairs.

Chapter Ten

ABBY

On Wednesday night, two days later, I found myself kneeling in Daniel's playroom for a demo with Nathaniel. My head was lowered and I closed my eyes as the almost highlike sensation I always got when we did something in front of people rushed through my veins. I couldn't explain why, but lately the need for that high was growing and I was glad Nathaniel had these opportunities for us to be in front of people. I was on a platform in the playroom, and that only added to my excitement. I felt as if I were onstage.

I didn't know what he had planned for tonight, but I had a feeling it was something different. He didn't have me naked this time. *And* he'd had me wait in a side room while he talked with the other Dominants in private before we began.

Now I heard the sound of Nathaniel's footsteps as they came near me. Then there was silence as he stood before me and I focused on the black leather of his shoes, which was all I could see with my eyes downcast. Excitement flooded my body.

"Hello, Abigail," he said.

"Hello, Master."

"Stand up for me."

I slowly rose to my feet and met his gaze. His lips were curved up in a sultry smile that hinted at deliciously evil plans.

"I have one command for you today that you are not to disobey," he said. "You are not to sit in the chair on the platform. Understood?"

I looked around. A chair sat to his side near the edge of the platform.

Simple enough. "Yes, Master."

"Tell me, what is the one thing you are not to do?" he commanded.

"I am not allowed to sit in the chair on the platform, Master."

"Excellent." He looked down to the crowd. "Cole?"

My heart jumped to my chest. Cole? Nathaniel was going to invite *him* to participate? No wonder he'd asked me to wait outside while he spoke to the crowd. He probably wanted them to make note of the look of complete shock on my face.

I watched as the man in question rose from the crowd and climbed the stairs to join us on the platform. He wore a gray three-piece suit and it was beautiful. After being married to Nathaniel for as long as I had been, I knew a thing or two about men's suits. The one Cole had on was clearly custom-made. It should have been ridiculous that he wore it to a BDSM meeting where he would be part of a demo session, but somehow on him it worked.

He appeared to know the impact seeing him dressed in such a manner had on me. The corner of his mouth lifted in a brief smile of acknowledgment before his expression once more took on the look I'd seen on him before in a playroom setting.

"Abigail," Nathaniel said. "I've asked Cole to run the scene from here. Any command from him you can take as a command from me."

The reason why I wasn't naked suddenly made more sense. "Yes, Master."

He nodded to Cole and walked down the steps.

"How are you doing today, Abby?" Cole asked.

"Slightly more anxious now, Sir."

He chuckled. "Because of me?"

"Yes, Sir. Your reputation precedes you."

"I'm sure you have nothing to worry about. Master West speaks very highly of you."

"Thank you, Sir." Nathaniel's indirect praise warmed me and made me want to show everyone it wasn't misplaced. Whatever Cole threw my way, I'd handle.

"Tell me your safe words."

"Red, yellow, and green, Sir."

"Very good. Go sit in the chair."

I actually took a step toward it before I remembered that was the one thing Nathaniel told me not to do. I looked at him for some sort of direction, but his expression gave me no hint as to what I was supposed to do.

"Are you hesitating, sub?" Cole asked.

"No, Sir." I shook my head.

"And yet you aren't moving. It was a very simple command,

one I would think a submissive of your experience would not find hard to carry out."

"Yes, Sir. But you said——"

He snapped his fingers. "Silence. I know what I said."

I was screwed either way. If I sat in the chair I would be breaking Nathaniel's command, but if I didn't I would be breaking Cole's. There was simply no way to obey.

You are not allowed to sit in the chair on the platform.

Unless . . .

I squared my shoulders and walked over to the chair. It was a metal folding chair, and it didn't weigh much. I picked it up and started carrying it past him to the stairs. A look of complete shock covered his face.

"What are you doing, Abby?" he asked.

"Master's command was that I was not allowed to sit in the chair on the platform, Sir. I'm going to put it on the floor and then sit in it, so I can obey *your* command."

There was subdued laughter from those watching and it occurred to me that my loophole was Not A Very Good Thing.

"Put. It. Down," he said in a harsh voice.

I put it down.

"Now sit in it."

I sat.

There was the *thump, thump, thump* again as he walked toward me. He crossed his arms and looked at me with blue eyes so cold I actually shivered.

"Do you think that's funny, Abby?" he asked. "To make the Dom you're in a scene with look like an idiot?"

"No, Sir."

"So why would you do that?"

"I was trying to follow your directions, Sir, and to follow Master's at the same time."

"Did your idea of following my directions make you feel better?"

"No, Sir."

"And you know what else?" he asked.

I was afraid to ask. I simply shook my head.

His lips curved up in an evil, wicked grin. "You're sitting in the chair Master West specifically told you not to sit in."

Damn. Damn. Damn. Damn.

He straightened up. "Fortunately, I wore the appropriate outfit for a discipline session."

Discipline? Nathaniel was going to allow this? I tried to catch his eye in the crowd, but Cole was in the way and I couldn't see around him.

My heart pounded in my throat, but I told myself if Nathaniel had a problem, he would put a stop to it. Cole hesitated, maybe waiting for me to safe-word, but when I didn't, he took a blindfold from his jacket pocket.

"I don't normally blindfold submissives for this, but in your case I think I will." He stepped back. "Stand up and hold on to the back of the chair."

I stood and quickly slid to stand behind the chair so I could hold the top of it with both hands. Within seconds, Cole had secured the blindfold around my head, covering everything in darkness.

With my sight gone, I strained my ears as hard as possible to hear something, anything that would give me a clue as to what was happening or what he had planned. There was a shuffling sound and two soft thumps behind me as if something was being dropped to the floor. Toy bags?

"Master West," Cole said. "Hand me the cane we discussed earlier."

Nathaniel didn't say anything, but Cole's simple request told me everything I needed to know. Whatever he was getting ready to do, he'd already cleared it with Nathaniel. I hated being punished with a cane, but this was for the demo and I'd been caned before. I knew I could handle it.

Though something told me it would be an entirely different thing being caned by Cole.

And there would be people watching and I wanted to make Nathaniel proud. Plus—and I knew it was crazy—it turned me on a bit to know I was being observed.

The crowd was so silent. I heard Nathaniel bring the cane to Cole and then the sound of Cole's footsteps returning to where I stood.

"I'll only do two. Hard and fast," Cole said. "This is for your disobedience."

I tensed my body for a second, then forced my muscles to relax. It hurt less that way. Cole whipped the cane through the air a few times. Damn evil Doms. I thought they did that just to get inside a submissive's head.

"No need to count," he said.

I curled my fingers, gripping the back of the chair as hard as I could.

I heard him take a step back. The cane whistled as he pulled back and then sang louder as it cut through the air on its downward path. I held my breath, waiting for impact.

It landed with a vicious-sounding strike and I grunted before realizing it hadn't touched me. Instead it had hit something slightly to my right.

What the hell?

I didn't have time to think anything else because it landed again with a hard smack to my left and I squealed.

I held perfectly still. That was two, but they hadn't landed on me. I didn't know if they counted or if he was simply warming up. At that moment in time, I didn't know much of anything. I wasn't sure I could speak my own name. Nothing made sense.

Cole lightly touched my shoulder. "Stand up and take the blindfold off, Abby. It's over. You did a beautiful job."

My hands trembled as I attempted to untie the blindfold, but my fingers fumbled and I couldn't get them to do what I wanted.

"Nathaniel," Cole said in a low voice.

Within seconds, familiar arms held me and ever so slowly the blindfold fell away. Nathaniel's warm eyes were the first things I saw and I smiled in spite of the conflicting emotions swirling around inside me.

"Can you make it down the stairs?" he asked, and I nodded.

Once we'd made it down, he led me out the door to a side room. He sat down on a plush couch and pulled me into his lap. I rested my head against his chest and closed my eyes. When I started feeling more like myself, I looked up at him and asked, "What was that?"

"That, my lovely, was a mind-fuck."

I opened my mouth to ask him more, but he placed a finger over my lips. "I want Cole to join us before we discuss."

I nodded. "Is he coming in here?"

"Yes, he wanted to give us a few minutes alone." He reached for a robe beside him. "Want to put this on?"

Even though I wasn't naked, I was still exposed more than I wanted to be after a scene was over. Especially if we were going to be talking about it. "Yes, Master."

I slipped the robe on, but returned to Nathaniel's lap. My shelter.

The door cracked open and Cole stuck his head in. "Mind if I come in?"

"If you're ready," Nathaniel whispered.

"Yes, Sir," I said. "Please come in."

Cole made his way to where we were. He still had on his three-piece suit, but his easygoing smile was back. He sat down on the opposite end of the couch. Close but not touching.

"I called Cole last week because I wanted to do a mentally challenging scene for the demo," Nathaniel said.

"Nathaniel told me the two of you haven't done much in the way of mental play," Cole added.

I shook my head.

"It's intense, like a physical scene, but in a completely different way. I find it utterly fascinating. With all our science and research, there's still so much of the human brain we don't understand. All the tiny details we take in and what we do with them and how we think."

"Is that why you wore a three-piece suit?" I asked.

"Partially," he said. "I knew it would surprise you and I wanted you slightly off balance. Not knowing what to expect. But this is actually what I wear to discipline sessions."

"Seriously?" Who'd ever heard of that?

"Seriously." He smiled. "Assuming I have time to prepare us both and it's not a matter of the submissive needing immediate correction."

I shivered as I tried to imagine one of his planned discipline sessions. There was no doubt in my mind it would be very calm, very controlled, and not easily forgotten by the submissive in question.

"I assume you usually use a cane in these sessions?" I asked.

"Yes, almost always." He shifted forward, placing his arms on his knees. "I've found mental play is often more intense because it can force a submissive to think through her motivation."

"Like Master giving me a command and then you commanding me to go against it?"

"Yes, rather like a catch-22. What command do you break? Which one would he want you to break?"

"Or maybe he doesn't care, because either way you're going to mess up," I added.

"Almost makes your head hurt," he said. "Of course, then you have the submissives who look for a loophole."

I'd been thinking about the commands and decided they had been carefully worded and stated a certain way on purpose. Cole made a living with words and if he'd helped plan the scene, only one thing made sense. "You knew I'd try to take the chair off the platform."

"I did. In fact, while you were in the side room before the scene, we told the group what we were doing and told them if you started to walk off the platform with a chair, they were to laugh."

"You guys planned *that*, too?" I asked, and behind me, Nathaniel chuckled.

"Yes, Abby. We planned everything. I wasn't completely certain you'd try to take the chair off the platform. I knew I would have to goad you a bit."

"Oh, right," I said. "I forgot that part for a minute, when you told me I'd been a submissive long enough to know what to do?"

"Mind-fuck disguised as humiliation."

"And you were never going to cane me?" I asked.

"Of course not. If you'd done something horribly insulting or disrespectful, I'd have let Nathaniel deal with it."

I twisted in Nathaniel's arms. "It seemed so real at the time."

"Ah," Nathaniel said. "Now, there's where you're wrong. It didn't just seem real. It was."

"Right now I feel like it was a play I wasn't given the script for."

"Don't you see?" Cole asked. "If you knew what was going to happen, *that* would have been an act."

"If you want," Nathaniel said, "I can have you bend back over the chair. The cane's still around here somewhere."

"No!" I held up a hand. "That's okay."

He lifted an eyebrow. "If you're certain?"

"Very, Master."

Cole checked his watch. "I have a call to make. Nathaniel, I'll call you tomorrow. Abby, thank you. You did really well for someone not experienced with mental play."

"Thank you, Sir."

Nathaniel waited until the door closed behind Cole before talking again. "So, tell me, how was doing a mental scene in front of a group compared to a physical one?"

"You mean, did the scene we just did turn me on like the ones we normally do?"

"Yes."

"Mmm." I leaned farther into his arms. "I was turned on kneeling and waiting. And then again, just a little, when I was bent over the chair. Even though it was Cole and not you. But during the actual thinking part? No, that didn't turn me on at all."

"Interesting. I wondered if it was enough to be in front of the group or if there had to be a physical or sexual component involved."

His words gave me momentary pause. He'd thought that much and that deep about what I needed and got out of a scene. But as soon as that thought popped into my head, it was replaced with *of course he does.*

I cleared my throat. "What do you think it means that the mental play in front of others didn't turn me on like the physical?"

"First of all, I'm not surprised that's how you feel."

"You're not?"

"No, remember the day in Wilmington when I had you be, what were your words, a coffee table?"

I'd been horribly bored, I remembered that. In my mind, I'd sat on the couch for hours balancing two glasses on my legs. Then when Nathaniel mentioned it was time for something else, I'd snorted. He hadn't been amused.

"I don't think I'll ever forget that day."

"There was mental play in that scene, too, and you weren't excited or turned on by it." He smiled, faintly, but still a smile. "In fact, I believe your exact words were 'What's hot about a coffee table?'"

"Nothing," I answered. "There's nothing hot about a coffee table. But you didn't answer the part about what it means."

He framed my face with his hands, making sure I kept my eyes on his. "It means mental play in front of people doesn't turn you on. And there's nothing wrong with that. It's just how you're wired."

I stroked his hand, touched by his words, and thankful that it did help me realize there wasn't anything abnormal about me. "You always know how to make me feel better. Thank you."

He shifted me so I could snuggle against his chest, and rested his chin on my head. "Every part of you, no matter how small or big or how it's wired, is what makes you the person you are. And that's the person I love. I won't have you thinking negative things about her."

I lifted my head for a kiss. "I love you, too."

Chapter Eleven

NATHANIEL

Abby didn't speak much on the drive back to Wilmington. Normally after a scene, she grew tired and would sleep, but apparently that was not the case when the scene was totally mental. It was almost as if I could see her brain working, still trying to process her time with Cole.

We had never done very many mental scenes. I thought to do one with the Partners in Play Dominants because it was different from what was normally demoed and I thought it would appeal to Abby's intellectual side. And, if I was being honest with myself, I was starting to grow a bit concerned about her seemingly increasing need for public displays. Would it stop, or would it keep escalating? What if one day being with me suddenly wasn't enough?

And what did it mean that she was turned on when she bent over for Cole? Did she want to be with another Dom?

I couldn't even think about that. I didn't know how I would handle it.

"Are you okay?" I asked when I heard her sigh deeply.

"Yes, Master," she said. "I'm still just thinking."

"Not tired?"

"No, Master. My mind is going in so many directions it won't calm down long enough to get tired. It's different this time from how it is after a physical scene. After being flogged or something, my mind is still in that fuzzy subspace hangover for a while. This mind stuff isn't the same."

"Was it something you wouldn't want to do again or that you might not mind doing again?"

"I wouldn't say I hated it. It's just so different." She laughed. "It's like my brain's been flogged."

"I think that's a very accurate description."

She looked out the passenger-side window as we approached our house. Still thinking, it appeared. And while I loved her intellect, I wanted to play with other parts of her tonight.

I pulled into the garage and told her, "Upstairs in the playroom. Naked. I'll let Apollo out and then I'll meet you there."

She looked sharply at me, obviously not expecting another scene. I didn't have any plans to go crazy tonight, but I needed her. Needed to control her pleasure. Needed her waiting for *my* commands.

She must have sensed how I felt because even though she pressed her lips together and seemed to want to argue or suggest something else, she nodded. "Yes, Master."

I took my time letting Apollo out and climbing the stairs, wanting to allow her time to prepare mentally.

She was waiting in the middle of the room for me and I let that sink in. *For me.* She was waiting for me. No one else. No people to watch. No demos to teach. This was her and me. Dominant and submissive. Coming together because it was what we wanted and what we needed from each other.

There was no other submissive, no other woman, who could affect me the way Abby did. There was something about her that made me calm and complete and I didn't know who I would have become without her in my life. She had given me so much, and I knew as sure as I was breathing that whatever she needed, if it was within my power, she would have it.

But for tonight, it would only be us. If I was craving having her at my command, more than likely she craved being under my control. I took a deep breath as I settled into my headspace and when I opened my eyes, I was ready.

Tonight I would once more take her to those places we only found together, in this room, and with her in my collar.

"Abigail." It was the only word I spoke, but it was the only one needed.

"Master."

"You did so well with Master Johnson. I'm so proud of you."

"Thank you, Master."

I stood silently, allowing us both to bask in our roles. It had to be difficult to submit to a different Dominant. Especially since I had been her first. She needed to know how much she pleased me. How proud I was that she went through the session with Cole, was even going so far as to be ready to let him cane her because she understood that I'd given my consent.

It had been hard as hell, watching her react to Cole's insistence that she sit in the chair. But I wanted her to experience what he offered. I knew it would be something she would find fascinating and think about for a long time, and write about. Whether she liked it or decided not to experience anything similar again, the session today would aid in her continuing journey of self-discovery and serve to make her stronger. And that would make us both stronger.

"You pleased me today, Abigail, so I'm going to reward you for being such a good girl."

"Thank you, Master."

I gave a slight chuckle. "Make no mistake about it, I'll be getting something out of your reward, too."

Though her head was bowed, I could hear the smile in her voice. "I wouldn't have it any other way, Master."

Hours later as she slept in my arms, I tried to plan for what I would do if this need of hers continued. If I didn't plan, there might come a time I couldn't meet her needs. It was hard for me to even think that, much less envision it happening.

The problem was solely with me. I didn't like another Dom controlling Abby and it didn't matter if it was a training session, a demo, or whatever you wanted to call it. The last few months had taught me I didn't like sharing her. It did nothing but remind me *why* I had made the rule that I wouldn't share my collared submissive. And if that made me a possessive, jealous dumb-ass . . . well, I was a possessive, jealous dumb-ass.

We didn't have another demo scheduled any time soon. The tri-state was having a workshop weekend they'd invited me to speak at. That was about a month away, though. But I did have my own playroom and could set up my own demo.

Lynne was due to come by over the weekend to meet the kids and talk with us. If everything went well, we could possibly have her watch Elizabeth and Henry the following weekend. She could keep them occupied or take them out somewhere while we were in the playroom.

Feeling a bit calmer and more at ease, I finally closed my eyes and allowed myself to sleep.

The next day at work, I made a list of who I'd invite to our demo. Not Simon this time, not with Lynne potentially in the house. That was an awkward situation we didn't need. I tapped my pen against the desk. Maybe Cole in Simon's place? I could invite Luke DeVaan and Jeff, and have them observe the two of us in the playroom, maybe ask them to be part of the scene in a nonsexual way. Three would be enough. The playroom wasn't *that* big, after all.

With that decided, I brainstormed about what to do. Abby had spent some time over the last few days writing about the mental play we'd done, but I didn't want to do another mental-only scene. What I wanted to do was combine mental and physical play. Give her a little of both and see how she responded.

I formed a skeleton plan in my mind and then called her. She answered on the second ring and we chatted briefly before I explained my purpose in calling.

"I have an assignment for you," I said. "You can either do it in your notebook or post it on the blog, but you have forty-eight hours to complete it."

"Sounds interesting."

I didn't give her assignments very often, but in this case, the topic and writing would serve to add to the mental aspect of the upcoming session.

"I hope you find it interesting. I think it's certainly an entertaining topic."

"I'm intrigued."

I chuckled. "The topic is predicament bondage."

With predicament bondage, I'd bind her in such a way that any movement would cause some sort of consequence. We'd done it a few times, but not often at all. Now that I'd put the idea in her head, she'd know we'd be doing a scene with it soon. And if I guessed correctly, she'd spend a lot of time wondering if the consequences would be painful or pleasurable.

"I know what you're doing, you know," she said.

"Oh?"

"You're mind-fucking me, aren't you?"

"I am, Abby. And the funny thing is, even though you know it's a mind-fuck, it's still working."

She muttered something under her breath and I laughed.

"See you in a few hours," I said.

As I suspected, she was very excited about inviting the men over to watch. I wondered if I was helping or hurting her by setting up this session and feeding this growing need of hers. But it was hard for me to deny her anything, and if she wanted public play, I wouldn't be a good Dom if I didn't meet that need.

To further get her into the right frame of mind, I had her set up the playroom the morning of our session. Lynne had hit it off great with the kids the previous weekend and they were excited she was coming over again. The new house was large and I'd designed it so that the playroom was as far from the children's wing as possible. Everything was separate, but I had installed both an intercom system and a security system so we would be notified, even in the playroom, if something was wrong or someone needed us.

Five minutes before the men were due to arrive, I sent Abby to the playroom to wait. We found her kneeling as I'd directed when the four of us stepped inside. I waved the men over to the three chairs I'd arranged for them, then walked over to Abby.

"Tell the gentlemen your safe words, Abigail."

"Red, yellow, and green, Master."

"Very nice. Stand for me, please."

She slowly stood to her feet. Her breathing had taken on the panting sounds she made when she was aroused, and though her head was bowed, I knew if I looked into her eyes, they would be lust-filled. She enjoyed playing in front of an audience, but just how much she liked it struck me in the chest.

"You're already so turned on you can hardly stand it, can you?"

"Yes, Master," she confirmed.

"Going to show these men what a good submissive you are?"

"Yes, Master."

"I have no doubts, my lovely. You've never disappointed me before."

I could see her body nearly humming with my praise.

I looked over the area she'd set up for our scene. As per my instructions, a St. Andrew's cross stood in the center of the room. All but a tiny circle of the floor surrounding the cross was covered in sharp points. Not sharp enough to break her skin, but it would be painful if she stepped on them. Not a problem if she could somehow find a way to remain in the small circle.

I would ensure that she couldn't.

When she moved the ropes between her legs, it would rub against her clit, which I knew she'd like. Being bound with a rope that excited her clit wasn't new to her, but being bound like that in a predicament situation was.

Once she was bound to my satisfaction, I led her to the tiny circle that was clear in front of the large wooden X. The circle was so tiny she had to stand on her toes. One by one, I bound her arms above her head, allowing enough slack to let her drop to her flat feet if she needed.

Then I turned to speak to the men. "We haven't done many scenes with predicament bondage, so this is relatively new for Abigail. It's not going to be comfortable for long being on her toes like that. But if she drops to her feet, she'll be standing on the sharp pegs. Plus, I've bound her with rope in such a way as to provide stimulation with every move." I turned back to her. "Are the ropes okay? Not too tight on your arms?"

"I'm as comfortable as can be expected, Master."

He turned back to the group. "Now we could just sit here and watch her, waiting for her to grow tired of standing on her toes. But she can have a bit of a stubborn streak, so I think I'll provide some incentive for her to move."

I was willing to bet they thought I'd flog her, or maybe use the cane. But when I went to my cabinets and pulled out a long feather, they laughed. Abby couldn't see it from her angle, so I moved closer to her.

"Personally, I think it's a lot more fun to use something other than pain to entice her to move. Of course, she may not agree." I held up the feather so she could see.

Abby groaned. She probably wished I'd use a flogger; she was incredibly ticklish.

"Are you ticklish?" I asked her for the benefit of the watching men.

"Yes, Master. Very."

"Mmm," I hummed. "This will be quite the challenge for you, then, won't it?"

"Yes, Master."

"But you like a challenge, don't you?"

"Most of the time, Master."

"Only most of the time?"

"My liking of a challenge is indirectly proportional to the amount of bondage I'm in."

The three men chuckled.

"Is that so?" I asked, and without waiting for a response, tickled her side.

She yelped and twisted, stepping on part of the peg-covered mat. "Ouch." She moved back into position, but doing so made the ropes shift. "Oh."

I tickled her again. "Bit of a predicament, wouldn't you say?"

She only sucked in a breath, but she still couldn't hold position. Poor Abby was so very ticklish. I took another feather and started tickling her with both.

I ran them down her back, around her waist, and under her arms. Just as I thought, Abby squirmed and danced, trying to get away from one feather, which only sent her into the path of the other. And each time she moved, the rope I'd placed around her clit had to be driving her crazy.

I decided to arouse her even more and circled her nipples while tickling right where the rope rubbed that supersensitive spot.

"You like that?" I asked.

"Oh yes, Master."

"You know our guests are watching you get turned on by my two feathers?"

"And the rope, Master."

I tickled her again so it moved against her. "Right, we can't forget the rope."

I fell into a rhythm, which allowed her to drift into subspace. Soon, I had her swaying back and forth and before too long, she wasn't even trying to stay on her toes. Her feet were on the pegs and she moaned in bliss every so often.

"What color are you, Abby?" I asked.

"Green, Sir."

"Shall I continue?"

"Mmm," she hummed, and swayed, causing the rope to hit a new spot. "Oh!"

"Is that a yes?"

"Yes, Master." She sounded dreamy. "If it pleases you."

I ran the feather down her side. She hummed and tried to get closer. Apparently, that shifted the ropes in a way they hadn't rubbed before and she sighed and began rocking back and forth again.

"None of that, now," I chided. "You don't have permission to come."

"Verflucht," she said, which I guessed was a curse word. But she stopped rocking.

I knew she'd start with the German at some point and I wanted to play with her mind a bit. So I glanced to my side and nodded at Cole.

"Watch your language. I know more German than you," he said.

"Entschuldigung, Herr," she said in apology.

"I was mentored in Germany by the most badass Dom you can imagine."

She swallowed a laugh at his accidental reference to the nickname given to him by submissives who'd played with him.

"Let's just say I know all the German words," Cole said.

She stopped trying to make the ropes move and went back to gently swaying. I kept her in subspace for a few more minutes and then began tickling her less and less. Her movements slowed and finally, I set the feathers down and unbuckled her arms from the cross. She dropped to her feet with an "Ouch!"

I immediately picked her up and carried her over the pegs until we reached a thick rug I'd placed on the platform. There I gently put her back on her feet while I undid the ropes. She let out a deep breath as they fell away from her.

"Move your legs, if you need to," I said. Though the sensation of the rope had been pleasurable while she was in the scene, she'd probably be in some discomfort once it was over.

"Do I need to massage your legs?" I asked.

"No, Master."

When I set up our new playroom, one of the things I'd done differently from our playroom in New York was add a large aftercare area. I'd furnished it with a plush couch and minifridge stocked with juice and bottled water. The night before, I'd set out a large blanket, and once we sat down, I draped it over her.

The three men took their cue to leave the play area. I'd told them earlier to wait for us in the kitchen and Abby had laid out snacks for them to enjoy.

Once they were gone, I turned my entire focus on her. One of our aftercare routines involved me rubbing her feet, so this was familiar and calming for both of us. She sighed as I took a foot in my hand. It was red on the bottom, but while the skin was tender, it wasn't broken. I massaged a soothing lotion into her arch, gently moving down to her toes and across the ball of her foot.

"You have the most amazing hands, Master," she said. "I've told you this before, yes?"

I kissed her big toe. "You have, my lovely. But feel free to tell me again."

"Your hands are amazing, Master."

"You're pretty amazing, too." I slowly worked the lotion into her skin and took a pair of supersoft socks I had waiting. I slipped one of them onto her foot.

"Makes me feel a bit like Cinderella," she joked as I placed that foot down and motioned for her to give me her other one.

"Does that make me Prince Charming?"

She brushed her hand down my arm. "You'll always be my Prince Charming."

We shared a smile as I cared for her other foot. Reconnecting like this after a scene always made us closer. Usually, we'd take our time and even curl up in bed for a catnap, but since we had guests, I thought it was time to make our way out of the playroom.

"Can we go check on the kids before we head to the kitchen, Master?" she asked.

"Of course. Are you ready to go now, or do you want to wait a bit longer?"

"I can go now."

I stood up and helped her into the outfit she'd brought down earlier. While we got her dressed in jeans and a soft sweater, I watched for any sign that would tell me her feet were in too much pain. Satisfied she was okay, I took her hand and we went to pop in on the kids.

Lynne, Elizabeth, and Henry were in what we called the nursery. It was really just the children's playroom, but neither Abby nor I was comfortable calling it that. Lynne and Elizabeth were playing house in the large dollhouse my cousin, Jackson, and I had made for her last birthday. Henry was pushing his dump trucks and tractors around. Abby giggled when she saw he had one of Elizabeth's dolls on top of the tractor, acting as if she were driving. Nothing like doing farm work in a silver cocktail dress.

I knocked on the doorframe. Elizabeth turned and, seeing us, hopped up and ran over to give us hugs. "Mommy! Daddy! Lynne is fun. Can she stay? For always?"

I kissed the top of her head. "We'll see. Are you playing dolls?"

"Yes, I'm the mommy, Lynne's the little girl, and Henry's the daddy. But he won't play with the boy doll, so Lynne's being the daddy, too."

Henry picked up the silverly clad doll and nodded. "Pretty."

"You can't wear a fancy dress on a tractor," Elizabeth told her brother.

He held the doll to his chest. "Mine!"

"Just let him play," Abby said. "At least he's not throwing everything in the trash can." She looked over to Lynne. "How's everything going? Do you need anything?"

Lynne and the kids had eaten lunch earlier. She'd told us they were going to play for a bit and then watch a movie.

"We're good," she said. "I promised cookies during the movie."

Abby nodded. "Elizabeth helped me make sugar cookies yesterday. I think we have a few left. Do you want me to set them out?"

"I know where they are, Mommy," Elizabeth said. "I can show her."

"Okay, princess. You two be good and I'll see you after the movie."

Abby smiled at me, content now that she had seen the children and satisfied they were happy. From everything I'd observed so far, it appeared hiring Lynne would be a great thing for everyone involved. I hadn't had a chance to talk to Simon yet, but I planned to soon. I didn't understand why he'd broken up with her. Especially since they had appeared to be so happy and compatible when we last saw them together.

But I knew as well as anyone that things weren't always as they seemed to be and people often did things for reasons not understood by those not involved.

And seriously, you have enough to deal with concerning your own relationships. No need to borrow anyone else's problems.

Cole, Luke, and Jeff were standing in the kitchen snacking

on the array of sandwiches Abby had left out for them. At our entrance, they stopped talking and greeted us, and then Jeff made Abby a plate.

She took it from him with a big smile and sat down. "Thank you."

"Can I get you something to drink?" he asked.

I wanted to tell him not to bother, that I'd get her a drink, but it occurred to me that this was probably his way of providing some sort of aftercare. No, he hadn't done anything in the scene other than watch, but if he needed to get my wife a drink, I'd let him.

I was reminded again of why I didn't share my submissives. I enjoyed being the one, the *only* one to do aftercare. Which was silly, I told myself. It was only getting her a drink. It really shouldn't bother me the way it did.

In fact, it had never bothered me before. Jeff had done a lot more with Abby when we were in Wilmington for the first time and I hadn't minded when he sat and talked with her once the scene was over. That day, I'd actually left them alone while I cleaned up and prepared the bedroom for the aftercare I had planned.

It raised the question, why was it different today?

I didn't have an answer for that.

Jeff and Abby talked for a few minutes with Luke and Cole joining in occasionally. I simply watched, but I noticed Cole looking my way a few times. It was a bit unnerving and I wondered briefly if he could read something in my expression.

Jeff glanced at his watch. "I hate to be the first one to leave, but Dena and I have an appointment this afternoon and I need to swing by the house to pick her up."

Luke stood up. "I need to be going as well."

Cole made no move to go and after the two other men left, he approached me. "Can I speak with you for a minute?"

Abby hopped up and started clearing the dishes. "Let me get these in the sink and I'll leave you two alone. I'll go see what the kids are up to."

"Something wrong?" I asked Cole after Abby left the kitchen.

"I was going to ask you the same thing. You seemed different today."

Was I that transparent? I shrugged. "Just a lot of things going on at the moment."

"Abby certainly appeared to enjoy herself."

I snorted. "She loves playing in front of people."

"And you don't?"

"No, I'm fine with it, usually." I decided to tell him some of what had been going on. My own feelings were somewhat bewildering to me, and maybe he had some experience with this kind of thing that he could share with me. "It's just that her need to play publicly is growing lately and I wonder if I can keep up with her."

"You mean, will she want to push the envelope faster and further than you're comfortable with?"

"Something like that. I'm just not sure what to do next. How to keep her on her toes and excited."

He nodded. "It's hard to be creative and think up new ways to torment our subs sometimes," he said with a grin. "And the two of you have been together a long time."

"Yes, exactly. And I'm afraid the things I do think up, *I* won't be comfortable with."

"Have you considered a threesome?"

I had always shot down the idea in the past. Me share Abby? No way. But instead of blurting out "Hell, no," I gave it some thought. She'd enjoyed the session with Jeff even though I had placed limits on what he could do. A threesome would be different.

Would a threesome satisfy her? Was it something she'd want? Maybe not a scene where she actually had sex with another man, because I knew there was no way in hell that would ever happen. But something like what we did with Jeff and maybe let him go a little further.

"A mild scene, perhaps," I said in answer to him. "Would you want to participate?"

"Oh no." He held up his hands. "It was merely a suggestion. I don't act as third in the group I'm a member of."

I nodded. "Makes sense."

Who would I invite into our playroom? Should it be someone she'd worked with? Or someone who was a complete stranger to her? Or would someone like Luke be better? A man she knew, but not too well and one she wouldn't see on a regular basis. Someone I wouldn't see on a regular basis.

I didn't need to think about what would be best for me. This would be for Abby and I needed to put my thoughts and emotions to the side for her. It was only fair she got to experience two men if she wanted. I was her only Dom and for me to limit what she wanted simply because I was jealous? That wasn't looking out for her. That was looking out for me.

I didn't think a stranger was the way to go, though. I did know men in the lifestyle whom she didn't, men I wouldn't have to worry about seeing often. But I didn't think Abby would be comfortable with someone she just met.

At the same time, I didn't think someone she was very familiar with would be a good choice, either. I could easily ask someone like Jeff to join us. They had played together before, they knew each other, and they were comfortable around each other.

But I knew Abby would end up feeling uncomfortable around him and I wasn't sure he'd want to join us anymore, since he was back together with Dena. Hell, this was uncharted territory for me. I honestly had no idea how she would react when it was all over. She might feel guilty and I needed to make sure I addressed that before we did anything. We would have to spend a lot of time talking about how she felt when the scene was over.

If I didn't want a stranger and didn't want someone she was too friendly with, that left a mere acquaintance. Simon was out. Neither one of us would feel right inviting him, not with Lynne living under our roof.

I ran through several names in my mind, but kept coming back to Luke.

He was the obvious choice. She knew him, she'd spoken to him, and he'd been in our playroom already when he took the pictures. Plus, I'd watched him in a scene before and he was more of a sensual Dominant. If I had to pick someone to join us, I'd choose someone like him over a Dominant like Cole. Cole had earned his reputation as a hard-ass in the playroom, and while I didn't have a problem with that, I didn't want someone like that to be her first experience with two men. Besides, it didn't sound as though Cole was an option. And, to be honest, he didn't seem to be the type of Dom to truly enjoy being a third. He'd want to be the one calling the shots.

The only downside to asking Luke was his history with Abby's supervisor, Meagan. Though whatever happened between them had taken place years ago, I needed to get her idea on adding a third and to make sure she was okay with who I asked. I thought it would be fine. According to Abby, Meagan had said under no circumstances would she ever get back together with *that man*.

I made a note to ask Luke what had happened between him and Meagan. I didn't think it would be anything beyond a typical breakup, but I wanted to be certain.

I would still ask Abby, though. I'd also give her the option to ask a stranger instead of Luke. This was going to be a big step for her, and I wanted to make sure she was as comfortable as possible. And a large part of that would depend on the man we asked to join us.

"If nothing else," Cole said, "perhaps you could increase the intensity of your public play."

He'd been so quiet I'd forgotten he was still here. But he had a good point. Maybe increasing what we did in public would be what she needed.

"I like the way you think," I said. Maybe adding a third was too much and increasing what we did publicly would be the best thing to do next. "In fact, I'm speaking at the tri-state group meeting in two weeks, the weekend after Jeff and Dena's wedding. There may be a chance to do something more public there."

If the upcoming meeting was like the last one, I wouldn't reserve a balcony this time. Instead maybe I'd keep her on the main floor in the courtyard and we'd put on our show. And I would call Luke soon.

I looked up as Abby came back into the room.

"Everything good?" I asked. Her eyebrows were wrinkled as though she was thinking hard.

"Yes." She nodded. "I had a call from Sasha. She wants to talk to me and I have a feeling I know what it's about."

"Miss Blake?" Cole asked. "Is she back in the group?"

It hadn't been hard for me to pick up on Sasha's interest in Cole. Outside of the subtle comments she made, I saw her interest the night she watched his demo with the lady who never returned.

Cole, on the other hand, wasn't as easy to read. On the surface, it was only a question. *Is she back in the group?* It could have been an *I'm interested because I'm now a senior member and she's part of the group.* Or it could have been an *Oh yes, I remember catching her before she fell to the floor and broke her nose.* But the question wasn't spoken like either of those. It was more of an *I'm going to act all nonchalant because I don't want you to realize just how much I remember about Sasha Blake.* Plus, there was the way he'd looked at her the night of the demo she watched. The sly smile and his obvious delight in her interest.

I glanced at Abby to see if she'd picked up on Cole's comment. Sure enough, her eyes had grown wider. She looked at me, obviously wanting to say something. I nodded.

"She's not an official member, Sir," Abby said. "Master and I are still working on requirements to join the group, and since she dropped out, she'll have to reapply. But . . ." She paused, glancing at the wall behind him, not meeting his gaze. "She did go to the last group play party. I was with her as she watched your demo."

"Oh?" he said with a smile.

I knew I hadn't misheard that one. The *Oh* that was not so much of an *Oh yes,* but more of an *I hope I left her hungry for more.*

"Yes," she confirmed to Cole. "In any case, she's not ready to join just yet. At least in my opinion."

With that, Cole rose from his seat and patted me on the back. "Time for me to say my good nights. I'm sure you and Abby will work everything out perfectly. I trust you two."

I smiled to myself as the outline of a plan took form in my head.

We showed Cole out and said our good nights. Abby and I went to sit in the living room, and I brought up the plan that was on my mind. She was surprised at first. But as I explained my thought process I could see her understanding what I was suggesting.

"You have played with other men in a limited capacity. It's not like the cane where this is completely new."

"You want me to give you names? I wasn't expecting that." She shook her head. "I think I'd rather you decide."

"I don't want a name necessarily, just your thoughts on a few things. For instance, would you want a third and in what capacity? And if you do, do you want it to be a stranger or someone you know? And if you think you'd like someone you know, would it be better for you if they were in the Partners group or someone you won't see frequently?"

"I haven't given this any thought." She was shaking her head gently. "You have to give me time to wrap my head around it. I don't think I want a third, but I do like the idea of increasing public play and I'm not opposed to doing more scenes with another Dom. But I don't want it to be any more than what we've already done with Jeff and the others. And I know I don't like the thought of a stranger. I mean, the stranger fantasy we do is fun. But I don't think I'd like to be in a scene with someone I don't know."

"That's what I was thinking."

"Those are my thoughts right now and as for who? Someone I know from the Partners group or the New York one." She picked a pen up from off my desk and spun it around. "Daniel and Jeff are out; they're in relationships themselves and neither of them wants to play with anyone else. That leaves Cole or William Greene or Evan Martin. I'm not sure the New York group is an option. We haven't met with them in forever."

"No to Evan Martin, he's a bit too flippant for my taste." He was a good Dominant, but I didn't care for his juvenile behavior outside the playroom. "William Greene I could talk to. Cole's out. He told me he doesn't serve as third for people he's in a group with."

"Just as well," she said, but didn't expand further. "And who were you thinking of if we went outside the Partners group?"

"There are several people I had in mind, but the one I think would be the best is Luke."

"Oh," she said, a look of mild shock in her expression. "I hadn't thought about him." She was quiet for a minute. "But he makes sense."

"You don't have to decide right now. I just wanted you to think about it."

"I wonder if it'd be strange if we asked someone from the Group. Would it make things weird when I saw them in the future? Like, would that be the first thing to pop into my head when I saw them?"

"It would only be as weird as you let it be. If you tell yourself it was just a scene, an experience, it might not be that weird. But you also need to think about the future. If we asked William and then months from now, he had a serious relationship, would you feel strange having played with him before?"

"I don't know. When we're with our New York group, we're with women you played with and it's not odd for me."

"Yes, but it's been years since I've played with anyone else." There were only two women still in the New York group whom I'd played with in the past. The rest had moved away or joined another group. "If we pick someone here in Wilmington, you'll see them frequently."

Talking about the New York group made me wonder if Charlene was in a group. Abby and I hadn't been to a meeting with them since before Henry was born. Was it possible she was in our New York group now? I probably needed to find out before Abby and I did anything with them again. And I didn't have to think about just how weird it would be if Charlene was in the group. Seeing one of my employees naked wasn't something I wanted to do. Not to mention, I didn't even want to think about what Abby would say if she saw her at a function.

Abby broke into my train of thought by saying, "I'm thinking it might be too strange to play with someone from the Partners group."

"In that case, what do you think of Luke?" I asked.

She was silent again before answering, "I don't know. Let me think on that. Would it create tension between me and Meagan?"

"You wouldn't have to tell her. In fact, I don't really see why you would. It's not any of her business."

She nodded idly. "How soon?"

How soon would you like? The question hovered on my lips. "I'm not sure. Why don't you think about if you'd like the third to be Luke and once we decide on that, we'll worry about a time?"

"Will you tell me what your plans are for the scene?"

I smiled in spite of my thoughts. "Have I ever told you ahead of time what I plan to do in a scene?"

"Well, no. I just—"

"Then why would I start now?"

She looked as if she'd just been caught stealing a cookie. I had to hand it to her, she usually tried to slyly get information out of me. It never worked. But she was persistent.

"You know me too well when I'm trying to be sneaky," she said. "Maybe I should distract you with sex next time."

"You're more than welcome to try." I stood up. "I'm going to take Apollo outside if you'd like to distract me in the backyard."

I hadn't gone too far down the hall when I heard her footsteps following me and I smiled at the thought of the fun we'd have outside.

Chapter Twelve

ABBY

The weather the weekend of Jeff and Dena's wedding was like one of those summer days you wished would never end. Though it had been a hot summer, the meteorologist's forecast predicted a comfortable seventy degrees with a light breeze. The reception was planned to be held outside at a country club, and Dena had been worried all week it would end up raining anyway.

"This is perfect weather for the reception," I said to Julie as we sat in a small room at the back of the church helping Dena.

"Did you and Nathaniel get married in the summer?" she asked.

"No." I shook my head. "In the winter, but our wedding was perfect. I wouldn't change anything."

"As it should be," she agreed.

I looked over to Dena. The wedding wasn't for another hour, but she was dressed and ready. Her makeup and hair looked perfect. Her outside was radiant. Inside was a different story. She shifted from one foot to the other, refusing to sit down, and her eyes kept glancing at the clock. I was just getting ready to ask her if she was okay when she spoke first.

"Say something," she begged us, looking from me to Julie to Sasha to her Domme friend, Kelly, and back to me again. "Anything."

"I don't know why you're so nervous," Kelly said, placing a hand on her shoulder. "You're finally marrying Jeff."

Dena shook her head. "I'm not nervous about Jeff. It's my dad."

"He decided to come?" I asked. Last I heard, Senator Jenkins had made it crystal clear he would not be present today. I wasn't sure why Dena's father didn't like Jeff. What wasn't to like about him?

"No, Mom called and said he was feeling light-headed and disoriented." She took a deep breath. "She knows today's my wedding day and that Jeff and I are going away for a week. I swear that man will end up in the hospital today just to spite me."

"Oh my God," Julie said, the rest of us being unable to find words. "How long have you known and why didn't you tell us?"

"I figured she was just making it up, but the longer I sit here, the more I think, *What if he's really sick and I don't go? I need Jeff.*"

"Have you told him?" I asked.

"No, I don't want it to spoil his day even if it spoils mine."

Kelly looked at me over Dena's head and mouthed, *Go get him.*

I nodded and left the room before Dena could try and stop me.

Nathaniel and Cole stood in the hallway outside the room Daniel and Jeff were in. The two men were laughing over something, but their expressions sobered when they saw me.

"Abby?" Nathaniel said, crossing the last few steps as quickly as he could. "What's wrong?"

I nodded toward the closed door. "Is Jeff in there? Dena needs him."

"Before the wedding?" Cole asked. "Isn't that against the rules?"

"Her mother called and said her dad is having some neurological symptoms. Dena didn't tell anyone and now she's freaking out."

"Bloody hell," Cole said.

Nathaniel knocked on the door. "Jeff? We need you out here."

The door opened and Jeff looked out into the hallway, all smiles and happiness. At least until he saw me. "Is Dena okay? Is it the baby?"

"Senator Jenkins," I said. "He—"

"He's here?"

"No, Dena's mom called and said he's light-headed and disoriented." At my words, he started walking down the hall to where the women were getting ready. I walked after him. "She just told us, I don't know how long ago she got the call."

He knocked on the door. "Angel?"

Kelly let him in, motioning for Julie and Sasha to join us in the hallway, leaving the couple alone. I saw Dena stand and Jeff's arms encircle her before the door closed. The rest of us stood in the hallway, not saying anything, not really knowing what to say.

I didn't know the senator. I'd only heard bits and pieces through gossip. I couldn't imagine he would pretend to have neurological problems just to cause his daughter stress on her wedding day. But that was the funny thing about people, you never really knew what they were capable of.

"If he's faking, I'll fucking kill him," Cole said. "Doesn't he know what he's doing to her?"

"He probably doesn't care," Daniel said. "It's killing *him* she's marrying Jeff. Hasn't even said anything to her about the baby, his own grandchild. And he has to know what losing the last one did to her."

"I just want her to be happy." Julie moved to stand next to Daniel and he put his arm around her. "That guy is toxic. And so is her mom for putting up with it."

"Let's not lynch the man yet," Nathaniel said. "We haven't heard the whole story and it is possible he's actually having some sort of neurological episode."

"Odds are he's faking. I've had his number for years. It doesn't surprise me at all he's pulling something like this," Kelly said.

"That may well be the case, but let's wait until we know something more definitive."

No one particularly looked as though they wanted to give the man the benefit of the doubt. For several long minutes we stood, silently watching the closed door and waiting not so patiently for it to open.

We all jumped forward when it cracked open and Jeff waved us inside.

"Dena called the senator's housekeeper," Jeff said. "Miss May has always held a special place in her heart for Dena."

"Thank goodness for Miss May," Dena said, and she looked so much calmer than she had a few minutes earlier. "I called her cell phone and made sure she wasn't near Mom and Dad. She said Dad took some new medicine and he's reacting badly to it, but they've called his doctor and he's going to be fine."

"Did your mom know it was only a side effect of the medication when she called you?" Julie asked.

"I don't know," Dena said. "And to be honest, I'm going to try and put it out of my mind." She smiled up at Jeff. "I think I've spent enough time on Senator Jenkins for one day. I have more important things to do."

"That you do, my Angel." Jeff bent his head, as if he was going to kiss her, but Daniel pulled him away.

"None of that just yet. Wait until you're pronounced man and wife," Daniel said, and led Jeff toward the door.

"Ass," Jeff said, but let himself be carried away. "I'll remember this."

When the men left, a calm peace settled over us. Dena was no longer stressed and she finally had the radiant look of someone about to marry her soul mate.

"It's time, you guys," Julie said, about fifteen minutes later.

We walked out alongside Dena with Sasha carrying her train. Because her father wouldn't walk her down the aisle, there had been much debate about who she should walk with. All things considered, she finally decided to walk by herself.

"I walk down alone, give myself to Jeff, and we walk out together," she'd said. "I like the symbolism of that."

She looked stunning as she walked down the aisle. She'd chosen a strapless gown that gathered high above the waist. The fabric encircling her torso gave the appearance of a corset, and also served to showcase the pleated folds that draped gracefully down her tall frame.

With her hair pulled up and her long neck adorned by Jeff's

black-and-silver collar, she looked like a goddess. Or an angel, as her soon-to-be husband called her.

The man in question stood at the front of the church grinning bigger than I thought he could. His eyes were locked on her as she slowly made her way down the aisle. Their emotion was so vividly displayed in their expressions, my heart ached with joy and I brushed a stray tear from my cheek.

"I love you, Angel," I saw him whisper.

I looked to my side and saw Nathaniel watching me. Like everyone else, I couldn't go to a wedding without thinking back to my own. We had married in the winter, in a church about the same size as the one we were currently in. I was a fortunate woman to have my husband of so many years still look at me with a love and desire that had only grown since our wedding day.

As Dena and Jeff repeated their vows, I whispered in my heart my own back to Nathaniel.

"Do you take this man?"

Yes, yes, a million times, yes.

"For richer, for poorer. In sickness and in health?"

Anyway, anytime, anyhow.

"To love and to cherish . . ."

With all that I am.

"Until death do you part?"

Until then and for whatever comes after.

Daniel came up to us at the reception. "You guys ready for the conference next weekend?"

"I can't wait," I said, before Nathaniel could say anything.

"Listening to Nathaniel give his talk, seeing everyone again and the party after? Yes, I'm so ready."

Daniel laughed, throwing his head back slightly. "I need to go get Julie over here and let your enthusiasm rub off on her. She's a bit apprehensive."

"Well, it's her first one, right?" I asked. "And she's never played outside the Partners group?"

"Both true," he said.

I looked up at Nathaniel. "Do you mind if I go talk to Julie?" I had seen her earlier with Sasha and Kelly. Right now the three of them were talking with Dena.

"Go on, my lovely. I'll be right here."

I rose on my toes and kissed his cheek and then trotted over to the girls. I hugged Dena first.

"Congratulations, Mrs. Parks. You look beautiful."

She positively glowed and happy tears filled her eyes. "Thanks, Abby. I feel like the happiest, luckiest, most fortunate woman in the world."

"As you should," I said with a smile, still remembering my own wedding day. "And I bet if we asked that handsome groom of yours, he'd say the same."

She looked over to where Jeff was talking with Cole. He must have felt the weight of her stare, because he turned his head and looked our way. His eyes met his new wife's and he mouthed, *I love you.* Dena blew him a kiss.

Cole, too, was full of smiles, though I did see his jaw tighten when he saw Sasha. I don't think anyone else noticed it. Surely not Dena, who suddenly said, "Okay, I have to go touch him, make sure this is real. Half the time I feel like I'm living in a dream."

She walked over to Jeff, who put his arms around her and drew her close for a kiss. He reached down and gently touched her belly. Dena nodded.

Beside me, Julie sighed. "They're so happy. It gives me chills watching them."

I smiled and nodded in agreement and we watched them for several minutes before I spoke again. "How do you feel about next weekend?"

"Half nervous. Half excited." Julie turned from the newlyweds. "How was it when you first played in public?"

I thought back to my early days with Nathaniel. "When people knew what we were doing or when we were so sly they had no idea?"

"Sounds like you have a few stories to tell."

I thought she would probably get a kick out of hearing about the Super Bowl.

But at that moment, Daniel came up. "I'm going to steal this gorgeous woman away from you, Abby."

"Bye, Abby!" Julie laughed as he took her hand and pulled her away, a huge grin on his face.

I had a feeling another wedding wasn't too far away.

Chapter Thirteen

ABBY

The Tuesday night after the wedding, Nathaniel collared me when he got home. He'd told me the day before he would do it because we were having Luke DeVaan over for dinner. Also as part of our experiment with different protocol levels, we'd agreed that Tuesday evening would be high protocol. At least it would be once the children were in bed.

So far it was okay, but I could already tell it wasn't anything I wanted to do on a more permanent basis. I felt it was too restrictive to do all the time.

After Luke arrived, I went to check on Lynne and the kids. We were doing a trial week, just to make sure we all wanted to have her move in full-time. So far, it was working out beautifully. Satisfied they were all happy and well into the bedtime routine, I slipped into the living room as silently as I could and dropped to my knees beside Nathaniel. He didn't stop talking with Luke, but rested his hand on the top of my head and stroked the back of my neck. My head was down, so I couldn't see Luke. I closed my eyes as the men talked and in doing so felt the stress of the day drain away.

"Thank you for joining us, Abigail," Nathaniel said sometime later. "Everything good upstairs?"

"Yes, Master," I said with my head still down. "The children are great and Elizabeth asked if Lynne could stay forever."

Nathaniel chuckled. "Lynne's part of our New York group. She's staying this week as a potential nanny," he explained to Luke.

"She must be the lovely lady I saw heading up the stairs when I arrived."

"Yes, that was her," Nathaniel said. "Apparently, everyone's hitting it off well." He stroked my neck one more time and said, "Do you need to check on dinner, Abigail?"

"Yes, Master. But I wanted to come in here first to see if you and Master DeVaan needed anything."

"Unless Master DeVaan needs something, I'm good. You can do what you need to do in order to finish dinner. We'll be in the dining room in fifteen minutes unless you tell us differently."

He'd told me earlier that even though it was a high-protocol evening, while we were eating dinner with Luke at the dining room table I could assume kitchen table behavior. I appreciated that he was stepping down the protocol level for dinner.

"Thank you, Master." I bent low and kissed his right foot.

"You're excused, Abigail."

I stood as gracefully as possible and went to check on dinner. I'd roasted a turkey using a recipe I'd gotten from Dena. She said Jeff made it and it was the best turkey she'd ever had. I had to agree, it smelled wonderful. Hopefully, it would taste just as good. I served it along with a squash and quinoa gratin and a big salad. I quickly set the table for three and then stood and waited by Nathaniel's chair.

"Everything looks wonderful," Nathaniel said when he entered. He nodded toward my chair and pulled it out for me.

"And smells divine," Luke added.

The men took a seat after I did and Nathaniel sliced the turkey. Then they filled their plates, and Nathaniel filled mine.

"Mmm," Luke hummed after taking a bite. "Tastes divine as well. Excellent turkey, Abby."

"Thank you, Sir. I'm so glad you like it. It's Master Park's recipe. Dena gave it to me."

"I'll have to thank both of them," Nathaniel said.

After we ate a bit more and made small talk about nothing in particular, Nathaniel cleared his throat. "Luke, why don't you tell Abby your idea about opening a club in Wilmington?"

Luke took another bite of his turkey. "You remember I'm taking over the club in New York you went to?"

"Yes." I took a sip of my water. "Someone needed to. It was a nightmare. Not the best clientele, either."

"Very true," Luke said. "I'm hoping to change that. Right now I've closed the place down. It'll need almost a complete gut job. Once I redo it, I'll be very selective about who I allow in."

A sudden image of the guy who had almost assaulted me the one time I was at that club popped into my mind and I realized I'd never found out his name or what happened to him. I wonder if Jeff knew, since he'd gotten me out of that bad situation when I met him there.

"I had a run-in with someone there. I don't know his name."
I wrinkled my brow, trying to remember what he looked like.
Of course I couldn't remember because I'd gotten so stupidly
drunk that night.

"All taken care of. Jeff Parks filled me in on the guy." Luke
caught my eye and smiled. "He's most definitely not allowed."

Luke's demeanor was totally charming and he spoke and
moved in a way that put me at ease. I felt certain he never had
trouble finding companionship.

"If you don't mind me asking, Sir. You restore and run BDSM
clubs *and* own an art gallery?"

His laugh was low and seductive and the sound sent shivers
up my spine. The right woman could get lost in that laugh. "The
art gallery and photography are hobbies. The clubs are a job. But
they're also a pleasure. Life is good when you enjoy what you do."

"I know exactly what you're talking about," I said. "I feel the
same way."

"I read your blog. Very insightful observations."

"Thank you, Sir."

"Though I must admit, I've yet to catch you on TV. Monday
nights are usually busy at the club."

"I'm only on for a few minutes and if you didn't know it was
me, you probably wouldn't recognize me."

"Keeping your identity private?" he asked.

"Yes, for a number of reasons, but mostly because of the kids,
and quite frankly my identity isn't really anyone's business."

His lips curved up into a smile. "How very true. I commend
you for finding a way you can get up on television every week.

The other thing I mentioned to Nathaniel is, I'm thinking about opening a club here. If I can find a partner, that is."

"Master and I were just talking the other day about how the Partners in Play group needed a home base."

"Yes, he told me that when he called."

I looked to Nathaniel. "Are you going to be a partner, Master?"

"I'm giving it some thought. I would like your opinion, though."

My heart swelled because I knew he was letting Luke know in a not at all subtle way that he valued my opinion and we made such decisions jointly.

"Off the top of my head, I can't think of a reason you shouldn't do it."

"Good," he said. "We can talk about it a little later, but I agree, I couldn't find any reason not to. Daniel's been very accommodating letting the group use his house so frequently, but I just think it would be better to have a centralized location that isn't a personal residence."

"Especially now that Julie's moved in and Cole's in the guesthouse." Would Cole be staying permanently? I hadn't heard about him moving anywhere, and I hadn't heard he was looking for a residence, either.

"Yes, it's a lot for one person."

"If you like," Luke said, "I can send you some general information on my plans."

"That would be great." Nathaniel wiped his mouth with his napkin and looked at the table. My eyes followed suit. It appeared that everyone had finished eating.

"Can I get you anything else, Master DeVaan?" I asked.

"No, thank you. I'm afraid I couldn't eat another bite. Thank you for the delicious dinner."

"You're welcome." I turned to Nathaniel. "May I be excused to clear the table?"

"Yes," he said. "Just put everything in the sink for now. I know you'll want to stop and check on Elizabeth and Henry, so meet us in the playroom in fifteen minutes. You can leave your clothing on."

"Thank you, Master." I gathered up the dishes and utensils and carried them to the sink. My heart pounded in excitement at the thought of going into the playroom with someone else there.

On my way, I passed by the room the kids and Lynne were in. They had made a seating area out of pillows and were reading a book before bed that they'd read at least two hundred times. Elizabeth could quote it. Lynne had got to one of our favorite parts and both kids howled with laughter. I saw Henry pop his thumb in his mouth. A few more minutes and I'd bet his eyes would start to grow heavy.

It was odd walking into the playroom fully clothed. But again, the entire night was odd. Lynne being here with the kids. Knowing it wouldn't be just me and Nathaniel. And most odd of all, kneeling in my clothes waiting for Luke.

The two men weren't silent when they entered. They were talking softly and something Nathaniel said made Luke laugh. I was surprised at the relief that swept over me knowing they were jovial, and my body relaxed further into its waiting position.

One of the guys, I assumed it was Luke because the steps sounded different than Nathaniel's, walked to where I was waiting. Another set of footsteps, Nathaniel's, I guessed, walked to the side of the room, before coming to join him.

"Head up, Abby," Luke said in a commanding voice that somehow still managed to be smooth and sexy.

I looked up and my gaze didn't land on Luke, but traveled to Nathaniel. I needed to see his face, to look in his eyes. He appeared calm and smiled just a touch at my perusal.

"Master DeVaan is here as my guest. Therefore you are to treat him as you would me."

"Yes, Master."

"He is aware of both of our limits."

I knew Nathaniel would never let another man touch me in a sexual manner. I also knew he would have had a long discussion with Luke before inviting him over. My Master was extremely picky about who he let into the playroom.

"Thank you, Master."

He nodded to Luke. "Master DeVaan."

"Stand up, Abby," Luke said. His expression was still easygoing, but his voice was definitely no-nonsense. From the corner of my eye, I saw Nathaniel step away. He didn't move far, but made his way to stand behind me.

Before me, Luke glanced once more to Nathaniel and then turned his attention to me. "Take your shirt off, Abby."

I quickly pulled my shirt over my head and let it fall to the floor.

"Very good," Luke said. "Hesitation is one of my pet peeves. Now remove your bra."

Somewhere in the back of my mind, I was thinking, *You just had dinner with this man. He ate at your dining room table and now you're taking your bra off for him.* But another part of my mind was getting turned on. Excited about where this would go.

The familiar rush I got when playing in public built within me. It was almost as if someone else invaded my body, as if I became a different person when I had an audience—even if it was just an audience of one.

I reached behind my back and unhooked the bra. Slowly, I drew the straps down over my shoulders and, just like the shirt, it fell to the floor. Almost instantly Nathaniel's mouth was on my skin, peppering kisses along my back.

"This turns you on, doesn't it, Abigail?" he whispered. "Stripping in front of someone, showing off your body, knowing he can't touch."

"Yes, Master." The cool air of the playroom made my nipples hard, aching to be touched. But I hadn't been instructed to move, Nathaniel was behind me, and Luke couldn't touch me.

"Finger yourself and show us," Luke said.

I slipped a hand into the waistband of my pants, reaching a finger between my legs to gather the wetness there. The temptation to stroke my clit was hard to resist, but I did.

Luke's gaze didn't move from mine. "Let me see."

I held my finger up.

"Very good. Now make yourself come," Luke said.

I moved my hand down again.

Luke snapped his fingers. "Stop. I didn't say you could use your hands."

I blinked. *What?*

"I want to see just how turned on you are right now. With your Master behind you, so close to your ass. And me in front of you, seeing your lovely naked breasts." His voice dropped another level. "I want to watch you work for your orgasm. I want to see you writhe as you try to catch it. As you attempt to give that clit the attention it desperately wants."

His expression was much more intense than I would have thought possible, especially when compared to his demeanor outside the playroom. Intense and unyielding. What would happen if I couldn't do it?

I wouldn't know until I at least tried. I doubted I'd be able to make myself come, but if they wanted me to attempt it, I was game. I looked over to the padded table, thinking that if I could get on my stomach . . .

"Standing right here," Luke said.

I couldn't help the *it ain't ever going to happen* look I threw his way.

"Your submissive appears to lack the proper attitude," he said to Nathaniel.

"Abigail," Nathaniel said, "you have two options. You stand there and make yourself come without your hands or I'll fuck your ass and make you come, but I'll fig you after."

I'd had ginger used on me exactly once and that was enough for forever, thank you very much. No figging. I'd try option one.

The image of him taking my ass over the padded table while Luke watched was vivid. I closed my eyes to concentrate on it while I pressed my thighs together, squeezed, and rotated.

"There you go," Luke said. "Tell us what you're thinking."

"I'm thinking Master has me bent over the table and he's fucking me with a vibrator. He says he's saving his cock for my ass and I'm going to be so tight when he thrusts inside me." I squeezed my legs tighter. "I feel him, his cock is right at my anus and he asks me if I want it soft or hard."

"What do you pick, Abigail?"

"I say hard, Master. Fucking ride my ass like you own it."

Nathaniel groaned and I couldn't help wondering if he was using his hands.

"Then you tell me to reach back and hold myself open for you." I shifted my legs and with a squeeze, I managed to get just a touch of fiction on my needy clit. "Oh, fuck yes."

I sucked in a breath and I heard Nathaniel's choppy breathing behind me.

"You say you have to make sure I'm ready, so you push a finger into me and I beg you to fill me. I need it. I need it." I rubbed my thighs together. What I needed was a hand. Right the fuck now.

"Finally," I continued, "you take your cock and push it into me. Not as hard as I'd asked, but not exactly slow, either. You tell me you have to get it good and deep inside and then you'll be fucking my ass."

I was so close to my orgasm, it was just within my reach; if I stretched hard enough I could get to it. Funny how I spent all those years working on delaying my orgasm and I had no tricks on making myself come faster. I rubbed my thighs together again, but it wasn't going to be enough. I needed more.

More.

More.

More.

Nathaniel's arms came around me and in one move, he pulled me to his chest while slipping his hands under my waistband and finding my clit. "You want more, Abigail? I'll always be happy to give you more. Come."

He rubbed the sensitive flesh roughly and I screamed a little as my release swelled up and washed over me faster than I thought possible.

"Again," he said. And he worked two fingers into me while rubbing my clit with his thumb.

"Oh God. Oh God. Oh God," I chanted as release two built up.

He was merciless and kept finger-fucking me even as I came around his hand. Panting heavily, I whispered, "Thank you, Master."

I had just sent my post for the WNN Web site to Meagan the next afternoon when I heard the garage door open. Frowning, I went to see what was going on and smiled when I saw Nathaniel.

"Hey," I said. "You're home early."

"I wanted to change up our routine," he said, grabbing me around the waist and pulling me close for a kiss.

His lips crushed down on mine and holy hell, I didn't know what had gotten into him, but I welcomed it. I tightened my arms around his neck and kissed him back.

His eyes were dark with lust when he lifted his head.

I dug my fingers into his hair. "You should change up our routine more often."

"I'm glad you think so." He slipped a hand under my shirt and teased my belly. "I called Lynne on the way home. She's going to keep the kids occupied. Meet me in the playroom in ten minutes."

We'd been in the playroom the day before, and he'd taken my collar off. Still, I wasn't about to turn him down. "Yes, Sir."

Nathaniel was waiting for me inside when I walked into the playroom seven minutes later. That in and of itself was enough to give me pause. Normally, I arrived first. I quickly made my way to him and knelt at his feet. Without the first few minutes by myself, alone in the room, I struggled to get into the right frame of mind.

"Take your time, Abigail," he said, picking up on my inner turmoil. "It occurred to me, we've fallen into somewhat of a routine and I thought it best I put a stop to that."

Though there was a part of me that craved routine, I knew he was right. It wasn't that our time in the playroom had become mundane, but I had begun to feel as though I knew what to expect. I would enter, he would meet me, I'd give him a blow job. Lather, rinse, repeat.

"After our first trip to Delaware, we put some rules in place to play more often and they're working well, but I think there's still room for us to do better."

I remained silent, knowing he was right. I loved the fact that he was being more spontaneous and changing things up. The day before with Luke had been different than our normal scene. And him coming home early was very different.

"What are you thinking, Abigail?" he asked.

"That you're right, Master. We have gotten into somewhat of a routine and I'm glad you noticed it and are trying to make sure we don't do it again."

"We'll discuss it more a little later," he said. "I didn't bring it up to talk about right now, but I saw your unease at the changes I made tonight."

"Thank you for explaining, Master."

"Move into your inspection position," he commanded.

Years ago, my body moved effortlessly from position to position without much thought on my part. Not so anymore. The combination of long periods in between play mixed with motherhood had slowed my movements. As I shifted into place, sliding my knees apart and holding my head back, I tried to think back to the last time he'd had me in my inspection position and failed. My back ached from the rarely used position and I kept shifting my knees until he spoke again.

"Stop. Move back into waiting."

I breathed a sigh of relief and moved back into the more comfortable position.

"That was almost painful, Abigail," he said when I finally held still. "I take responsibility for this as well. But it's going to be up to you to correct it."

He walked over to the cabinets lining the wall. He didn't have anything in his hands when I walked into the playroom, so he was probably getting a cane or a crop.

"I've set a timer for fifteen minutes," he said. "In that time I want you to move from your waiting position to present position to inspection and back again. Your focus is to make your movements graceful and smooth. Time starts now."

I went back to my waiting stance, held still for five seconds, and then moved forward to present, with my upper body to the floor, and back to inspection. My inspection and present positions were uncomfortable if I stayed in them for too long. I felt so exposed and open.

Which is the point, Abigail, I could almost hear him say.

The very first time he showed me the inspection position, I had failed to wax appropriately. Now, even as uncomfortable as it was to display myself the way he wanted, I breathed a sigh of relief knowing he would find my body meticulously prepared for him. I held still for another five seconds and then moved back into my waiting position.

He didn't say anything, though I was certain he was still in the room. I took time to ensure that my posture was perfect before I continued.

"Very nice," he said a few minutes later. I wasn't sure how many minutes I had left, but I wanted them to be perfect.

"You're getting your posture right," he said. "Now see if you can smooth out the transitions between them a bit more."

After six times of going back and forth, he approved. "Excellent work, Abigail. Now work on speed."

My arms and legs trembled slightly from the unexpected exercise. I wasn't out of shape, just out of practice moving from position to position. I was in my waiting position when the timer went off, so I stayed still.

"Remember what I had you do when you were out of practice kneeling?" he asked, his feet coming into view as I looked toward the floor.

"Yes, Master." I remembered with excruciating detail. "You had me kneel for three hours. But it was broken up."

When he went to the conference that morning, so many months ago, he'd left with instructions that for three hours, I was to alternate kneeling and free time. Five minutes each, then ten, and finally fifteen. I hoped he wasn't going to have me do something similar for the positions. That had been an extremely difficult exercise.

"Did you find that exercise helpful?" he asked.

"Yes, Master. Eventually."

"Excellent. Because I want you to practice getting in and out of your positions. I won't make you do the three-hour thing again. I think fifteen minutes each day will do. I'll let you know when you can stop. Any questions?"

That didn't seem too bad. Fifteen minutes a day was extremely doable. My muscles were already a bit sore just from what he'd had me do so far, so I knew repeating the exercise would strengthen the muscles that had grown soft.

"No, Master."

"Good. Now since we're changing things up a little today, I'm not going to have you serve me orally."

I understood at least in part why he decided to change things up in the playroom, but I didn't like not being able to take him in my mouth first thing. Much like kneeling and waiting for him to join me in the playroom, serving him orally helped me get into my mind-set. The ritual we'd established helped me take my thoughts away from what was on my mind and turn my focus toward him.

"I am, however, going to put your mouth to work. Look at me."

I lifted my head and met his gaze. Like always, the intensity of his expression while he was in the playroom took my breath away. The corner of his mouth quirked up a tiny bit in an *almost, but not quite* smile. He took something out of his pocket and held it out. It looked like a replica of a cock.

"You're going to keep this in your mouth until I tell you to take it out. You are also to treat it like you would my cock. Which means no dropping and no biting. The material is made to show teeth imprints, so I'll know if you bite down on it."

Nathaniel was my first Dom and I'd never sucked someone off while being pleasured. Well, unless you counted the times we went sixty-nine. But to be situated between two men like the woman at the BDSM convention? I'd never done anything resembling that. It was as if he was letting me get a feeling for how it was with two men.

"Open," he said, and he slid the toy past my lips. "There you go. All the way. Just like it was me."

It filled my mouth more than I thought it would. It certainly was big enough to be his cock.

"Suck it," he said. "Suck it like it's my dick and you have to get it hard."

I took more of it in and sucked hard.

"There you go. That's it." He took it out unexpectedly. "That's what you're supposed to do whenever this is in your mouth. Now I want you to go drape yourself across the bench."

As I positioned my body across the bench, I realized that he planned to re-create the whole scene we'd witnessed at the club. Or as much as he could by himself. I allowed my mind to wander down paths I'd marked as no trespassing. I closed my eyes and pretended I was the woman in the courtyard that night. With Nathaniel behind me and a shadowy man in front of me.

He padded over to me and the cock pressed against my lips. "Suck it good and hard."

It felt weird having the toy in my mouth, so I allowed myself to slip back into the fantasy where I imagined it was real. I licked the shaft, making sure it didn't fall from my lips. I'd just got a good rhythm started when Nathaniel stroked my backside.

"Keep sucking," he said, and before I could guess why he would repeat himself, he spanked my ass. Hard.

"Mrpf," I said around the object in my mouth.

"Don't stop sucking and don't drop it." He rained more swats on my backside.

It wasn't long before the familiar warmth his touch created started to spread throughout my body. He wasn't being gentle, and each smack landed on a different area, so within a few minutes, my entire butt was pleasantly sore.

He came to the front of the bench and took the toy out. "Ask me to strap your ass."

Fuck yes. "Strap my ass, Master."

"Not good enough. Beg me."

"Please, Master, use your strap on me. I need you to use it hard." I widened my legs, just a touch. "Please."

I didn't realize he was naked until he pressed his cock to my lips. "First, I'm going to fuck this mouth."

That was all the warning I got. The next second, he was pushing into my mouth with a hard thrust. "There we go. Suck that cock, Abigail. Suck your Master's cock."

He went so deep with his next thrust, he hit the back of my throat. I relaxed it so he could go deeper.

"Fuck yes," he moaned.

He only pumped a few more times. Waiting, I guessed, because he didn't want to come just yet. Which meant he had more things in mind. He jerked out of my mouth, breathing heavily.

"Your mouth is so good, but I'm going to be buried in your

pussy when I come today." He pushed the toy back in my mouth and then started with the strap.

Oh, hell yes, it felt good. Sharp and hard. Then he'd press a hand to my skin and the warmth would diffuse throughout my body. Helped by his other hand, which he trailed between my legs to tease my entrance.

I hummed around the fake cock in my mouth.

"That doesn't sound like sucking." The strap hit my backside harder than it had been striking. "Suck."

I went back to sucking, but it was hard to concentrate on that when he was making other parts of me feel so good. I sank back into my fantasy, pretending the shadowy man was in front of me. I worked my mouth harder.

Nathaniel's fingers pushed inside me. "Mmm, now you're ready."

Again, there was no warm-up, no hesitation, just his spoken word followed by an all-consuming thrust. I almost bit the toy, but caught myself in time.

Behind me, his hands grabbed my ass and I groaned because the sharp pain left by his strap meshed with the sinfully sweet push and pull of him in and out of me. Together it had me seeing stars.

"Work that mouth around that cock," he said. "Imagine you're being fucked by two cocks. Two cocks filling that naughty body." He grunted and shoved inside harder.

It didn't take much for me imagine it. I could see the scene that played out in the courtyard in my head. It took nothing to picture me in place of the woman, held between two strong men, both of them using me for their pleasure.

Nathaniel smacked my ass again and I moaned, almost dropping the cock. He started circling his finger around my clit, brushing it with every other thrust. Fuck, I was so close.

My eyes flew open. He hadn't given me permission to come and my mouth was full, so I couldn't ask.

He kept up his rhythm with both his hips and his fingers while I started reciting German in my head. I squeezed my eyes tight as an orgasm threatened to overtake me. Oh, hell, I couldn't stop it.

"Come."

With his permission, I dropped my control and within seconds, my first release was shaking my body. My nose flared with my heavy breathing, but I didn't drop the toy.

"Fuck yes," he said, and thrust once more, spilling himself inside me.

He stayed buried in me for only a few seconds before pulling out and walking to my head and removing the cock. I took several deep breaths. Nathaniel took a nearby cloth and gently wiped my mouth.

"Sore here?" he asked, touching my lips.

"No, Master."

"Good." He glanced down at the toy. "No bite marks, good job. I imagine that wasn't easy."

"No, Master," I said. "But it occurs to me, you must have to trust someone a lot to put such a sensitive body part in her mouth."

"Just like you have to trust someone a lot to give him your submission?"

I smiled. He never let me forget how he treasured my submission. "I guess it is a lot like that."

Daniel and Julie rode with us to Pennsylvania for the tri-state conference that Friday afternoon. Daniel had called Nathaniel earlier in the week to ask about traveling with us. Nathaniel told me later he thought riding with us would help alleviate some of Julie's fears.

"Who are your kids staying with this weekend?" she asked not long after we left Wilmington.

"Lynne. It's her first time keeping them overnight while we're away."

"Is that hard?"

"Yes, but I don't think it ever becomes easy to go somewhere and not take your kids. Even when they stayed with Nathaniel's aunt, they were on my mind a lot."

Julie had met Lynne when she came by the house a few days ago. I didn't tell her Lynne was also a submissive, though Nathaniel and I had discussed letting her attend a group meeting if she wanted to. If she decided she wanted to go, Julie would learn then.

"Lynne seems to get along great with the kids," she said.

"Yes, and they love her. It's working out so well. Even having her living with us twenty-four/seven."

I had worried about having a live-in nanny. All the worry had been for naught, though. Lynne fit into our household so seamlessly it was already difficult to imagine what it would be like without her. I'd feared she'd be introverted and sometimes she was, especially around Nathaniel. But not when she was with Elizabeth and Henry; she was clearly happy and relaxed with them. She was so natural with the kids, and I was so glad we'd found a way to help her achieve her dream of being a teacher.

"I'm glad it worked out for you," Julie said. "Dena's been struggling trying to decide what to do when the baby comes."

"She told me. It's a hard decision."

"Last time she discussed it with me, she said she was leaning toward quitting."

"Really?" I asked.

Julie nodded. "I couldn't believe it, to be honest. She's always loved her job. But the more I thought about it, the more I really couldn't see her still working. I think she'll stay home, at least for a while."

"Makes sense. I don't see her giving up law forever."

"The one thing I know won't happen, though, is her becoming a judge like her father wants."

"I hope he comes around after the baby's born," I said, thinking about what a help Nathaniel's family was.

"I wouldn't count on it. He's still pretty upset she married Jeff."

I didn't say anything else. How would it have been if my father didn't approve of Nathaniel? My mother had died years ago and my father still lived in Indiana where I grew up. We had a nice relationship, and he visited a few times a year and we went to see him when we could.

"You would think he'd suck it up for a grandchild," I said.

"You would think." Changing the subject, she asked, "Did you and Nathaniel stay overnight when you came to the conference before?"

"No, we just came for the day. Nathaniel said there are rooms in a side building to stay in overnight. Kind of like a hotel, but not really."

"When's he giving his talk?"

"Sunday afternoon. Tonight and Saturday night, if it's like last time, there'll be a party in the courtyard."

"That sounds like fun."

"We watched it from a balcony last time we came. It was fun, but it'd be a lot more fun if we stayed in the courtyard," I said. "We wouldn't even have to play. I'd be fine with dancing."

"I'd love to dance. It's been ages." Julie's eyes grew large. "Oh! I heard there's a chance the owner will be building a similar space in Wilmington."

"You haven't heard the latest?" I asked, and she shook her head. "He *is* building a similar space. He's going to start when he finishes the remodeling of the club in New York. Nathaniel's going to be a partner."

"Really? That's so exciting!"

I nodded. "I think it's going to be exclusively for the Partners in Play group."

"That's even better. I mean, I don't mind having everyone over for meetings and parties, but after a while . . ."

Because he had the largest house in the group, plus a stocked playroom, *and* a guesthouse, most of the group's meetings were held at Daniel's house, so I knew where she was going and completed her sentence, "It gets old."

"Very. I know Daniel will never say anything. He feels like it's something he should do."

"It's a big responsibility and really too much to expect one couple to handle all the time."

"At least now I know it won't be forever and our time's limited. That'll help."

Before too long, we were pulling through the iron gate. We stopped while Nathaniel gave our information to security.

"I like how safe this is," Julie whispered.

"Me, too." I knew anything Nathaniel was involved in would also have top-notch security in place. "In fact, Nathaniel's going to bring up security with Daniel on Sunday morning when they meet to discuss changes to the group."

Both men had agreed to set aside a few hours to discuss potential changes for the Partners in Play group. I was looking forward to the new regulations. Hopefully, they'd make everyone feel more secure.

The guard let us through and we took the driveway that led to a big stone building. But Nathaniel didn't stop. Instead he drove around it to the separate facility we'd be staying in overnight.

The place was spotless. Painted with a light grayish blue and with a small fountain in the far corner, the building felt light and airy and calming. The floors were a light gray stone. It certainly didn't look like any BDMS club I'd been in before.

"Master DeVaan said to apologize that he's not here to welcome you personally," the front desk clerk told us. She looked over all four of us as she checked us in. I wondered if she was in the lifestyle. I didn't try to guess what role she took. I'd learned through the years, I guessed incorrectly most of the time. Currently, she looked as though she could fall on either side with a black T-shirt, hair pulled back into a neat ponytail, and her fingernails filed short and painted a neutral color. "There was a snag with the evening's entertainment and he's taking care of that."

"It's no problem," Daniel assured her. "We'll find our way around."

The clerk nodded and lifted a folder. "Master West, I put a schedule in your packet. Your talk is highlighted with the time and location."

Nathaniel thanked her and we made our way up to our room, telling Daniel and Julie we'd see them later. The color scheme from the lobby carried through to the room, which was similarly decorated in blue-gray. It was a good-sized room and held a king bed. Nathaniel pointed out the hidden loops at the corners.

"For tying people up," he said.

Of course there would be ties. It was a BDSM club.

"Want to go look around?" he asked.

"Sure."

He took my hand and for the next hour, we explored the property. My favorite area was the courtyard outside our balcony. A redbrick patio was done in a herringbone pattern and surrounded by willow trees. The branches swayed in the light breeze. At one end, a long buffet was being set up with tables and chairs nearby for eating. The other end, however, had a much different purpose.

While we watched, a handful of men were transforming the patio by adding benches, whipping posts, and a St. Andrew's cross. I closed my eyes, imagining playing on some of the equipment while others looked on. I really hoped Nathaniel decided to play in the courtyard. It would be filled with people and, if it was the same as the last conference, hypnotizing music. To play in public with that atmosphere would be so much fun.

"Did you reserve a balcony?" I asked.

"No, we have one in our room. I didn't see the point in reserving one."

His answer was matter-of-fact and didn't really tell me what I wanted to know. I sighed and opened my mouth to ask him if we could skip the balcony in favor of the courtyard, but he shook his head and put his finger over my lips.

"I'm not telling you my plans. Don't ask me."

He hadn't collared me yet, so I thought about asking him anyway, but decided to trust him instead.

More people were arriving, and I recognized a few of the Partners in Play group. Evan and William arrived together and not long after they came in, Kelly arrived alone. Jeff and Dena weren't coming and Cole was out of town. We walked over and made small talk. They all mentioned how they were looking forward to Nathaniel's talk on Sunday.

For once, Evan and Kelly didn't argue. At most of the group functions we'd attended in Wilmington, they seemed to bicker a lot.

I mentioned it to Nathaniel when they left to see the rest of the property.

"Maybe being out of town is good for them," he said.

"We should keep them out of town, then," I joked.

He laughed and then said he wanted to see the room he'd be giving his talk in, so we went into the main building to find it. The talks were to be held off the main lobby in large rooms set up with rows of chairs, like a theater. We went into the one he'd be speaking in and Nathaniel chatted for a few minutes with the woman setting up the sound system. Once everything was confirmed to his liking, he wrapped his arm around my waist, pulled me close, and kissed me.

"Let's go get ready," he said.

The music's *thump, thump, thump* slowly worked its way from my ears, to my mind, and gradually eased into my muscles, loosening them, filling my body, and I soon found I was unable to do anything except sway to the beat.

While we had been eating dinner, a dance floor was put in the courtyard, flanked on one side by the play area and on the other, the eating area. Currently, the bulk of the people were on the dance floor. Men and women of all ages—from twenty to retirement—were dancing, and it didn't seem to matter who they danced with. Men danced with men and women danced with women, and in one corner, a group of three men danced with one woman. Tonight, everyone was wearing masks and I thought maybe that accounted for the uninhibited mood.

Alcohol wasn't allowed, so everyone was sober, but the very air seemed to be intoxicating. Even Nathaniel, who didn't care much for clubs, was tapping his foot. He wasn't acting as though he would be making any move to the dance floor, though. Daniel stood at his other side and Julie looked up expectantly.

"I don't think this is my type of music, kitten," he said. "If Nathaniel's okay with it, why don't you and Abby go dance?"

I glanced at Nathaniel and he nodded. "Go on, my lovely. I'll get more enjoyment out of watching you than joining in myself."

Julie and I didn't have to be told twice. She reached for my hand and we made our way onto the middle of the dance floor.

Julie wore a half mask of navy and gold that matched the flirty skirt she wore. Her cheeks flushed a light pink as she turned toward me.

"I haven't danced like this in forever," she said.

I was wearing my black lace, one-sleeve dress. It was the same dress I'd worn to that seedy club in New York. But I chose it because it matched the black mask covering my face as well as the black leather collar that was very obvious with the low neckline of the dress and the way my hair was pulled up.

"Me neither," I said.

We didn't talk after that. The music was simply too loud. But I could feel her laughter as the crowd pushed us together. I closed my eyes and let the music sink into my body, allowing it to overtake me. My hips undulated and as the song went on, I felt as if I were the only person on the dance floor.

My eyes flew open as someone swung me around and I found myself facing a large wall of a man. I took a step back, my eyes searching the crowd at the edge of the dance floor for Nathaniel. I expected him to motion me back, but instead he nodded. To my left, Julie was dancing with another guy I didn't recognize. When she saw me looking, she shrugged. Apparently, Daniel hadn't minded, either.

It made me feel wanton and wild. I didn't recognize the woman I became on the dance floor. Whoever she was, she was free and uninhibited. Very similar to when Nathaniel and I played in front of people. I wasn't sure why, but even though I felt like someone else, for some reason I still felt safe and secure. I couldn't make sense of it, but I didn't worry about it, either. I didn't know the large man dancing with me, but he made me feel sexy and sensual—not attracted *to* him, but just feeling sexy in my own skin.

I threw a look over my shoulder and I knew what it was. Though Nathaniel was watching me with that intensely sexy look of his, others in the room were, too. It was the same as having sex in public. Something about people watching me, wanting me, but unable to touch me. Hell, part of me thought it made me sound like a freak. And I was having too much fun to feel like a freak, so I decided not to think about it anymore. Instead I looked back to Nathaniel.

He watched me with a look of unadulterated lust and longing. He no longer tapped his foot, but stood completely still, his eyes locked on my every move. I circled my hips, dipped my knees, and swayed with my arms over my head. For him.

Over his shoulder, I noticed a group of strangers watching. For them.

But wasn't that wrong?

I closed my eyes once more and imagined I was a harem girl, dancing for Nathaniel, my sheik. In my mind, I was naked and taunting him with my body. Showing him how I could pleasure him later with the moves of my hips.

I wasn't sure how much time passed, but as it did, I grew more and more turned on. Needed him more and more. Craved his touch. Yearned for his command. And it suddenly hit me that the people watching saw how much dancing for him turned me on and that made me want to dance even more. For him. For them. They blurred together.

The music slowed and as it changed, I looked for Julie. When I found her, I motioned that we should head back to our men. I didn't want the dancing to end, but I knew I couldn't slow-dance with another man. Julie slid away from the guy she'd been dancing with and we slowly walked back to the edge of the dance floor.

"I can't believe Daniel and Nathaniel allowed us to dance with those two guys," she said.

We took one last look back to where we'd been dancing. The two men were now dancing with each other. Julie raised an eyebrow and I simply shrugged. *Who knew?*

As soon as I got within touching distance, Nathaniel took me in his arms, pulled me close, and whispered coarsely, "That was damn near the hottest thing I've ever seen."

"I danced for you," I said, pushing my hips against his, feeling his erection. "It was all for you." Well, not all of it, but most of it. Maybe.

"I think I understand it now," he said. "At least in part."

"The dancing?"

"No, we'll talk about it later."

He pulled me in front of him so my back was to his chest. "Right now we're going to watch for a few minutes. Then I'm showing you what happens to sexy submissives who tease their Dominants."

"I look forward to it, Master."

He ran a hand down the front of my body, brushing my breasts. "Did you enjoy putting on that little show?"

"I enjoyed dancing for you, Master. Knowing you were watching turned me on."

His hand moved lower, inched by my belly button, making its way to where I yearned for him. "And did you know that nearly damn near every man in this place was watching you? Getting turned on by the way you moved that hot little body? Imagined it was them pressed up against you?"

"My mind was on you, Master. Wanting you to get turned on. Wanting you to imagine how you'd feel pressed up against me. I danced for you. But," I whispered, "I knew they were there. I knew they were watching and saw me getting hot for you."

His finger slipped even lower, so near my clit and yet not touching it. Just teasing. "It worked. I'm so turned on right now. Your little show made me so hard I might just bend you over a table and fuck you in front of everyone."

It wouldn't be so crazy. Already there were couples engaging in various sexual acts all around the courtyard. To our left, a woman knelt between a man's knees giving him a blow job. In another corner a man had a woman pressed against a wall while he fondled between her legs.

I fluttered my lashes at him. "Yes, please, Master."

Nathaniel brushed aside the fabric of my thong and dipped a finger into my arousal.

"The thought of me taking you like that turns you on, doesn't it, naughty girl?"

I couldn't very well say it didn't, not when he could feel how wet I was.

"Oh yes, Master," I said, grinding my pelvis against his hand. "It makes me so wet."

His breath was hot in my ear. "What turns you on more, dancing with the other guy for me or thinking about my taking you in front of everyone?"

"You taking me, Master." Then to prove my words, I circled my hips again.

"Better watch it, Abigail. You don't have permission to come. Though I bet these people would love to watch me spank your ass."

I stopped my hips and waited. Maybe he'd let me come soon. He removed his hand from my dress. "Hold that thought."

"Hold that what?" I asked. Did that mean . . . ?

"Is my naughty girl curious?"

"Very, Master."

His expression was pure evil enticement. "Too bad."

He turned to his side and I realized Daniel had signaled for him. While the two of them spoke softly, I took Julie a few steps away.

"What are you guys doing?" I asked.

"We're going to go back to our room. You?"

"I think we're staying down here. At least I hope we are."

She winked at me. "He knows you well. I'm sure you'll have fun."

"I bet Daniel has something very exciting planned for when you get back to the room."

"I think he does." Her voice dropped. "And I have a pretty good idea what it is."

"Oh?"

"He's been preparing me for anal sex." She bit her bottom lip. "I'm not sure it's what he has planned for tonight, but I bet it's sooner rather than later."

"Trust me, if Daniel's anything like Nathaniel—and so far, he has been—he has everything all planned out. And when it's all said and done, you'll probably end up loving it. Craving it even."

It should have felt strange to be talking about anal sex while standing near a dance floor, but it didn't. It was partly because Julie and I had grown close as friends. But probably it was also because sexual tension was so thick in the courtyard. Besides, I felt certain that if I walked over to the play area, someone would be having anal sex. Possibly lots of someones.

"I'll just have to take your word on that. I don't see me ever craving it."

"Trust me," I said. "I wouldn't lie to you, especially about something this big."

"It's Daniel's something big I'm worried about," she said, half joking.

"You'll be fine," I said. "Matter of fact, call me in the morning and tell me how right I was."

"It makes me feel better hearing that from you. It's not like I don't trust Daniel. It's just I've never had anyone take me there before. You know?"

"Yes. My first time was actually when we were out of town as well." I thought back to the Super Bowl weekend years ago, when we'd just gotten together and his cousin, Jackson, played pro ball. "I was scared to death, but he took it slow, making sure I got pleasure out of it, and to be honest, it was rather sweet."

"Sweet? I don't know if I believe that."

"It hurt a bit, too. Even with the preparation."

"That I believe."

"You ready?" Daniel asked, coming beside Julie and putting his arm around her waist.

"Yes, Master." She looked up at him with trusting eyes and I knew everything was going to be all right.

"See you later, Nathaniel. Abby," Daniel said as they walked away.

"Follow me," Nathaniel said after they left.

He led me away from the dance floor and over to the playing end of the courtyard. I froze momentarily when we made it to the spot between the two groups. I couldn't look at just one scene. There were too many and I wanted to watch them all.

From what I could see, there were at least five couples in the middle of play that I saw from where we stood. One man was talking with another while a naked woman knelt at his feet giving him a blow job. The two men Julie and I had danced with were taking turns flogging a blond woman. I watched them for a bit. I'd seen a few threesomes play before, but I'd never witnessed tag team flogging. I imagined it felt pretty good from the breathy moans coming from the woman.

"That looks intense," I whispered to Nathaniel, and was going to ask him if he'd done anything like it, but his expression stopped me cold.

He was watching the threesome as well, but he looked shocked. No, it wasn't shock, it looked more like guilt. Which didn't make any sense. Why would he feel guilty over a flogging scene? I looked at the two men again, but they appeared to know what they were doing and the blonde didn't seem to be in pain. Quite the opposite actually.

"Master?" I asked. "Is everything okay? Do you know them?"

He startled and glanced down at me. "No, not at all. I was just thinking."

"About what?" Whatever it was looked too serious for a party.

"About where the best place to fuck you would be."

He spoke it a bit too quickly, but I didn't call him on it. I highly doubted he was thinking of places to have sex with *that* look on his face. I didn't want to dwell on it, so I hooked a finger through his belt loop and pulled his hips to me.

"What did you decide on, Master? I'm here to serve you in any way I can."

He nodded to his left. "I want you facing that wall. Naked."

Yes! Finally!

I shoved his odd expression even farther back in my mind and focused on the fact that we were finally going to do what I'd been wanting for so long. What I'd been fantasizing about.

I moved with seductive strides to the wall he'd indicated. Halfway there, I peeked over my shoulder to see if he was following. He was, but his head was turned so he could keep his eyes on the threesome.

He caught me staring and I swore he looked guilty again. But just for a split second. His countenance changed and he spoke in a low voice. "Keep going."

I wasn't sure what his obsession with the threesome was, but I wasn't going to let it keep me from enjoying myself. Especially since he wasn't sharing what was going on. I walked the rest of the way to the wall and turned to wait for him.

I'm not vain, but I knew I'd attracted some attention and there were several men watching me. *At least I had someone's undivided attention.* I unbuttoned my shirt and was down to my bra by the time Nathaniel made it to me.

He stood in front of me and I undid the clasp at my back. "Will I be enough to keep your attention, Master?" It was a bit bratty, but his focus on the threesome irked me.

"Maybe," he said. "You got anything under that bra that can keep me interested?"

"Just these." I slid the bra off my shoulders.

His dark, lust-filled eyes were all the encouragement I needed. His and the handful of other men watching.

I felt excitement flutter in my belly and once more it was as if I was playacting. Almost like a role play. I lifted my hands to cup my breasts. "Will these work, Master?"

"I don't know. Pinch them. Hard."

I rolled my nipples between my thumb and forefinger before giving them a pinch.

"Did it hurt?" he asked.

"No, Master."

"Then you didn't do it hard enough. Do it again. Make it hurt."

Normally, I'd obey, but I wanted to make sure *I* had his entire focus. "If it pleases you, Master, I'd like for you to do it."

He didn't hesitate, but sprang forward, pushing my back against the wall and palming my breasts with rough hands. His lips crushed mine.

He pulled back long enough to ask, "Are you sure this is what you want?" and I was pretty sure he wasn't talking about the way he pinched my nipples.

I rolled my pelvis against his. "Yes, Master. I want them all to see you take me."

"I bet you do." He fumbled with the button on his pants. "I bet you can't wait to show off how much you like my cock." He pushed down on my shoulders. "Suck it."

I dropped to my knees, and his fingers twisted around my

hair as I took him in my mouth. He thrust forward and I barely had a chance to inhale before he hit the back of my throat.

"That's it." His hands tightened in my hair. "Take it just like that."

I worked my mouth around him, taking him deep, showing him and everyone watching how much I loved to serve him, how serving him turned me on. I closed my eyes and relished the sharp tugs he gave my head as he worked his hips.

It wasn't his plan to finish with me on my knees and before he came, he pulled out. "Stand up."

I leisurely rose to my feet and I no longer had to worry about his attention being elsewhere. He watched me with such intensity I knew I was the only thing on his mind. I slowly licked my lips. "I love your taste, Master."

He gave me a wicked laugh. "Hands on the wall. Bent at the waist."

I took the few steps to the wall and situated myself, looking over my shoulder when I was in place. "Like this, Master?"

I kept my eyes on him, but from the periphery I noticed we'd attracted a handful of onlookers.

"Someone's being a little sassy tonight, aren't they?"

"You bring it out in me, Master."

And he knew it, too, judging from the way the corner of his mouth quirked up. "Face the wall."

I'd rather be facing the crowd, so I could see their reactions to what we were doing, but I turned and faced the wall.

"Good thinking on my part not to have you wear anything under this skirt."

Cool air brushed my skin as he lifted the skirt, and desire

swelled low in my belly because I knew my ass was bared for all to see. I jerked when he smacked my backside and then groaned at how good it felt.

"You're such a bad girl getting turned on by having your ass spanked in public." He smacked it again. Harder. "Aren't you?"

"Yes, Master. So bad."

He rained smacks across my flesh and I couldn't keep the moans of pleasure to myself. "Green, Master," I said when he stopped.

"No," he said. "No more. I'm hard as hell and I'm going to get some relief now."

As he moved against me, I realized he hadn't even taken his pants off completely. But they were clearly open enough because less than a second later, he thrust into me. He went so deep and felt so good my eyes rolled to the back of my head.

"Oh, hell yes, Master."

His only response was to grab my hair with one hand and jerk my head back as he drove into me again. "Quiet."

I bit the inside of my cheek to keep from making a sound because *oh my God, he felt so good.* He kept one hand in my hair and worked the other one between my legs to tease my clit. And the entire time, he continued his pounding rhythm, making good on his promise to seek his own relief.

"Get there, Abigail."

It wouldn't take me long. I felt my release grow closer with every thrust of his hips and each teasing sweep of his fingers. And still he didn't let up.

The crowd around us started murmuring and in the distance I heard the unmistakable sound of a woman's orgasm. *They are watching us. Watching me. Almost. Almost.*

"Come."

A few more teases of his finger and my climax crashed over me. He grunted in victory and gave my hair one final tug before allowing his own release.

The space around us seemed suddenly much more quiet and it finally hit me that the music had stopped. The only audible melody was the sound of pleasure from the couples around us and our own pounding hearts.

Nathaniel groaned behind me, but pulled himself up and smoothed my skirt down. I wasn't sure I was physically able to move. He rubbed my arms and took my hands. "Are you okay?"

"More than okay, Master. Just on pleasure overload."

He kissed my neck. "Let me help."

His touch no longer bore its earlier hastiness, but instead was gentle and controlled. He eased me up and away from the wall, picking up my discarded bra and shirt, and helping me back into them both.

The crowd, aware that we were finished, began talking among themselves and stepping away. Slowly, the noise level grew again. Or maybe it was only that my heartbeat slowed back to its normal rate.

"Ready to go to our room?" he asked with a soft kiss to my forehead.

His question made me realize how tired I suddenly felt and I wanted nothing more than to be in bed, held snuggly in his arms.

I swayed slightly. "Yes, Master."

He slipped his arm around me, holding me close and secure, and we headed toward the courtyard's exit and our waiting room. As ready as I'd been hours before to be part of the crowd, I surprised myself with how ready I was to escape it.

And I wasn't positive, but I was fairly certain, right before we left the crowd completely, I sensed him turn his head. Looking back to the spot where the threesome had been.

Because we didn't have anywhere to be the next morning and no one to wake us up, we stayed in bed longer than normal. It'd been so long since we woke up to each other. Hunger finally drove us out of bed and we dressed leisurely and hit a local café for brunch.

Nathaniel's talk wasn't until the next day, leaving us plenty of free time. We arrived back at the hotel after eating and stopped in the lobby to decide what sessions we wanted to attend. We stood off to the side, our arms brushing as we looked over the schedule.

The elevator doors pinged in the background and I would have continued looking over the schedule if the lady who stepped off hadn't laughed. But she did and Nathaniel's body stiffened at the sound. It was such a contrast to the easygoing attitude he'd had all morning that I glanced up and followed his eyes. What I saw hit me in the gut.

"That looks like Charlene," I said.

Whoever she was, she hadn't seen us yet. She was too busy laughing at something one of the two guys she was with said. I tilted my head. The same two guys from both the dance floor and the threesome scene Nathaniel had been obsessed with.

And he hadn't said anything yet.

"It *is* Charlene."

"It appears that way." He spoke in that monotone voice I hated and his face held no expression.

The group of three moved closer to us and I knew exactly when she saw us. Her lips curved up into a smile that could only be considered evil and she excused herself from the two men.

"Nathaniel," she said. "I thought we might bump into each other. I was surprised, though, to see you watching our little scene last night."

Heat consumed my body. *She* was the reason he watched the threesome so intently the night before.

Nathaniel didn't say anything. That pissed me off, too, until I saw him motion one of the men over. "Permission to address your submissive?" he asked the man Julie had danced with.

"I don't care," the man said. "She's not mine. We just hooked up for the weekend."

That dimmed her high-wattage smile just a bit.

Nathaniel nodded and turned to address Charlene. "Because of our working relationship, I would prefer we stay away from each other as much as possible in situations like this."

"Of course," she said. "Hello, Abby."

Before I could reply, Nathaniel held up his hand. "You do not have permission to speak to my submissive."

"My apologies." She looked me up and down before heading out the door with the two men.

My body shook as the threesome walked away. *What. The. Fuck?* Charlene was a submissive? And Nathaniel knew?

It doesn't mean anything.

I snorted at my brain's attempt to reason with my emotions. It sure as hell meant something. If it meant nothing, Nathaniel would have told me last night what he'd seen.

He's around submissive women all the time.

Yes, but he doesn't work with them and have weekend meetings with them and they don't fall all over him.

You told him you trusted him.

That was before I found out Charlene was also a submissive. Besides, the fact that I trusted him didn't change the fact that I didn't trust her.

Wonder how long he's known.

That was a good question. Did he know when he hired her? Or did he find out later?

Does it matter?

It did. For some odd reason, I needed to know how long he'd known she was a submissive.

"Fucking hell," I said as understanding hit me. "You knew. You knew she was a submissive."

"Let's go upstairs," Nathaniel said.

I didn't want to go upstairs. I wanted to go somewhere and be by myself so I could process this new information. But I was in a relatively strange place and I didn't know it well enough to determine where I might find a quiet spot.

I did know that we should get out of the lobby, so I gave Nathaniel a curt nod and breezed past him to the elevator bank. I might be going upstairs, but I wasn't going to touch him.

When we got to our room, I suddenly felt exhausted and I plopped down on the couch and crossed my arms.

"How long have you known?" I asked.

"I found out the weekend we moved that she was a submissive."

Not too long ago, then. "So you didn't hire her because you knew she was a sub?"

"I don't make it a general practice to hire someone based on their sexuality. Opens you up to lawsuits."

"But the fact is, you knew and you didn't tell me."

"To be honest, there never seemed to be a good time to say, 'Hey, by the way, Charlene's a submissive.'"

"So you decided not to tell me anything. Because *that's* so much better."

"Frankly, my employees' sexuality is none of your business."

I opened my mouth to argue, but stopped. There was more to it than me wanting to know about his employees' sexuality and he knew it. The fact was, there would always be animosity between me and Charlene. It didn't have to be right and it didn't have to make sense. It just was. And no matter how often Nathaniel and I argued about her, discussed her, or whatever you wanted to call it, I would never like her.

The best thing for me to do was to shut up and deal with it. "You're right. It's none of my business. I won't mention her again, much less talk about her."

Those were the words I spoke, but inside, I was chanting:

Charlene's a submissive and Nathaniel knew.

Charlene's a submissive and Nathaniel knew.

Charlene's a submissive and Nathaniel knew.

Then I asked myself if I was going to let her ruin my entire weekend.

No. No, I wasn't.

"What's first on our schedule tomorrow?" I asked Nathaniel.

"Don't you want to talk about this?"

"You just, very eloquently I might add, correctly informed me that your employees' sexuality was none of my business. You know Charlene's a submissive. She knows you're a Dominant and that's how we're going to leave it. That's all there is to it."

He looked at me with a raised eyebrow. He didn't believe me. He knew as well as I did that that wasn't all there was to it. Maybe I'd bring it up later. When I wasn't feeling as emotional about it. The last time I'd gotten into a heated discussion about Charlene, I ended up on the receiving end of a discipline flogging.

Technically, what earned me the flogging was calling Nathaniel a liar while I wore his collar. But I blamed that on Charlene, too.

"In that case," Nathaniel said, "there's a session on electrical play I wanted to attend starting in fifteen minutes."

That night the dance party was even louder and more crowded than the night before. I was glad. I didn't want to run into Charlene at all, and the more people between us, the better. The afternoon had been awkward with Nathaniel. The joviality we'd had earlier in the weekend was gone.

But I had said Charlene was a done and finished deal, so I couldn't very well keep bringing her up. Maybe, I thought, if I refused to mention her name, and tried not to think about her, she wouldn't bother me as much.

It hadn't worked so far.

Julie and Daniel had been unsuccessful in lightening our

mood. They'd tried during an early dinner, finally giving up when it became obvious neither Nathaniel nor I wanted to have the mood lightened. Currently, they were dancing together. Daniel must have decided he didn't want to spend another night watching his woman dance with another man.

Julie looked just fine with that. Though she'd danced with the stranger the night before, she was definitely less inhibited with Daniel. Her dance was hypnotic to watch and there were more eyes than just Daniel's following her every move. My feet itched to join in.

Nathaniel wouldn't be dancing with me. Not only did he look completely uninterested, but I'd recently spied Charlene step onto the dance floor with her two men. After the run-in this morning in the lobby, there was no way in hell Nathaniel was going to set foot on it with her there.

I closed my eyes and let the music sink into my skin. I wanted to dance. It was so easy to remember the feelings I'd had the previous night. The freedom, the power, the pleasure. I wanted to feel them again.

"May I go dance, Master?" I asked. Obviously, he wasn't going to voluntarily tell me to go dance.

"Yes."

I waited for him to say more. To tell me who I could dance with or how long I could dance. Something. But there was nothing. Just that one word.

With a shrug, I made my way to join in with the dancers.

Something almost magic hit me as soon as my foot touched the dance floor. Probably it was only that the music was louder and I was feeling the excitement and joy from all those bodies.

I swung my arms over my head and started swaying in time to the music.

"You dancing?" a middle-aged Dom asked me.

I couldn't talk to Doms in a club without Nathaniel's permission, so instead of verbalizing my response, I answered with my body and moved closer to him. He kept his distance, aware because of the collar I wore that I belonged to someone else. Still he danced with me, and several of our moves received a few catcalls.

Not long after we started our dance, another Dom joined our twosome and I laughed to myself when I realized I matched Charlene for the number of men I was dancing with. I looked across the dance floor to see if she was still there, but I couldn't find her.

"She yours?" the new Dom asked the one I'd been dancing with.

"No," he replied. "I thinks she belongs to the tall guy in the back with a scowl on his face."

That certainly sounded like Nathaniel.

A faster song started and our little group grew by another guy. *Three.* I'd never danced with three men at one time before. The new guy was young and he could move. I inched closer to him to match what he was doing.

"That's it," he said. "Move those hips."

I didn't reply, but moved them slow and sultry, exaggerating my movements in a suggestion of more intimate activities. I ran my hands down my body and across my chest, rubbing my nipples.

This was what I needed. This time to let go and dance and be free. To be watched and to feel sexy and wanted. To let the music sweep me away.

"That's enough, Abigail."

I opened my eyes and found Nathaniel in front of me. Although the music still played, the three Doms had left.

Damn him for stopping my fun.

"Is something wrong, Master?"

"Do you plan to dance with every male in the place?"

Was he serious? *He* was pulling the jealous card? After Charlene? *The nerve.*

"Only the Dominant ones, Master."

"Are you purposely trying to irritate me?"

I put my hands on my hips. There was no way I was going to stand there and listen while he acted all jealous. I'd only been dancing. "You said I could dance, Master. You didn't give me any restrictions or instructions. With all due respect, if you didn't want me doing something, maybe you should have told me."

He lowered his voice. "With all due respect, my ass. I shouldn't have to tell you I don't want you dancing with half a dozen men at one time."

"Three is hardly half a dozen, Master."

He stared at me for a long minute, his lips pressed into a thin line. "Go kneel next to the willow tree in the far left corner," he finally said.

I huffed, but followed his command. Our confrontation had garnered some attention. *And not the good kind.* I walked quickly, but with enough attitude so he'd know I was pissed.

He wasn't far behind me and he stood over me almost as soon as I went down on my knees.

"People are watching," he said. "Not exactly the type of attention you like, is it?"

"No, Master."

"Maybe you should have thought about what kind of attention you wanted before you got up and decided to dance with half the men at the party."

I really didn't see what his problem was. He didn't seem to have minded the night before when Julie was with me and we danced. But I had his collar on, I'd already been bratty, and it didn't feel like the right time to point out how inconsistent he was being.

I saw a pair of shoes walk up in my peripheral vision and stop nearby. *Great, more onlookers.* I enjoyed sexy times with people watching, but I didn't enjoy sharing with them when I got in trouble.

"You want to see what it's like to be with another Dom?" Nathaniel asked. "Is that what this new fascination with playing in public is leading to?"

"No, Master." Where had that come from? How did he jump from playing in public to me being with another man? Surely he hadn't got all that from my dancing.

"I don't know if I believe you."

"I don't know how to prove it, Master."

"You there," Nathaniel said, and I realized he was talking to the man who stood nearby. "Want to help out?"

Oh my God, what is he doing?

The stranger grunted and from the sound alone, I couldn't tell if it was an affirmative reply or a negative one. His shoes came closer to me, which I took to mean he'd agreed to be part of the scene.

"This is one of the men you were dancing with, Abigail."

I'd have to take his word for it. I hadn't exactly been looking at the guys' shoes when I was dancing.

"I think he wanted to make sure you were okay. You have permission to speak to him."

I kept my gaze focused on the floor. "I'm very much okay, Sir. Thank you for checking."

"Is that your idea of thanks?" Nathaniel asked.

What the hell did he want me to do? Kiss the guy's feet in thanks? "How should I thank him, Master?"

"Properly," a gruff voice I recognized from the dance floor said.

My heart pounded and the blood rushing through my body buzzed in my ears. Everything seemed to fog over.

Did he mean what I thought he meant? And Nathaniel was going to allow it?

Somewhere in front of me a zipper was being lowered.

Though the fog that was still clearing in my brain, I suddenly became very aware of what and who was in front of me. It was a stranger and he was unbuttoning his pants. I didn't want to look up and see him. I could do this, but I didn't want to see his face. For whatever reason, that seemed important.

Slowly, he took his jeans down and I focused on his cock. It was sizable, and very erect. And pierced.

"You're pierced." I felt my cheeks flush as soon as the words left my mouth because of course he was. And of course he knew it.

"The submissives at the club seem to like it," he said in a matter-of-fact way. But he might as well have poured ice-cold water over me because that simple sentence brought the image of one specific submissive kneeling at a club.

Charlene.

And it wasn't a stranger she knelt before in my mind. It was Nathaniel.

Time stopped as I pictured him taking his pants down and her licking her lips, desperate for him. He stroked his cock. "Ready for a taste?"

But when she opened her mouth to engulf his cock, it wasn't Charlene. It was me. I was Charlene.

The vision disappeared and the only thing in front of me was a cock that wasn't Nathaniel's.

Oh my God. I was Charlene.

"Stop. No! Red."

"What the hell, man?" the stranger asked, and I realized I hadn't been the one to safe-word. Nathaniel had done it.

"We're leaving," Nathaniel said, and his voice was shaky.

So he was upset. Good. I would hate to be alone in my pissed-off state.

"Whatever," the stranger said. I kept my eyes on the floor as he zipped his pants back up and left.

"Are you okay?" Nathaniel held out a hand to me, but I jerked away from him.

"Don't touch me," I said. "You were trying to turn me into her."

"What? Who?" Nathaniel asked. "What are you talking about?"

"Charlene," I said, putting as much disdain as possible in that one word.

"What?" he asked again.

"How long have you really known she was submissive? You've known all along, haven't you? And I bet you thought that if you could convince me to do a threesome, I wouldn't be able to say anything if you wanted to play with her."

"I don't know what the hell you're talking about."

"Look at it from my perspective. If you allow me to play with other men and you even go so far as to introduce a third, is it so far out there that you would come to me and say, 'I'm bringing another woman into the playroom. You shouldn't have a problem with it, since I brought another man in it for you'?"

"You've got it completely wrong. I don't want Charlene. If I wanted to be with another woman, there are easier ways to go about doing it. *And* I don't want to share you. I don't want to bring anyone into our time. But I saw the look in your eyes. You needed more and more and soon you'd have wanted to try two men at a time and I *was willing to do that for you. Not because I liked it. I hate it. I would do it for you!*"

"Excuse me," a Dungeon Monitor said. "Is everything okay here?"

Shit. I'd forgotten we were surrounded by people. The guy was looking at me, waiting for a response.

Of course a DM would stop by. Someone had safe-worded and then we'd been arguing.

"Everything's fine." I stood up. "We're actually headed to our room."

I started walking toward the exit, not checking to see if Nathaniel followed. I heard him say something to the DM and then follow behind me. He didn't say anything, though. In fact, there wasn't a word said until we made it into our room. Then I finally turned to face him.

"What the hell was that?" I asked once he had closed and locked the door.

He turned around and I was momentarily stunned. He was so pale.

"I'm so sorry, Abby."

He was sorry and I was fucking furious. "You should be. You had no idea who that man was. How dare you let him tell me to *thank him properly!*"

"There's no excuse for what I did. None." He ran his hand through his hair. "I don't know what got into me. It was watching you dance with those men and they kept coming up to join in. And I knew you liked being watched and I thought since you were dancing maybe you wanted to try a threesome and the thought of it killed me."

"Because I enjoyed dancing, I obviously want to have sex with a stranger? That doesn't even make sense. I have no clue how you thought that because I was dancing with a man I also wanted his dick in my mouth."

"I know. You're right."

"Damn straight, I'm right." He walked to the couch and sat down. I kept standing. "And tell me one more time how you found out Charlene was a submissive."

He exhaled deeply. "The weekend we moved, I was meeting with her about the nonprofit. She asked if we could have dinner and I told her no. She kept asking. I finally let her know, in no uncertain terms, that I would be eating alone and to stop asking about it. She replied back with a 'Yes, Sir' that left me with no doubt she was submissive. Just as I'm sure she had no doubt I was a Dominant."

"If that's the whole story, I still don't understand why you didn't just tell me."

"It seriously didn't cross my mind. It was that unimportant to me."

"Then why were you staring at her scene like you were last night? That's hardly the behavior of someone who finds the entire subject unimportant."

"I wanted to make sure it was her."

"And you didn't want to wait until she wasn't in the middle of a Dom sandwich?"

"Like I said just now, I wasn't thinking clearly."

It would be so easy to forgive him. To say the words and go on with our weekend. Sweep it under the rug and pretend it didn't happen. But I couldn't do that. We'd worked too hard at our communication for me to let him go that easy. "You not thinking clearly could have put me in a dangerous position. What if I'd done it and he had a disease?"

I didn't think it was possible, but he went even paler. "I called a stop to it."

"I was seconds away from doing it myself. That's beside the point." I held a finger to his chest. "You're the Dominant. It's up to you to make sure we're doing what we want to do, not just guess and throw something together at the last minute."

I'd rarely seen him so dejected and part of me hated it because I knew how deep his self-loathing could go. But the bigger part of me wanted him to hate what he'd done. What he'd almost had me do.

"I don't want anyone other than you. Ever," I said. "I don't want or need to experience a threesome. Yes, I enjoy playing in public, but that's an entirely different thing and they are not related."

I wanted to tell him to grow his petty, jealous self up, but decided that would be pushing it since I didn't handle Charlene all that well. He could, technically, tell me to do the same thing.

"I'm taking a shower and going to bed," I said, then left him with hands on his knees, looking as though his world had just fallen apart.

Chapter Fourteen

NATHANIEL

I didn't sleep that night. For a long time I sat on the couch, thinking about how badly I'd fucked up. Abby had been having fun and dancing. If I hadn't still been irritated over Charlene, I'd have joined her. As it was, I stood watching her dance with other men and grew more and more agitated by the second.

Abby was a beautiful woman. Of course she'd captured the attention of the crowd. And yes, her dancing had been on the risqué side, but hell, we were at a BDSM club and people were having sex not twenty feet away.

I'd acted out of anger and that was something I should never do. Abby's trust in me was far too important and precious for me to jeopardize it with anything less than my full self-control. I'd gone too far tonight and I didn't know how to make up for it.

After a while I went into the bedroom. She hadn't closed the door, so I peeked in and saw she was sleeping. But it was more than that—she was sleeping in one of my white dress shirts. The sight of her in bed, in my shirt, with the knowledge of what I'd almost had her do, struck my heart as if someone had stabbed me.

I knew she loved me. We'd had difficult times in the past and we'd always worked through them. I just wasn't sure she *liked* me very much at the moment. I didn't like myself very much.

I knew all too well that it took only a mere whisper of doubt to bring down something it had taken years of trust to build. My heart ached with the knowledge that there might be a whisper of doubt in Abby's trust in me now. I only hoped I could make it right before it did irreversible damage to what we'd spent years building together.

When she'd first left me right after our relationship had started, it crippled me. But now, if anything happened to us, it would do more than cripple me. It would destroy me completely. Before I'd only been with her for a few months. Now we had years of shared experiences, heartaches, and joys. And I'd been a damn fool to risk all that for nothing. *Nothing.*

When it became too much to think about, I turned my focus to the upcoming meeting with Daniel. The Partners in Play group trusted me, too. And though Abby was far more important, I'd made a commitment to them and I needed to be prepared.

I'd told Daniel I had my list of suggestions ready and we'd planned to spend an hour or so going over them. We'd originally thought to have both Julie and Abby with us. Their thoughts and ideas as submissives—one newer in her journey and one with more experience—were needed on all accounts. Abby knew my suggestions; she'd helped me with them. Together, we'd talked about what we needed to put in place to make group members feel safe and secure. I pushed aside the thought that maybe the group needed to get rid of me. After all, who really wanted to listen to me after what I'd put Abby through hours earlier?

The list of my suggestions blurred before me, and my stomach hurt. It was impossible to concentrate on anything other than Abby. With a sigh, I put the list down and picked up my speech. I stared at it for thirty minutes before I realized I hadn't read a single word. I wasn't even sure how I'd be able to face the gathering tomorrow, much less give a speech.

The clock said it was four o'clock. Years ago, before Abby entered my life, it was nothing for me to be awake at this time of morning. But when she moved in with me, I'd grown used to going to bed with her and falling asleep listening to her breathe and with her soft warmth surrounding me. The nights became more than a time to sleep or work; they'd become a time to reconnect and revive.

Now the night was lonely and without her in my arms, it was only dark.

I put the speech away. That wasn't going to be worked on, either.

I went back into the bedroom and knelt beside the bed where she slept. Careful not to wake her, I gently lifted the hair that had fallen across her face.

"I love you," I whispered. "And no matter what it takes, I'll make this right."

She sighed in her sleep. And while I realized that, though there were many things I could put into place or change, there was one item I could take care of right away.

"Where's Abby?" Daniel asked the next morning. He and Julie had met me in the courtyard where it was quiet. The play equipment had been put away and the only music was the occasional sound of a bird chirping.

"She's talking with Lynne and the kids." Much easier to say that than to tell him the whole truth. *I fucked up last night and Abby isn't talking to me.* "Julie, if you'd like to see her, why don't you go on up to our room? She'll let you in."

Julie nodded and gave Daniel a kiss before heading upstairs.

"Is she coming down when she finishes?" Daniel asked.

"I honestly don't know."

He leaned back in his chair and his eyebrows furrowed. "You don't look like you slept last night. Do you want to talk about it?"

"Not really. No."

"Offer stands."

"Thanks. I appreciate it."

This morning had been hell. She'd spoken to me only to say she wasn't ready to talk about anything and that she would let me know when she was. I didn't have a chance to reply before she pulled out her laptop, slipped on her headphones, and started writing.

And I stood there ready to discuss what I'd done wrong and the decisions I'd made in the early-morning hours, and simply nodded.

Across the table, Daniel took a deep breath. I wasn't fooling him. He clearly knew something had happened between me and Abby. "Okay," he said, accepting that whatever it was wasn't up for discussion. "I know you've talked to Luke DeVaan about building a club for the Partners in Play group. What do you think about incorporating the bulk of these changes when that opens?"

My mind had been on nothing but Abby for the last twelve or so hours. Now, forced to think about something else, I felt relieved, but also just a bit guilty. Guilty, because how could I focus on anything with things as they were between me and Abby?

"I think that will be fine." I forced the situation with Abby out of my head for the moment. "As long as we don't allow anyone new until then."

"That's exactly what I was thinking and why I suggested we wait. I think it'd be good for the current members to grow more connected, stronger as a group. Maybe I'm being too optimistic, but I think with a stronger group dynamic, everything about the group strengthens." He shrugged. "I think that's worth taking a break from adding new members for."

"In that case, a lot of the other things we came up with will be taken care of by the new building. We'll have video cameras installed. Someone dedicated to front desk duty. There will actually *be* a front desk. All doors will have built-in windows so rooms can be checked at any time. And there'll be a separate aftercare area."

"I really like the things you're adding to the new building. This is exciting."

"And, like Abby pointed out to me, it's important that you and Julie won't be burdened with the responsibility of hosting the group so often."

"We didn't mind."

"I know, but it's still a lot for one couple."

He didn't argue with that. "What are some other ideas you had?"

"We propose anyone wanting to join has to be recommended by a group member. Then once someone is applying, he has to meet with a senior member. And the new member has to be observed in play by a senior member. Even then, once admitted, he or she is a probationary member for a year."

"This sounds really good."

"Thank you. We also thought about having an electronic database of member information and checklists. It would be handy to have that information readily available and it would give us the ability to match people up. The downside is having all that information in an electronic database might make some people uncomfortable. We need to come up with a way to code everything to guarantee anonymity."

"I knew you were the right man for this. I believe all these things will go a long way to ensure that everyone is safe."

His words punched me in the gut. I wasn't the right man for the job, and I certainly hadn't kept Abby safe.

"Nathaniel?" he asked. "Are you okay? Did I say something?"

"I fucked up."

"Oh?"

"With Abby. Last night." I shook my head. "I don't know how to fix it and she's not talking to me."

"I'm sorry."

"It was so bad. We caused a scene and everything. The Dungeon Monitor came by to check on us because we were creating such a disturbance."

He gave a low whistle.

"Yeah," I said softly. "After that, we went back to the room and she told me off again and went to bed."

"From the way you look, you didn't sleep at all."

"I used to do it all the time."

"You were probably ten years younger."

"True, I don't remember it feeling this way."

He chuckled. "Hell, if I tried to do the things I did ten years ago, I'd be in a serious mess."

I tried to smile, but it hurt too much.

"I can't say I'm the expert when it comes to relationships. I've never been married and I've never been with anyone for as long as you've been with Abby. But I do know this: she loves you madly and deeply and I can't imagine anything you've done will cause her not to anymore."

I wasn't sure he was right about that. He didn't know what I'd done and I didn't feel like telling him. Not because I was afraid of how he would see me; I couldn't imagine him thinking less of me than I thought of myself. I just couldn't stand to say the words. If I did, I'd relive every torturous second.

"Thanks," I said. "We'll see if she talks to me when I go back to the room."

"The good thing about being here is there's really nowhere for her to go. I doubt she'll leave you here with no transportation."

The Abby I knew wouldn't, either, but I'd hurt her badly last night. There was no way for me to know what I'd inadvertently turned her into.

She wasn't in the room when I went back upstairs. But a quick check assured me she hadn't left. Her clothes were in the closet and her toiletries were in the bathroom. She hadn't even taken the car. The keys were still on the table where I'd left them.

While I waited for her to get back, I called home and spoke to Lynne and the kids. They sounded so happy. It had truly been a godsend to find Lynne to be our nanny. Elizabeth was as bubbly and bright as ever. Henry was speaking more often in shorter sentences. Sometimes it made me ache because they seemed to be growing so fast. I knew I'd turn around and find they were teenagers.

An hour before I was due to give my speech, she still hadn't shown up. I gave serious thought to searching the grounds until I found her. But I knew she needed time and distance and though it went against everything inside me, it was important that I gave her that.

I finally put my speech notes away and took a shower. Then I walked down to the conference room. It didn't feel right to have so much alone time. Even when I traveled for work and she couldn't come with me, we were always connected somehow through text, or e-mail, or something. This distance from her felt as if I'd lost part of who I was. Which made sense. After so many years, I was no longer only Nathaniel West. I was also Abby's husband, Elizabeth and Henry's dad, and Abigail's Master.

Today, it felt as though two of those were missing. As I walked to the conference room for my speech, I vowed I'd find her afterward and we would talk this through. I'd listen and let her rant and yell at me because I more than deserved it. Then we'd sit down and work our way through it as we had done with other problems in the past.

Because I'd made it to the conference room early, it was

relatively empty. I went to the platform and put my notes down. An employee came in and we did a sound check. Once that was done, there was nothing left but to wait.

Just get through the speech. Then you can find her and head home.

Home. Tonight we would be home. After a car ride back to Delaware with Daniel and Julie.

I didn't even want to contemplate how awkward that potentially could be.

People started drifting in. I was the last speaker on the schedule, so I'd thought many people would be heading home and I'd have a small audience. I guessed wrong. There were a lot of people gathering. As they did so, it wasn't too hard to pick out the ones who had witnessed my fight with Abby the night before. They strolled into the room and did a quick double take when they saw me.

Yes, I wanted to say. *It's me. The ass from last night. Come in and sit down. You know you're even more interested now in what I have to say.*

I was surprised no one left after seeing it was me. Maybe they wanted to stand around and give me hell after the speech. I certainly deserved that. Or perhaps they were interested in what the ass from the night before had to say.

It never occurred to me that Abby wouldn't show up. The entire day I'd operated with the assumption she'd be at my speech. Yet when I stood up after being introduced, I did a quick glance around the room and didn't see her.

I looked down at my notes, staring at the words I'd written until they blurred and I couldn't see them anymore. Someone in the back coughed. I sighed. I really didn't want to be up here.

"Thank you all for coming today," I said. Better to get the

speech over and done with. Then I could find Abby and we could leave this place. "Today I'm going to talk about the building blocks of a strong D/s relationship."

I almost snorted. *Right.* This should be good. Even I didn't believe this one.

The back door creaked open and my breath caught as Abby walked in. Head down, she took a seat in the back. I tried my best to see her expression, but there were too many people in front of her and I could only make out the top of her head.

But regardless of her mood, she'd come. We were in the same room. It wasn't much, but it was a start. The same person coughed again. I tore my gaze away from Abby and saw that not only was everyone looking at me, they were looking as if I had three horns growing out of my head.

Right. The speech. Damn it.

I cleared my throat. "Like I said, today's topic is the building blocks of a strong D/s relationship."

Two women in the front row started to murmur to each other. I glanced back at Abby to make sure I didn't conjure her from my imagination. The person in front of her leaned over and for a second I could see one of her eyes peeking out at me. I knew she'd slept; I'd seen her sleeping. But it didn't appear to have been restful sleep. There were dark circles around her eye and it was red, as though she'd been crying. Even so, she was beautiful.

Satisfied that she was really and truly in the back, I picked up my notes. I could do this.

But the cards mocked me. I ripped the notes in half.

There was a murmur of surprise from the audience. The two

women in the front row stopped talking. In fact, I suddenly had everyone's complete and undivided attention.

I forced a smile, but I don't think it worked. "If any of you were at the courtyard last night, you know as well as I do that I have no business talking about how to build a strong D/s relationship. How to completely fuck up the best thing in your life? Yes. How to scare the living hell out of your submissive? I'm your man. But a strong relationship?" I shook my head. "You better look elsewhere."

I wadded up the torn pieces of my speech and placed the paper ball it made on the corner of the podium. "Love is a funny emotion. Not funny in the ha-ha sense, but funny in what it does to you. For over ten years I participated in the BDSM scene and never fell in love. I cared for the women I was with. I wanted their pleasure, but I didn't love them.

"There's freedom in that type of play. You have no sort of expectation beyond the scene you're in. There's no deep emotional commitment. And another upside is that the person you're with can't hurt you. Well, he can hurt you physically, but if you don't love him, the emotional hurt isn't as damaging to you. If you want freedom, forget love.

"When you love someone, you have the ability not only to harm their body, but to cut their soul to pieces. And though those cuts may heal, they leave scars behind. With enough scars, you stop feeling anything at all. The skin's too thick."

I looked to Abby's right and saw that Julie and Daniel were sitting next to her.

"If you're smart," I said, "you'll play without love."

I paused to let that sink in.

"Love makes you do things you never thought you'd do," I
continued. "It keeps you up at night. It makes you sick and drives
you crazy. And when you combine it with the intensity of a
BDSM relationship? Forget it, you're just asking for trouble. It's
much safer to play without love."

The two ladies in the front row looked confused. I couldn't
gather the courage to look at Abby yet.

"I played for over ten years without love. But for the last ten,
I've played with love. I'll tell you the truth. Love is hard. Love
takes work. And sometimes love truly sucks." I grabbed the
edges of the podium, looked down at the crumpled paper of my
speech. "But I would trade twenty years of no love for one hour
with it. Because in my experience, there is nothing more beautiful, more worthwhile, more rewarding, or more precious than
being with the one you love.

"I'm not smart. I'm not safe. And I'll trade every bit of my
freedom for the prison of love." I looked back into the crowd and
found Abby. She was looking at me with tears streaming down
her face. "I can't talk about building strong D/s relationships,
because I royally screwed mine up. But I can talk about what I
know, and I know that life is nothing without love."

There was more I wanted to say. More I needed to say. But
grief and guilt crushed me and it was all I could do to grab hold
of the podium so I wouldn't stumble. I dropped my head.

"I'm sorry," I whispered, and stepped back from the micro-
phone.

I had to find Abby. I made my way down the stairs off the
platform. As I walked toward her, some part of me heard the
crowd's applause and felt the pats on my back and shoulders as I

passed people. Some of them even spoke, but there was only room for one word in my world.

Abby.

I hurried as best I could to where she sat, dodging the people who crowded my way wanting to talk, because all they did was block my view of her seat. I probably wasn't even very nice and I knew I didn't speak back. As I pushed my way past a huge mountain of a man, her seat came back into view.

It was empty.

I stopped cold.

She's left me.

My body turned to ice and I couldn't breathe.

She's left me.

I struggled to inhale.

She's left me.

"Nathaniel."

My head shot up and to the right. And in the middle of the aisle, standing with wet cheeks and outstretched arms, was my universe, my everything, my love.

"Abby," I managed to get out as I crossed the remaining steps between us with four long strides. "God, I'm sorry." I took her in my arms as hers slipped around me. I held her as tightly as I could, overjoyed with the privilege to do so. "I'm sorry. I love you so much."

She sniffled. "I love you, too."

I couldn't say anything else. The most important words had already been said. There would be time later for words. *Please let there be time later for words.* What I needed was to hold her. To have her in my arms. To feel her breath on my cheek and her heart beat in time with mine. Everything felt right again while we were in each other's arms.

She pulled back, but instead of stepping away, she tipped her head up. "Kiss me."

I could do nothing else other than brush my lips with hers. Once. Twice. And on the third pass, she grabbed my hair and held me in place while she kissed me thoroughly.

The crowd around us once more broke into thunderous applause and she smiled against my lips. She gave me one more kiss and pulled away, making sure she had my attention.

"I'm ready to talk," she said. "And more important, I'm ready to listen."

I took her hand and entwined our fingers. "Let's get out of here."

Chapter Fifteen

NATHANIEL

We didn't speak as we made our way back up to our room, but she didn't take her hand out of mine. Once inside, I led her to the couch and sat down, still holding hands.

"You were a complete asshole last night," she said.

"Yes."

"That for one second it even crossed your mind to have me give someone else a blow job?" She shook her head. "I don't know what upsets me the most: that you considered it or that I did."

I would never get the image out of my mind of her kneeling while that man undid his jeans.

"I was getting ready to safe-word," she said. "You beat me to it. Can you tell me why? Why you thought I wanted that?"

"Seeing you dance and having fun with those men did something to me. You were enjoying yourself and I realized it was more than people watching you, because you were getting into the dance with that younger guy. We'd talked about a threesome, and I thought maybe it was the next step you'd want to explore."

"But you made that decision without talking to me."

"I was wrong." Playing with others wasn't a hard limit for her. But our assumption had always been that if there was another party involved, they wouldn't touch her in a sexual way. But that had always been more my defined limit. We'd never discussed the exact lines of her limits.

"Damn straight you were." She squeezed my hand. "But it wouldn't be fair for me not to admit that a lot of my actions yesterday were because of Charlene. The fact is, I'm never going to be okay with her. And we both have to accept that."

I recalled the decisions I'd reached in the early hours of the morning. "Charlene's not going to be an issue anymore."

"You can't fire her because of me. And if you did it now, she could file a claim."

"I'm not going to fire Charlene. She's too good at her job. The nonprofit has never seen growth like it has under her direction."

She wrinkled her forehead. "Then how is she not going to be an issue?"

"There's no law that says the nonprofit's headquarters has to be in Manhattan," I said. "I've decided to move it to Boston. Charlene has family there. And I'm not going to have direct contact with her. I'm going to have her report in to one of my senior executives."

"You don't have to do that for me."

"I'm not," I said, and at her frown I added, "I'm doing it for us."

I watched as the full meaning of what I'd said sank in, and I saw the relief slowly seep into her expression. The frown disappeared and the wrinkles in her forehead vanished. But they came back too quickly.

"What if she doesn't want to move?"

It was my turn to squeeze her hand. "I spoke to her this morning. She's thrilled. In fact, she's already left and is taking a few days to look at real estate there."

"What if . . . ," she started, but shook her head. "Nah, it's not important."

I'd known her far too long not to know what her question was, and likewise, I knew it was very important.

"If she had said no, she would have been told to look elsewhere for a job," I said. "There is no business or nonprofit or position or employee more important than you. Never doubt it."

She didn't have to say anything, but the tears in her eyes spoke volumes. I kicked myself for not doing something before now.

"We have to discuss last night," I said, knowing there was more that had to be said.

"I thought we did."

"Not everything." I took her other hand. "What I did was seriously wrong and it's not enough for me to simply say *I'm sorry.* I want you to flog me. Or cane me. Whatever you would prefer."

She gasped. "I can't do that."

"You can."

"I've never used a flogger or a cane."

"First time for everything."

I'd anticipated her response and I was glad she took some time to think before she spoke again, but I'd be the first to admit that I didn't expect what she said next. "I can't. For me to do that to you would be more of a punishment for me than one for you."

Of course. That made sense. "I see," I said. "I didn't think of it like that."

The wicked gleam I loved so much danced in her eyes. "I wouldn't, however, have any problem with you writing two thousand times *I was an ass to make assumptions and I'll never do it again.*"

I swallowed the wrong way, setting off a coughing spell. "Two thousand times?" I finally wheezed out.

"Do you think that's not enough? I'm not a Dominant, so I don't know. Would three thousand be better?"

"If you want me to do three thousand, I'll do it."

"Oh, I know," she said, so animatedly I was afraid to ask.

"What?"

"How about you write the number of lines *you* think is appropriate to make up for what you did?"

"That is an evil way to set it up," I said. She looked very, very pleased with herself, so I added, "But it's so creative I'm going to have to remember it."

I laughed at her look of shock and then pulled her close for a quick kiss.

"One more thing," I added. "Playing in public. After last night, I want to put guidelines in place."

"Like what?"

"I know you enjoyed the scene with Luke and the one months ago with Jeff. And you liked it when there was more than one man watching. I'm fine with scenes like that, but I think it would be wise, at least for the foreseeable future, if we only invited other people to participate in limited, nonsexual ways, when we're at our house."

"Anytime we play in a public setting, it's just us," she said.

"Yes."

"I don't have a problem with that." She raised an eyebrow. "You are okay playing in public?"

"I am. I enjoy it, too."

"I'm glad we're in agreement."

"I never want to experience another twelve hours like the last," I said, growing serious. "You're so much a part of me now, it'd be easier to lose a limb than to live without you."

"I don't even want to imagine life without you."

I drew her to me and as our lips touched, I felt we had finally come full circle. We had hurt each other and hurt ourselves, but now we'd found each other again and we could heal. I didn't know why I thought our journey would be easy. She had told me once before nothing worth anything was easy.

I supposed that meant we were priceless.

We arrived back in Delaware stronger than we'd been when we left. We'd walked through the fire once again and instead of perishing in the flames, we'd been strengthened like tempered steel. With our lines clearly drawn concerning what we would and would not do in public, I discovered it was a lot of fun exploring the edges of those lines.

Tonight, three weeks after the conference, we were doing a medical scene role play for the group. I would no longer share her, even in a nonsexual way, in public, but she still got off on exhibitionism. That being the case, she had to be excited about the scene we were about to do. From where I stood, at one end of Daniel's guesthouse garage, it appeared as if everyone in the group was watching.

I pushed the sleeves up on the white lab coat I wore and turned to Abby. She was on an examination table, naked and waiting.

"What's your name?" I asked.

"Don't you have it written down in the chart, Doctor?" she asked, and the gathering crowd laughed. "You'd think that's one of the first things they teach you in medical school. I certainly hope you didn't come in here to remove my gallbladder. I heard about that on TV once. All these medical mistakes."

I smiled. I loved it when she acted like a brat during our role play. "Patient is noncooperative." I acted as if I were writing it down. "And no, I'm not taking out your gallbladder. In case you didn't notice when you walked in, I'm not a surgeon. Now, why don't you tell me, in your own words, why you're here today?"

We hadn't rehearsed our answers, so I had no way of knowing what she would say. *This should be interesting.* Ad hoc role play was fun. With Abby's limitless imagination, there was no telling what she'd come up with.

"My Master made me come here."

"I see. And what was your Master's reason for that?"

"Well, we were getting ready to have sex the other day. It was our first time and I refused to let him touch me after I saw how big his cock was. I said it wouldn't fit. He said it would, and now I'm here. I told him I needed medical proof."

"You need me to make sure your Master can fuck you?"

"Yes, but I'd sort of hoped he'd be the one here and not me."

"Why would he be here?"

"So you could tell him his dick was too big. That's what I thought the medical examination would prove."

"That he had a big dick?"

"Not just big. *Ginormous*."

"Unfortunately, that's not how it's going to work. Since we can't do anything about his ginormous dick, we'll just have to make sure you can take it. Let's start by having you slide all the way down to the edge of the table. I want your ass almost off. Feet in the stirrups."

She mumbled under her breath, but scooted down and adjusted her feet, giving me and our watching audience a perfect view of her exposed pussy.

"Everything looks good from a visual standpoint," I said. "But I can't say with any certainty until I do a more thorough exam. Have you had sex before?"

"Yes."

"First I'm going to see how responsive you are. You're going to feel me touch you." I ran a hand down her leg, and back up, teasing her. She wiggled, trying to get me closer to where she wanted to be touched. I smacked her inner thigh. "Stop." She started to say something, but I cut her off. "Quiet. Let me concentrate."

I resumed my slow stroking of her legs. I let my fingers trail up and down, arousing her, and making sure each one of her nerve endings was on edge.

"There you go. Feel how turned on you are?" I asked. "I've barely touched you and you're desperate to be filled."

She didn't say anything.

"Aren't you?" I asked.

"Yes, Doctor."

"Not quite as mouthy as you were, are you?"

"No, Doctor."

Satisfied with her answers, I ran a finger along her wet slit and circled her clit. Her hips jerked slightly.

"It appears you have no trouble getting aroused. That should make your Master happy." I repeated my actions a few more times, never pushing into her and never touching her clit directly.

"I think it's time for my next test," I said. "Do you know what that is?"

She shook her head.

"Louder. My interns can't hear you."

"No, Doctor. I don't know what you're going to do next."

Not letting her have very long to think about what it might be, I bent down and sucked her clit into my mouth. She bucked against me, and I forced her hips back to the table. I lifted my head long enough to say, "Move again and see what happens," and then went back to torturing her sensitive flesh with my mouth.

I stayed there for several long minutes. I didn't want her to fail in withholding her orgasm, but I wanted to push her to her limit. I licked and nibbled, and every once in a while, I'd suck her clit back into my mouth. I pulled back when her trembling legs indicated she probably wasn't going to be able to hold out much longer.

"Tell me." I walked away so she could see me and I unzipped my pants. "Is your Master any bigger than me?"

Her right eyebrow lifted. "No, Sir. I believe you're bigger."

"So if I can fit inside you, he should be able to?"

"I don't think——"

I shoved my hand over her mouth. "You're not here to think."
She shook her head.

"Your Master called me," I said. "He said I was to fuck you as part of my examination. But only with my fingers." I zipped my pants back up. "Which means, you'll just have to dream about having a cock as big as mine inside you."

She hadn't expected that and from the look on her face, she wanted to whine.

"Poor thing," I said. "But don't worry, I can make you feel good with only my fingers." I teased her slit again. "But your Master said you weren't to come and that if you did, I could punish you however I saw fit."

She did let out a groan then.

"Yes, and I spent a long time finding the perfect finger of ginger. And I peeled it and made it nice and smooth. And it's just waiting for you mess up."

"Won't happen, Doctor."

"We'll see about that." I hooked two fingers inside her. "That's two. Should I go for three?" I started pumping slowly. "Yes, you're tight, but stretching to take my fingers."

Her eyelids fluttered closed.

"Feel good?" I asked. "This will feel better." I slipped a third finger inside her and started moving them in and out. "Yes, you'll be able to take your Master just fine."

"Does that mean you're finished, Doctor?" Her shallow pants told me she was getting close to her climax.

"Oh no, I'm not close to being finished." I slipped my fingers out and held them to her mouth. "Clean them."

She sucked them into her mouth and it took all my strength

not to unzip my pants again and replace my fingers with my cock. Instead I commanded, "Enough," and moved to the side of the table. "I forgot to check one thing."

"I'm not sure I can handle one more thing," she moaned.

"Oh, you can and you will." I moved to the side of the table. Her eyes traveled with me. She was trying to anticipate what I was going to do now. I didn't make her wait too long, but leaned down and sucked a nipple deep and hard before pulling back and slipping a clamp onto her.

"Holy shit," she said.

"Does that make you more or less turned on?" I asked.

"Is this still part of the medical exam, Doctor?"

"No, this is just me enjoying your body."

"I hardly think that's fair."

"I really don't care. Answer the question."

"More, Doctor."

"Good girl." I sucked the other one in my mouth and then bit and decorated it with a clamp, too. "More or less?"

"More, Doctor."

She was just about where I wanted her. I moved back between her legs and blew on her clit, smiling when her hips jerked.

"Ready to come?" I asked.

"Yes, please, Master."

She'd given up all pretense of the role play. Perfect. "Good. Now we're going home."

Her eyes had been half-closed, but at my statement, they flew open. "Wha—"

"Shh." I placed my finger over her lips. "Quiet girls get rewarded."

She whimpered.

"Get up and get dressed. As soon as you're ready, we'll head home."

I wasn't sure she'd ever gotten dressed so quickly. She even took the clamps off herself, which was something she normally asked me to do. I was talking with Daniel and Jeff, saying good-bye, and she was at my side, restlessly shifting from one side to the other. I slid my arm around her waist and let my fingers stroke her lower back.

"I'm not sure, but I think you're purring," I whispered in her ear.

"That's me sending you a subliminal message saying I'm ready to leave, Master."

Poor Abby, I'd really worked her into a hot mess. "Look, there's Cole. I wanted to speak to him."

She said something in German under her breath. I was pretty sure the English translation was something like, "For the love of all things holy, let's just get the hell out of here."

I slapped her butt. "I'm kidding. Let's go."

"Thank you, Master."

Our house was about a twenty-minute drive from Daniel's, and my plan was to work Abby into such a frenzy of lust she would damn near combust when I pulled into our driveway.

"Did you enjoy the scene?" I asked.

"Yes, Master. So much."

"Good. What was your favorite part? I know for me, I particularly enjoyed the whimper you made when I sucked you."

She lifted an eyebrow, as though she was onto me. She probably had a good idea I was going to play with her mind the entire way home. I would have laughed, but she chose that minute to take her shirt off. Of course, she didn't have anything on underneath it, and the car swerved for a second as her breast came into view.

"What are you doing?" I made myself focus on the road.

"I'm getting hot. Don't you think it's hot in the car, Master?"

"It is with you taking your shirt off."

"Mmm." She tipped her head back on the headrest. "And I was feeling just a bit itchy."

"Itchy?"

"Yes, Master. Here." She started stroking a nipple. "Yes. Right there. Ah, that feels much better."

"Abigail," I warned.

"You have a tiny bit of sweat on your forehead, Master."

"I don't doubt it."

"I can't imagine what's got me so itchy. Are you itchy?"

Focus on the road. Focus on the road. Focus on the road.

"No," I said. "I'm not itchy."

"You're hard, though, Master. I can see your erection from here. Want me to take care of that for you?" Her hand drifted to my thigh and inched upward.

"Not in the car."

"I think we should definitely do it in the car." She stroked me through my pants. "Let me see how much power you have under your hood."

"That's a horrible pun."

"I know. I can't come up with good ones when I'm this horny. All I can think about is how much I want to have this inside me."

"I'm driving, Abigail."

She unzipped me. "Pull over."

We were on a secondary road and because it was so late, no one else was out. I spied a clearing up ahead and sped up to get there. "You want me to take you in the car?"

"In the car. On the car. Against the car. Either one or all three."

I pulled well off the road, but still next to it, and turned the engine off. I didn't want to catch the attention of anyone who might happen to be driving by. "Backseat. Now."

She fumbled with her seat belt. "I didn't think you'd actually do it."

"Then you vastly underestimated me. Knees on the seat. Face the rear window. Lift your skirt." I pulled my cock out and fisted it. "Hurry."

"I can see out the back window like this," she said, positioning herself and giving me a fine view of her butt. I suddenly wished I had lube in the car.

"I'm fucking your ass once we get home." I moved behind her, desperate to sink into her. I looked around first, made sure there wasn't anyone nearby and no approaching headlights. "Did you do this in high school, Abigail?"

"Never, Master." She moaned as I pushed inside. "I was a good girl."

"Until you met me," I said with a smile.

"Yes. I'm so, so bad with you."

"Good." I pushed deeper. "I like knowing I'm the one who corrupted you." I held her head down and started thrusting. "Just like this. Fucking you in the backseat of the car. Good girls don't get cock in the backseat of the car, do they?"

"No, Master."

I spanked her. One hard smack. "Scream for me. Show me how glad you are I pulled over. Prove you're a bad girl who deserves to get cock in the backseat."

I placed a hand on either side of her and starting working my hips as hard as possible, drilling into her. Each thrust pushed her body against the leather and by the third stroke, she was grunting.

"More, Master. More."

I smacked her ass again.

"Yes. Yes. Yes," she chanted in time with my thrusts. I held still when I was as deep inside as I could go. "Oh, hell, uh, yes."

"Come for me one time." I teased her clit. "Then not again until I take your ass."

I started thrusting again, but kept a finger on that sensitive spot, knowing it would have her reaching her climax within seconds.

Somewhere a police siren started wailing. I looked around. *Shit.*

I sped up my thrusts, knowing there was no way I could stop. "Come for me."

The siren became louder and Abby lifted her head at the same moment red and blue lights came into view, rushing down the road toward us. I rubbed her clit harder.

"Oh, oh yes." Her head tipped back and her muscles clenched around me as she came.

With her satisfied, I sped toward my own release, keeping an eye on the police cruiser and watching as it came closer.

Almost.

Almost.

Almost.

"Oh, fuck!" I shouted, releasing deep inside her while at the same time I wrapped my arms around her and forced both of us down on the backseat, seconds before the police car whizzed by.

"Damn, that was close." I was still breathing heavily and my heart was racing, but I untangled us from each other and smiled as she twisted around to face me.

"I thought they were coming for us." Her cheeks were flushed in that *I've been thoroughly fucked* way. I'd have thought almost being caught by the police would have scared her, but she looked damn near radiant.

I pushed the hair back from her forehead and kissed her. "They must have heard you've been bad."

She laughed. "That would have been funny."

"No, I don't think it would have been."

"Yes, it would have been."

I pulled back and studied her. "What am I going to do with you, Abby West?"

She tried being serious, but she couldn't stop the traces of a smile in her voice. "Not more than five minutes ago you said you were very explicit about your plans."

"In that case we better get going." In the distance another siren sounded. "And quickly, before I'm caught with my pants down. My enjoyment of exhibitionism doesn't extend to being ticketed for public indecency."

We straightened our clothes, made our way back to the front seat, and had just pulled back onto the road when the second police cruiser showed up in our rearview mirror. As I moved to the side to let it pass, I glanced at Abby and took her hand with a smile.

"Here's to cheating the public indecency charge one more time," I said.

"We're going to be caught one day."

"Nah, not with my mad skills."

"Especially with your mad skills." She entwined our fingers. "Take me home, Master."

"Home." I brought her hand to my lips and kissed her knuckles. "Because I have promises to keep."

Epilogue

ABBY
Two months later

I looked out the kitchen window to where our friends had gathered together on our patio. Jeff and Dena's ultrasound earlier in the week had shown them that they were having a girl. To say they were excited was an understatement. I decided the news called for celebration and invited everyone over.

Nathaniel came up behind me and put a hand on my shoulder. "Everything okay?"

"Yes, just thinking about how fortunate we are to have so many good friends."

"We certainly are."

I turned around to face him and looped my arms around his neck. "Think they'd miss us if we didn't go back outside?"

"Probably. You came inside to get the food for everyone."

I punched his chest. "Spoilsport."

He laughed and leaned down to kiss my cheek. "Let me help you carry this out and later tonight I'll make it up to you."

"Deal," I said.

We carried trays of sandwiches, fruit, and cheese outside. Our guests already had drinks and were spread out around the backyard. Everyone who loved Jeff and Dena had shown up. Daniel and Julie were talking with the couple in question. The four of them stood near the garden, and once Daniel saw us, he waved and they all headed our way.

"Food looks great," he said.

"Dig in," I said. "There's plenty here and more inside if this runs out."

I set the trays down on the table and started passing out plates.

Dena rubbed her belly. "Good because the baby's hungry." Jeff came up behind her and kissed her head. She leaned back against him.

"Everything's so peaceful here," Jeff said. "This is an outstanding property. You're going to love it here."

"We already do," I agreed. "I love coming out here and just enjoying the stillness."

That stillness was suddenly broken by a sharp cry.

"Oh my God. Snake!" Lynne pointed toward a large oak tree about twenty feet from where we were.

We all looked in that direction. I couldn't see a snake, but I certainly saw *something*. But from where I was, it appeared more like a ball. A ball that was twisting and turning and fighting with something.

Dena gasped. "It's a kitten! It has a kitten!"

As soon as she said it, I saw the frightened eyes surrounded by matted fur. My hand flew to my mouth.

"It just fell from the tree," Lynne said. "Has the snake killed it?"

"Not yet, but probably very close." Cole had been talking with Kelly, but he walked toward Nathaniel. "I'll get it. Do you have a shovel?"

Nathaniel nodded. "Come with me."

As the two men ran toward the garage, we all watched, helpless.

"I hope it's not too late," Dena whispered.

I thought as long as the snake was writhing around the way it was, the kitten was probably still putting up a fight. As long as the snake didn't stop, there was still breath left in the cat.

Cole appeared, shovel in hand, and headed toward the snake. Nathaniel was right beside him, also holding a shovel. They approached the fight, planning what they are going to do.

"I'll go for the head," Nathaniel said. "You try to get the kitten."

The two men worked in unison, on opposite sides of the snake, not talking much, but moving together in a way that almost looked choreographed.

"If I get a clear shot, I'm going for it." Nathaniel's shovel hovered near the snake's head.

I held my breath. Odds were good the kitten wasn't going to make it. By now we could see that the snake was tightly wrapped around it. Even if it was still living, which seem impossible, there was no telling how long it'd been without oxygen.

"Almost. Almost." Nathaniel shifted his weight. "Now!"

He attacked the snake and within seconds, Cole attempted to grab the kitten.

"Got it!" Cole finally said. "Still alive."

"Thank goodness," Lynne said.

"He's really shaken up." Cole came toward us, kitten in hands, while Nathaniel disposed of the snake.

"I would think so," I said. "Being attacked by a snake. Do you need anything?"

"No, he's still running on an adrenaline high, trying to get away from me. Poor thing's going to crash later." Cole tried unsuccessfully to get the kitten to calm down. "I hate to put him down. He'll run off and we'll never see him again. He needs first aid, someone to love, and a bath."

"Good luck giving a cat a bath," Dena said.

"Hand him to me."

Everyone turned to where Sasha stood across the patio from Cole. She'd been so quiet all afternoon, I'd forgotten she was there.

She crossed the patio to Cole and held out her hands. "Give him to me."

Cole was fumbling, trying to keep the kitten from falling. "I thank you for your offer to help, little one, but this cat's feisty." He raised an eyebrow. Her bulky jeans and slouchy shirt couldn't hide the too-thin frame and the dark shadows around her eyes. "With all due respect——"

"I said give him to me," Sasha repeated in a firm voice. I didn't know about anyone else, but I didn't know Sasha could be that forceful. She motioned with her hands again.

Cole must not have known she could be that forceful, either. His eyes grew wide with shock and he nearly lost his grip on the wiggling creature in his arms. "Sasha," he said in a low voice.

But Sasha was determined and without waiting for him to offer or agree, she simply reached for the kitten and took him. Gathering the frightened animal tight to her chest, she dropped her face into his fur and whispered things I couldn't make out.

Cole didn't move from where he stood, though I wasn't sure if it was because he was still in shock over her actions or if he wanted to be close in case she needed him.

After a few minutes she lifted her head and Cole laughed. "Bloody hell, he's purring."

Sasha only beamed in response as Cole reached out and stroked the kitten's dirty fur. "How did you do that?"

"I don't know," she confessed. "I just saw him struggling and then he was free, but he didn't know it. I think it's because you're a bit intimidating, Sir. And I thought to myself, 'I know exactly how that kitten feels,' and I just had to hold him and tell him. I had to let him know he was safe and everything was going to be all right."

"Damn," Nathaniel whispered so they couldn't hear. "I didn't know she could speak that many sentences at one time."

"You and the kitten are kindred spirits, little one. That was good thinking," Cole said, and locked eyes with Sasha. The look that passed between them was so intense that for a second I couldn't breathe and my skin prickled with gooseflesh.

"Wow, I've never heard him call anyone 'little one' before," Daniel said. "Wonder what that means."

"Nothing," Julie whispered. "It means nothing. He called her that the first time he met her. Right before you whipped Peter."

We'd been whispering so Cole and Sasha wouldn't hear, but watching them, I thought we could have been yelling and they wouldn't have paid us any attention. They were speaking softly, the kitten held between them. Then Sasha suddenly looked our way.

"He's a stray, right?" she asked, looking between me and Nathaniel. "He's not yours?"

"No," Nathaniel confirmed. "We only have our dog, Apollo."

"I can keep him?" She was no longer the determined woman who'd confronted Cole, but once more tentative and unsure. "I'd like to have someone to care for."

"I know the feeling," Cole mumbled behind her.

"Of course," Nathaniel said, and then smiled. "We just won't tell the kids. Elizabeth would love a kitten, but we can't have one with Apollo around. He's too old and set in his ways."

"Thank you," she said, and dipped her head into the kitten's fur again.

"I think," Nathaniel said in a soft voice so Cole and Sasha couldn't hear, a slow smile covering his face, "I've just decided who I'll recommend to have retrain Sasha."

Julie and I spoke at the same time.

"Oh, hell no."

"That might be the worst idea you've ever had."

But Jeff was nodding and Daniel's head was tilted in thought.

I looked once more to the couple bonding over the bundle of fur. The tentative submissive who'd stood up to someone intimidating in order to calm a kitten. And the man I knew to be ruthless who'd looked on her with kindness and a hint of something more.

"He'll break her," I whispered.

Nathaniel shook his head. "She'll heal them both."

Turn the page for a sneak peek at the

next book in Tara Sue Me's Submissive series,

The Master

Available in February 2016

from New American Library.

She was going to have to book an extended session with her therapist.

Sasha Blake closed her eyes and tried to take deep cleansing breaths like she'd been told to do when the familiar panic started to take over. But the sharp claws of fear and dread grabbed onto her chest and the simple act of inhaling took more strength than necessary.

"Sasha?" Nathaniel asked. "Are you okay?"

She cracked one eye open. The Dominant in charge of running the meeting looked at her with concern. She focused on him and did her best to ignore everything and everyone else.

"Yes, Master West," she said. "I'm fine."

Fine. Her pat reply to everything. She was fine. Work was fine. Her back was fine. And being told the Partners in Play senior members had decided she could rejoin the BDSM group after a retraining with Cole Johnson?

Abso-freaking-fine.

She was sitting in a small room off to the side of Daniel Covington's playroom, where group meetings were held. Only the senior members were present, which meant there were only about ten people sitting around the oval table at the moment.

The side of her face tingled as if someone was staring at her and she slipped her hands under her thighs to keep from rubbing the spot. She used more discipline than what should be necessary to keep her gaze directed on Nathaniel and not to let it wander just a touch to the right where he sat.

Items numbered one through five hundred twelve to discuss with her therapist: Cole Johnson.

Based on conversations she'd had recently with Nathaniel, his wife, Abby, and her own best friend, Julie, and Julie's Dominant, Daniel, she'd expected to be offered a retraining. She'd even looked forward to it: experiencing the thrill of letting someone else take over, rediscovering the peace that came when she knew her Dom would do anything to protect her and—she wasn't even going to pretend otherwise—having earth-shattering orgasms.

It'd not once crossed her mind—not even in her wildest, craziest, never-gonna-happen-might-as-well-fantasize-about-it dreams—that the group would pick him.

Cole.

Sasha shivered just thinking his name. An alien spaceship must have transported her to an alternate universe because that was how hard it was to believe Cole was going to retrain her. He was an altogether intriguing man, one who had quickly captured her attention. But though he was usually laid-back and easygoing, talk among the group's submissives pointed toward a hard and unyielding Dominant in the playroom.

She didn't have to glance to Nathaniel's right to know who she'd find watching her. She pictured him all too clearly in her head. Dark tousled hair, devilish blue-green eyes, and a body that seductively hinted at sexual pleasure with every carefully controlled move. And then he'd speak in that oh-so-smooth British accent.

Yes, she'd call her therapist tomorrow.

"Are you okay?"

Sasha jumped at the sound of her friend Dena's whisper.

"I'm fine," she said, repeating the same lie she'd told Nathaniel. Dena narrowed her eyes in disbelief. "Hmm."

But Sasha was stopped from saying anything further by Nathaniel dismissing the meeting. Perfect. If she moved quickly enough, she could probably be on her way without having to talk about anything.

Unfortunately, Dena was onto Sasha's ploy and grabbed her arm before she could get away. "Not so fast. I want to talk. It's been a long night for you. How do you feel about Master Johnson?"

Sasha's body shook a bit. She had to leave before the panic came back. But Dena looked determined and she wouldn't let her leave that easily.

"Conflicted." Sasha took a deep breath. "He's not who I imagined would be suggested." She didn't add that he was the very last person she imagined would be suggested. She narrowed her eyes. "Wait a minute. You're a senior group member. Did you know?"

"No, I excused myself when the topic came up for discussion. I knew I couldn't be objective."

"And Jeff?"

"Yes, I'm sure he knew."

Sasha put her hand on her hip. She found it hard to believe Jeff, Dena's husband, wouldn't have told her, even if she'd excused herself from the discussion. Which made her wonder if Julie knew? After all, she lived with Daniel.

She turned to find the lady in question making a beeline toward her.

"I had a feeling that was going to happen," Julie said. "Are you okay? If you don't want Cole, I'll—"

"Julie. Dena," the smooth British accent she heard in her dreams said.

Sasha spun around and found Cole standing off to her side.

"Sasha."

He spoke her name like a caress. Soft and gentle and tender but with an underlying strength that couldn't be denied and with sensual promises woven in every vowel sound. She had an overwhelming desire to hear him say it again.

She opened her mouth, but nothing came out. *Damn it, this is why I should have left right when I stood up.*

"Master Johnson," Julie and Dena said in unison.

"Master West," Cole said to Nathaniel, who stood a few feet away with his arm around Abby. "If I may, I'd like a word in private with Julie and Sasha."

Nathaniel didn't answer right away but eyed Sasha up and down, as if making sure she was okay. He frowned. Hell, did she look that bad?

"Fifteen minutes," Nathaniel said. "You can use the kitchen. Master Covington?"

"I'll come get Julie then," Daniel said from his spot beside Abby.

Cole extended his arm. "After you, ladies."

They made it into the kitchen without speaking. Cole pulled chairs out for both of them and then settled into his own. He smiled and Sasha found herself questioning the things she'd heard about him.

This was the badass Brit?

"Anyone care for a drink?" he asked. "I should have asked you before sitting down."

"No, thank you, Sir," Julie said.

"I'm fine, Sir," Sasha quipped.

At her off-the-cuff reply, Cole narrowed his eyes and his smile faded away into a frown of displeasure. And in that moment, Sasha knew everything she'd heard about him was true.

Cole Johnson kept his gaze focused on Sasha long enough for her to understand he recognized her answer for what it was. He suspected she'd been fighting back a panic attack and was most likely anything but *fine*. Against his better judgment, he decided not to call her on it. This time.

He wondered what he'd gotten himself into.

When Nathaniel approached him about it, he'd agreed almost at once. In his mind he pictured Sasha as he'd first met her: a scared submissive dealing with the aftermath of a scene gone bad. He remembered catching her the night she almost fell and how she'd been warm and responsive in his arms. That is, until she'd realized where she was and used her safe word to get away from him.

In India weeks later, he had been surprised at how often he found his mind wandering back to the troubled woman with the expressive green eyes and a will of steel. And he couldn't deny he'd been secretly pleased when he heard a rumor she was thinking about rejoining the group. He'd been a Dom long enough to understand the strength involved in going through a traumatic scene and returning once more to the community. He respected that strength. He also had a strong desire to control it.

He cleared his throat. "We only have fifteen minutes and I'm positive Daniel is keeping an eye on the time, so let's chivvy this along." He leaned back in the chair so he could watch both women. "It appears as if my reputation precedes me and you're both, no doubt, wondering what the group was thinking with their recommendation."

Humor flashed in Julie's eyes along with something else, but she wasn't saying anything. She hadn't been all that shocked when he'd been named. Unlike Sasha, who at this moment stared at him like she'd dash out of the room if he said, "Boo."

He drummed his fingertips on the table. There was a time to push a submissive—this was not one of those times. He needed to draw her to him, to gain her trust, make a connection.

"How's the kitten?" he asked her.

Last weekend Nathaniel and Abby had a party for Jeff and Dena. While everyone was outside, a snake attacked a stray kitten. Cole and Nathaniel had rescued it, but afterward they couldn't calm it down. Cole had held the wiggling mass of fur at a loss about what to do until Sasha simply took the frightened kitten from him and had the creature purring within seconds. It'd been that confidence she showed, the way she pushed aside her fear because her desire to help the kitten was more important, that had made him accept the group's request to retrain her.

As he'd suspected, at the mention of her rescued kitten, Sasha's face lost all traces of worry and fear and a tender smile took their place. "She's doing great, Sir. Plays a lot, eats a lot, and sleeps in front of the refrigerator."

He couldn't hide his smile at her excitement over the little ball of fur. "I'm glad she found you. Sounds like the two of you have hit it off."

She nodded. "I like having her around. I mean, I know she's just a kitten, but it makes the apartment not so lonely."

From the corner of his eye, he saw Julie discreetly check the time. Daniel would be back soon.

Cole cleared his throat. "I can understand your surprise at the group's recommendation, Sasha." She opened her mouth like she was going to say something to the contrary, but he shook his head. "No need to hide your feelings. You were quite gob-smacked when Master West made his announcement."

She pressed her lips together, and with that small move, he caught just a glimpse of the feisty submissive he'd heard she was before the Peter incident.

He leaned forward. "The simple truth is, I require a great deal from my sexual partners and you're not prepared to meet those demands. That's the main reason I was selected for you. Since I know your body is off limits, I'll take my time getting your mind prepared to submit again."

Her jaw dropped. "What?"

"What's the body's most important sex organ?" he asked.

"The mind," Sasha said.

"Right. And we hear it so frequently, the answer is often given without thought." He watched her fingers inch forward on the table slightly. She pulled them back and repeated the motion several times until Julie stopped her with a hand. He continued. "So let's take a moment to think about it. Sex starts in the mind. Submission starts in the mind. As a Dominant, I have to earn my place in your mind before I can earn the right to take you physically. Am I making sense?"

Her voice was calm when she replied, "Fuck the mind before you fuck the body?"

He held her gaze for a long moment until she lowered hers. "Yes, precisely. Which is why I won't be fucking your body. Just your mind, Sasha."

She let out her breath in a half-swallowed sigh and looked at the table. "I understand, Sir."

He bit back his laugh. She might understand, but she wasn't happy about it. "Any questions?"

Sasha shook her head.

"No, Sir," Julie said. "Thank you for explaining."

Daniel walked into the kitchen and stood in the shadows behind Julie.

"When I work with a new submissive," Cole said, "I want to weave myself into her thoughts so that each movement she makes is made with me in mind. I want her to feel my presence when we're apart as strongly as she does when we're together. I'll do it slowly, Sasha." He allowed his gaze to wander over her body. She was a striking woman. "So methodically, you won't notice. And no, I won't fuck your body, but I believe you'll find our mental play nearly as intimate, if not more so, than physical play."

Tara Sue Me wrote her first novel at the age of twelve. It would be twenty years before she picked up her pen to write the second.

After completing several traditional romances, she decided to try her hand at something spicier and started work on *The Submissive*. What began as a writing exercise quickly took on a life of its own, and sequels *The Dominant* and *The Training* soon followed. Originally published online, the trilogy was a huge hit with readers around the world. Each of the books has now been read and reread more than a million times.

Tara kept her identity and her writing life secret, not even telling her husband what she was working on. To this day, only a handful of people know the truth (though she has told her husband). They live together in the southeastern United States with their two children.

CONNECT ONLINE

tarasueme.com